A Scoop Of Love

by Unoma Nwankwor

A KEVSTELGROUP BOOK

PUBLISHED BY KEVSTEL PUBLICATIONS

KevStel Group LLC

Lawrenceville GA 30046

ISBN 978-0-9890738-6-8

ISBN 978-0-9890738-7-5 (Ebook)

First printing January 2015

Printed in the United States of America

www.kevstelgroup.com

Praise for Unoma Nwankwor

"Unoma sets up each scene in **When You Let Go** with an emotional punch that will keep your heart racing to the finish line. Warning: You will lose sleep trying to get there!" ~**Pat Simmons, award-winning author of The Guilty series.**

"When You Let Go is a true testament of the power of God within ourselves and our marriage. Although, we are tested every day, it is up to us to lean on our faith to get through those difficult times and offer forgiveness to those who may have hurt us in the process. Amara and Ejike's faith was tested throughout this novel but once they learned to put God at the forefront of their household, they were able to weather the storm." ~ **Diva's Literary World**

"I love how Unoma Nwankwor weaves the distinctive, spicy flavor of West Africa into her novels. I feel right at home with the food, pidgin English, quirky expressions, and cultural norms. I'm also enjoying watching her grow as an author. ~**Sherri L. Lewis, Bestselling Author and Missionary**

"In **An Unexpected Blessing**, Unoma Nwankwor has penned a sweet romance with an important message about love and acceptance. She's definitely a writer to watch." ~**Rhonda McKnight, Black Expressions Bestselling Author of What Kind of Fool and An Inconvenient Friend**.

"What woman hasn't felt the pangs of unfulfilled desire? In **An Unexpected Blessing**, Unoma Nwankwor weaves deception, cultures and the intrigue of love for a romantic journey that spans two continents and challenges the cornerstone of faith."~ **Valerie J. Lewis Coleman, best-selling author of The Forbidden Secrets of the Goody Box TheGoodyBoxBook.com**

"I read **An Unexpected Blessing** and I must admit I loved it very, very much. I look forward to reading your next novel."~ **Diane Ndaba, reviewer Africa Book Club**

"**An Unexpected Blessing** is such a beautiful story had me over here in tears!"~ **Yvette Bentley of Words to Life LLC**

"Unoma's writing reads effortlessly. There is the perfect infusion of faith and international flavor. Readers are quickly swept up on a romantic literary adventure. **The Christmas Ultimatum** is a great read for anytime of the year"~ **Norma Jarrett Essence Best Selling author of Sunday Bruch**

"I loved it. **The Christmas Ultimatum** is my first read from Unoma and it won't be my last. I enjoyed the international favor she gave to the story. There is nothing sexier than a Christian man who goes after who and what he wants. Kudos!" ~ **Pat Simmons Award winning author of the Guilty Series**

Dedication

To my husband Kevin, and my kids—Fumnanya & Ugo.
Because of them, I am.

Acknowledgments

To my Lord and Savior Jesus Christ. I thank you for paying the ultimate price that I may have life and for your grace which I do not deserve. Thank You for the gift of writing and I humbly pray I continue to be a vessel in this journey.

To my family, my husband Kevin who is my number one fan, cheering me along every step of the way. I love you and thank you. To my kids Fumnanya and Ugo, my gang, my pookies, my munchkins they keep me sane when insanity sometimes abound. I love you both more than words can express. I pray for God's continued protection over you.

To my parents and mother in-law, *Daalu*. Thank you for your constant prayers and speaking words of life, courage and hope upon me.

To my readers, author friends and sistah writers thank you, thank you. Sometimes support doesn't always come from the people or places you expect but trust in God and He will send the right people to you.

Note from the Author

The Sons of Ishmael series tells the story of three brothers who should have been sons of favor but their lives took an unexpected turn when their father made a decision that molded their future. Or so they thought.

Just like Ishmael in the Bible, our circumstances in life can change quickly, and sometimes for the worse. That is when we should draw near to God and seek His wisdom and strength.

We may be tempted to become bitter when bad things happen, but that never helps. Only by following direction from God can we get through those valley experiences.

Follow Rasheed, Jabir & Kamal; the Danjuma brothers as they try to live in the present still harboring pain from the past and the ladies that will finally make them see that it is best to let go.

There are some questions at the back of the book, so you could discuss them with your friends or just read through by yourself. If you have additional questions you can reach me at unwankwor@kevstelgroup.com or www.unomanwankwor.com

Now kick back, relax and mentally step into the world of Rasheed and Ibiso.

Chapter 1

Rasheed Danjuma sighed aloud at the sight of another unwanted email from the law offices of Ezekiel and Stanley. These lawyers were beginning to work his last nerve. He placed his finger over the touchpad of his laptop, directed the cursor to the delete icon and pressed it.

It had been six months since Zayd Danjuma, the man that contributed to his genetic makeup, had passed away. And his lawyers were still hounding him. Rasheed had thought his non-attendance of the funeral service was a clear indication of his disinterest in anything they had to say about his so-called father.

Determined not to let the email ruin his day, he picked up the receiver and dialed his assistant's extension. She picked up at the first ring.

"Yes, Rasheed?"

"Have you heard anything back from those clients in the United States?"

"No, I didn't," she said. "But while you were on your conference call, your mother called."

Rasheed felt a strange rise in his stomach. His mother almost never called him on his office phone unless she wanted to reach him in a hurry. "Did she leave a message?"

"No, she just said to let you know she called."

"Okay, thank you." He disconnected the call.

Rasheed walked over to his jacket and pulled out his cell phone. Looking out of the large window of his Hyde Park office, his sense of unease grew. He checked, and there were three missed calls from his mother. His voice mail was empty. What was going on?

He dialed his mother. She answered on the third ring.

"Mama, you tried to reach me. Is everything okay?"

"*Nna,* I really don't know how to answer that."

His mother used her term of endearment, *Nna,* for her sons when she wanted to ask for something she knew they didn't want to give.

"What is it?"

"Those lawyers from your father's estate came to see me today," she said. "Rasheed, I don't want those men in my shop or house. I'm asking you again to come home and see what they want."

Rasheed's jaw set. How dare those lawyers hound his mother? Why was it so important that he and his brothers attend the stupid will reading? Even though it had been twenty-five years since their father had walked out of their lives, the memory of that morning was still vivid. Their father didn't care about them in life, so why was he so concerned about their well-being in death? Squaring up against those lawyers himself was one thing, but when they involved his mother, it was totally different. He wouldn't have it.

"You mean they came to your shop?" Rasheed asked as though he didn't hear her the first time. Anger shot through his feet as he began to pace the length of his office.

"Yes." His mother's voice sounded shaky. "It's one thing for them to call, but to show up, I don't appreciate it. They almost scared my customers away."

After his mother had retired as a school administrator, she decided she couldn't sit idle. Her love of fashion led to the opening of a boutique in the heart of Abuja's business district. Within months, the business had flourished. Rasheed had supported her because whatever made his mother happy made him happy, too. After many years of living in pain, she deserved to live her life in peace. They all did.

Rasheed's mind went back to the email he'd received earlier in the day. Since these lawyers were playing hardball, it was clear he had no choice but to travel to Nigeria. "If those lawyers call you again, tell them I'll be there soon."

His mother's sigh expressed her relief. "God bless you, my son."

"It's okay, Mama. They better make it worth my while. If not, I won't be held responsible for my actions."

***

Beat from what had turned out to be a pretty long and rough day, Rasheed disarmed the alarm code after walking into his condo. From the orangey citrus scent, he could tell that the housekeeper had come by earlier. The two-bedroom, 2,000 square-foot flat located in the heart of Kensington Gardens was his personal oasis. He was sold on the place the minute he saw the private balcony right off his bedroom. He dropped his briefcase on the leather couch, kicked off his shoes, and headed for the kitchen. After taking a long drink from a cold bottle of Heineken, he loosened his tie and settled into his favorite wingback chair.

As it usually did, Rasheed's mind went back to work. It was the last year of his contract with Nylon Consults and his plan was to leave the company on a high note. His University of Edinburgh degree had served him well as he had signed a lucrative deal with them seven years prior at an Alumni event. By some stroke of luck—although his mom would call it grace—he had risen to the rank of VP/Process Consultant and was enjoying the many amazing perks that came with the job. Within the short time, he had gotten to travel all around the world at their clients' expense. Although most of his days were spent cooped up in hotel rooms with Excel spreadsheets, he enjoyed what he did. But that didn't stop him from wanting to own his own consulting firm one day.

Rasheed grimaced. If he wanted to own his consulting firm, he couldn't afford to mess up like he had done earlier in the day. His failure to close on what would have been a very lucrative business deal had meant a huge loss of commission for him. That never happened.

After emptying the bottle, Rasheed stood and made his way to his home office. He still had work to do.

He powered on his laptop and a few seconds later, opened the

Microsoft Power Point document he was working on. It was the budget for this year's Turning Destiny camp. Every year, he volunteered at the camp put together by the local youth center. If he was headed to Nigeria, he had to tidy up the presentation and send it to the center's director, Mrs. Wright.

The camp was a cause dear to his heart. Its sole focus was pairing fatherless sons with male role models they could look up to. The workshop taught these boys that they had the power to change their destiny through programs that built self-esteem and confidence. That camp had been his saving grace. His mother enrolled him for the camp when he had begun to rebel due to the absence of his father. So it was his turn to give back and he did in a big way, with time and money. Now he would miss the most important event he looked forward to every year—when the boys graduated from the program and were sent back home better equipped for life—because a man had grown a conscience in death.

His fingers tapped hard on the keyboard as he worked. He struggled to keep his mind from drifting to where he dreaded to go—the early hours of that morning in Central London.

Rasheed woke up to the sound of hushed voices. He rubbed his eyes before looking around the cold, dark room. Soft snores confirmed his twin brothers were fast asleep.

Sliding off his bed, he walked to the door and pressed his ear against it. Rasheed frowned when the voices became familiar. It was rather early for them to be having an argument. It was pitch black outside and for the most part, the neighborhood was still asleep.

At ten years old, he had become used to the hushed arguments between his parents. It happened like clockwork right before it was time for his dad to go away again.

"You can't do this to me," he heard his mother whisper. "You promised this time would be it."

"Please don't make a scene—"

"What scene? I'm just tired of this," she said.

"Our children are sleeping. They'll hear you."

"Eh hen, let them hear. We've been doing this for a while now. You keep

Chapter 2

For a mid-March morning, the northern city of Abuja was windier than usual. Ibiso Jaja unlocked the doors to her dream. Her heart pounded from an adrenaline overload every time she entered her bistro—Bisso Bites.

There was noise coming from the kitchen, which meant that Amina Gombi, her cook and manager, along with her sales girl were already on the job. They always arrived early so they'd be ready when the eatery opened by noon.

She walked to the kitchen. "Good morning, ladies. How's everyone doing?"

"Morning," her staff crooned. They spent the next few minutes talking about the menu for the day and their commutes to work.

"I'll be right back. Let me check my email." Ibiso walked out of the kitchen to her office. She sat her cup of tea on her desk and noticed the envelope in her chair. The girls must have left it there for her. She had seen enough of these envelopes over the past few months to recognize that it was from Hassan Properties Management.

Her heart knocked against her chest as she read the heading of the letter; Six Month Notice. She scanned the contents. Nothing there was foreign. It reminded her that she had exactly six months to comply with the 800,000 Naira increase in rent or relocate her business. The deadline had been extended once for her, so she knew there was no longer any wiggle room. No more pleas of a single woman trying to make it. She had exhausted that line and was sure Alhaji Hassan wouldn't condone any more excuses.

If she wanted to keep the dream restaurant she had opened two short years ago, she had to come up with a way to pay the new lease. She couldn't start over—not now. It had taken her too much time, sweat and tears to get here. And in all honesty, this location she had in Garki was prime real estate.

Business had been slower than usual contract wise, considering her last two outside gigs had been cancelled. But Ibiso knew Bisso Bites had potential. God had given her a special talent and gift—to mix various foods and spices that sang a sweet melody to one's soul. She took pride in her ability to cook wholesome dishes in a non-traditional way. According to her customers, she provided tasty, nutritious dishes that were also pleasing to the eyes. That dream would fizzle as quickly as it started if she didn't come up with the additional money. Where was she supposed to get that kind of cash?

She took her laptop from her oversized tote and powered it on. Then she typed in her bank's web address and logged into her accounts. A deposit of 200,000 Naira turned her frown into a smile. Even though it couldn't all go toward the outstanding balance, as she needed some of it for operating expenses. It was something, and she had to make it work. She couldn't go back to Port Harcourt. That was not an option. She'd sooner beg for money on the streets of Abuja before she went back to her brother and asked for a handout. She was going to work twice as hard – anything to keep her dream alive.

Satisfied with her new resolve, Ibiso took a big gulp of her Tetley tea. Old habits die hard. Her eighteen month stay in England attending culinary school had her addicted to tea. She brewed herself a large cup every morning before she left her apartment. The weather in Nigeria didn't call for it, but she had somehow gotten accustomed to its taste.

She checked her email and social media accounts. In the few minutes that followed, Ibiso scheduled some posts with pictures of the dishes she made the day before. As she left her office to join the ladies in the kitchen she prayed, *"Father God, you know my condition. Abeg come to my aid. Guide and direct my path this day. Amen."*

***

Several hours later, Ibiso took off her shoes and settled on her orange sofa. It had been another great day. She moved the green and brown striped throw pillow to the side so her body could sink deeper into the couch. She crossed one leg over the other knee and massaged her feet. She had been standing all day.

As expected, the crowd started trooping in right after they opened the doors. The special for the day, Jollof rice with spicy snails, chopped spinach and fruit salad, had sold out before the end of lunch.

In addition to various pastries, Bisso Bites also offered lunch and dinner packaged meals. She always planned a special meal for the day, various secondary dishes and the standard snacks like scotch eggs, kebabs, chin chin, and meat pies. Her best friend, Boma Kadiri, loved the idea of offering customers the option of light snacks or full meals. Ibiso loved it, too. No matter what her customers wanted it, the main goal was healthy and convenient meals.

Ibiso missed her friend, but couldn't go back to Port Harcourt where Boma lived. Everywhere in that city reminded her of Tokoni, the ex-boyfriend she met after her return from England. Caught up in an intense and fierce romance, she had relegated her dreams of opening Bisso Bites to the back burner and followed him to Lagos. Her family was furious, especially her big brother, Sodienye. He was the closest thing to a father since their dad had passed when she was fifteen. Her brother felt he was the boss of her and had her life all planned out, to include marriage to one of his friends he considered "good." Tokoni's appearance had shattered that plan.

Boma had her reservations, too. "Let me get this straight," she had said. "You mean you're giving up your life here in Port Harcourt to follow a man who hasn't put a ring on it?"

"Stop being dramatic, you know Tokoni is the real deal. This will show him how committed I am to us," Ibiso said.

"You're kidding right? What did your brother have to say?" Boma sounded astonished.

Ibiso hadn't wanted to relive the conversation with her older brother and her mother because it was worse than she expected. Her mother had begged the "enemies that have possessed my only daughter" to leave her alone. And her brother had given her a one hour lecture about self-respect. She had turned a deaf ear. She was in love and happy.

"He makes me happy, gives me joy. I'll be fine."

"First of all happiness is temporal and only Christ can give joy. I've told you that time and time again," Boma had said.

Boma's words had turned out to be as true.

It had been three years since they broke up and Ibiso was still mourning the loss of what could have been. Tokoni got up one morning and ended the relationship. He told her he was no longer ready to settle down. He needed to get even further in his career and acquire even more accolades and money than he already had. He gave her the "there is still a lot I need to accomplish before marriage" line.

Once the fairy tale ended, the depression had kicked in. Ibiso couldn't go back home. Her brother forbade her to since she defied him and left in the first place. According to him, there was no longer a place for her in the Jaja household.

With Boma by her side, Ibiso had found her way to Jesus Christ. She had indeed begun to experience true joy, but not without challenges. At thirty-three, she never wanted to relive the last three years of her life. However, she was thankful for the journey because it had brought her to this point. Now she needed 700,000 Naira to stay there.

Fighting her anxiety, Ibiso gathered her purse and laptop bag and headed to her bedroom. She loved her apartment. It was simple, elegant and functional. The space had a predominantly white decorative backdrop, but Ibiso made it warm and inviting with modern, multi-colored furniture pieces and African art that hung on the walls. The two-bedroom apartment signified a fresh start for her.

Ibiso peeled off her pink capris and tossed her turquoise blouse over her head. She walked into the bathroom, thankful that the next day was Saturday. On the weekends, Ibiso wasn't as hands on. She would sleep in while Amina opened up. The only time she got up early was when she had to make a delivery to the local charity she gave back to or when she had a client to cook for.

Otherwise, she used the weekend to prepare the menu for the week ahead.

Moments later, she came out of the bathroom refreshed and not so defeated. She found herself humming Don Moen's song, 'God Will Make A Way."

Ibiso knelt to pray. Tomorrow she would begin strategizing. She needed to scout for outside clients. She would do her part and allow God to do His.

Chapter 3

A month later, Rasheed Danjuma made his way through the busy gate of Heathrow International airport, with his hand luggage and laptop in tow. He checked his Android. There was nothing yet from his potential client in the United States. Any other time, he'd be worried because he knew he had put together a great proposal. But with more immediate problems to handle, their delay was a good thing.

He rehearsed the plan in his head again—see about this will business, make sure his mother was okay, and be back in no time.

Rasheed handed his boarding pass to the flight personnel and gave her his signature smile, showcasing his pearly whites and one cheek dimple. He was aware of his looks and was often amused at the attention and special favors it got him. The attendant nodded her head, giving him consent to go through.

"Have a safe flight," she said.

If he didn't have enough on his mind already, he would have stopped to ask for a name and a number. But the realization of what his trip home entailed caused him to refocus immediately.

Rasheed settled into his business class seat on the British Airways Boeing 750 to Abuja, Nigeria. He stretched out his long legs which his mother always called "basketball legs." He then removed the blanket from its nylon casing and covered himself.

He hadn't had a good night's sleep in a long time. For the most part, his restlessness was due to the anxiety of what lay ahead. He cringed any time he flew back to Nigeria. He only began making frequent flights home when his mother decided to move back years ago. His younger brothers loved it. Jabir and Kamal always saw it as a time to kick back and relax from the hassles of college. For him, it always brought back memories and emotions that cut deep.

Pain. Humiliation. Rejection. Those feelings bombarded him any time he flew back home. The memories of more than two decades ago were still fresh in his mind.

His father didn't come back the following month as promised. Nor the month after that, but he called often. Every Sunday, Rasheed looked forward to the call from Nigeria. Then just like that, they stopped. The calls just stopped. Days turned into months, months turned into a year. Then one day his mother booked a flight to Nigeria so they could go in search of his dad. She took him with her, leaving the twins with her best friend.

The day after they arrived in Abuja, his mother took him to a house that was ten times the size of their small flat in London. She pressed the bell on the gate and the gateman appeared through the side entrance.

"Madam, gud evenin."

"Good evening my broda," his mother replied.

Rasheed looked puzzled. The British accent his mother had seemed to have disappeared as she spoke in this broken language he couldn't understand.

"Who you dey find?"

"Erm...I'm looking for one Mr. Zayd Danjuma. Does he live here?"

The gateman's eyes light up. "Ah! Na my oga be dat."

Rasheed saw his mother smile, and he smiled too. This must be the right place. He would soon see his daddy.

"Is he in?" his mother asked.

Rasheed couldn't figure out why the man hadn't opened the gate to let them in. This was his daddy's house.

"He no dey but madam and the pikin dey."

Rasheed felt his mother squeeze his hand a little tighter.

"Madam?" She asked.

"Yes, Oga's wife. Hold on make I call am."

His mother raised her hand to protest but the man had darted into the house.

Moments after, a woman, who had her head wrapped like those women Rasheed watched in Indian movies, came out of the house. She had a little girl hoisted on her hips. The grip his mother had on his hand began to hurt.

"Mama, you're hurting me."

She relaxed the hold on his hand. "Sorry love." Despite her wobbly smile, he could feel her trembling as the woman approached.

"Kasali, you this man. Open the gate for her," the woman said in an annoyed tone. "Why would you leave her standing outside?"

"I'm sorry, madam," the gateman said and hurried to open the gate wider for them to enter.

Rasheed and his mother stepped into the compound. The lady met them halfway.

"Hello, my name is Aisha Danjuma. I'm told you're looking for my husband. He is not home yet. Who are you?"

Husband? What is she talking about? Surely she isn't referring to my daddy, Rasheed thought to himself.

"Hello, my name is Obiageli…"

A horn blared. The gateman ran to open the bigger gate to a sleek looking Mercedes Benz. When the car came to a standstill, the door opened and Rasheed saw his dad. He wanted to bolt towards him but his mother held him back.

"Mama look, it's daddy."

His mother remained silent and stayed glued in place. Rasheed broke free and darted towards his dad.

He expected to be hoisted up in the air, but was surprised when his dad just patted him on the head. Rasheed turned around just in time to see the look of shock on his mother's face and the corresponding look of disapproval on the other woman's face.

The events that happened next were still a blur, but before he knew it there was shouting, crying and then he and his mom were back in Central London.

The year that followed was unbearable for Rasheed. His six year-old brothers—Jabir and Kamal—asked him questions that his mother was too distraught to answer. Some days she was so depressed, she forgot to pack their lunches or make dinner on time.

Rasheed hated his father for ruining their lives.

Then, one day, his mom moved them to East London. They started a new school and made new friends. Although she did everything a mother would do for her children, she spent the majority of her days on auto-pilot. Never again was she the light-hearted cheerful woman he once knew. He heard her cry every night when she thought he and his brothers were asleep.

From that point on, only one thing drove him – the need to elevate their status in society. Never again would his mother or brothers be rejected because of their rank in society or religion. His brothers would go to the best schools and it wouldn't have anything to do with Zayd Danjuma. Nothing consumed Rasheed more than the desire to succeed. And his hate for his father fed that need.

***

The pilot's voice roused Rasheed from his slumber. "Ladies and Gentlemen, thank you for joining us today on British Airways to Abuja, Nigeria. The local weather is 32 degrees Celsius. We hope you enjoyed your flight and will join us again. Once again, welcome to Abuja, Nigeria."

Rasheed couldn't believe that he had slept for the duration of the six and a half hour flight. His body had given into his exhaustion. He meshed his 220 pound body deeper into the chair. He put his headphones on, and braced himself for landing.

Two hours later, Rasheed looked at his watch again. He wished he had insisted the twins fly to London and they all fly to Abuja together. Or that he hadn't agreed to their insistence he wait for them at the airport. Rasheed turned his focus to the information board again. The flight from Amsterdam should arrive in half an hour. Then he'd have to wait some more for them to go through customs. He had landed in Nigeria a while ago and was tired and hungry. *Bad planning Rasheed, bad planning.*

He took a sip from the bottled water in front of him. His thoughts drifted to the reason he was here in the first place, Zayd Danjuma. He was a coward. He couldn't stand up to his family. Instead he succumbed to their demands to take a Muslim wife from a well-bred household and take over the family business. To top it all off, Zayd didn't even have the decency to tell his mother, but had kept her hidden in the UK while living his double life.

Rasheed knew it was not nice to talk ill of the dead, but no there was no law against thinking bad about them. He despised the ground that man had walked on and if it hadn't been for his mother, he wouldn't be here right now. He would be back in his cozy flat in London or better still, courting a new client.

Minutes later, Rasheed looked up from the *Guardian* newspaper he had busied himself with. He smiled when he saw his brothers approaching. The last time he had seen them was three years ago when their mother was in England celebrating her sixtieth birthday. They had come from their base in the United States. It had been just like old times, all three of them with their mother in London.

The Danjuma brothers got close and exchanged hugs. Rasheed was still amazed by how the twins were so alike in physical appearance but very different in character and personality. Jabir, the older twin, was more outspoken, flirtatious and care-free. He practiced medicine in Detroit. Kamal was more reserved. Although he was a trained architect, he didn't work in his profession. He spent some time discovering himself before deciding he wanted to become a professional soccer player. Rasheed knew his brother always had the talent but a profession pushing a ball around with his feet wasn't what he had in mind when he helped him through school.

"So we finally gonna do this?" Jabir asked.

Rasheed adjusted the strap of his laptop bag on his shoulders. "Yes, they're now harassing mama—"

"And we all know you don't mess with mama. Your first wife," Kamal joked.

Rasheed's nose flared in feigned annoyance. His mother was his responsibility. He promised himself that she would never be troubled or lack anything. That was a vow he didn't take for granted.

"Cut it out. Mama is my responsibility, not my wife." Rasheed folded his newspaper and placed it under his arm. He began gathering his other things.

26

"Oh yes Kammy, don't forget. Stone Cold here doesn't do the relationship thing," Jabir said, using Kamal's pet name.

"You guys just shut up and let's go. I've been salivating over the pounded yam I'm sure Mama prepared, but had to wait here for you knuckle heads."

"Alright, let's do this." The twins said in unison.

Rasheed hated it when they did that which was quite often. They drove him crazy but kept him sane at the same time. His family gave him a purpose for living. Just like him, the twins had grown up too fast. Despite the normal teenage episodes, they made him and his mother very proud. Rasheed was eager to be done with this thorn in his side—the will reading—then spend quality time with his family before they all went their separate ways again.

Chapter 4

Rasheed tapped his fingers on the window pane while his eyes wandered into the distance. The city looked different every time he visited home. There was always one new enhancement or the other. New buildings seemed to go up at rapid speeds and the business district was expanding. Abuja, the planned city located in the center of Nigeria, was home to several parks, green areas and landmarks. The most important and visible landmark was Aso Rock where the Federal Government sat. Abuja had taken over the title of capital of Nigeria from Lagos a while back. The town was charming and at the time Rasheed's mother had wanted to move back home, he decided that Abuja would suit her best rather than her hometown, Enugu, in the eastern part of Nigeria. He thought that if his father's other wife could live in Abuja, so could his mother. At first his mother had protested, but she began to love her life there as a school board administrator.

As the driver of his Range Rover zoomed down the highway, Rasheed squeezed his mother's hand. He lowered the window to let in the cool breeze from yesterday's rain. It was still early so the sun hadn't taken full effect yet.

"Mama, are you okay?"

"Yes, dear. I just want to get this over with." Her mood was pensive. She turned around to look out the back window.

"Don't worry. Jabir and Kammy are right behind us." Rasheed assured her. "Okay?"

She remained silent.

"Left to me, I wouldn't be going to this thing, but I don't want anybody to call you again about this matter. That man just donated sperm—he isn't my dad."

"Naetochi *nwa m*, please hold on to your temper when we get

there. I've been telling you about this temper thing. It's been years, but you're still so angry. Let it go."

Rasheed knew that anytime his mother called him by his Ibo name that she had a speech behind it. How she and his father fell in love was still a wonder to him. They both attended the same school in England. She is Ibo, he was Hausa. She is Christian, he was Muslim. Her family is poor, his is rich. If they were in Nigeria, that would have been a hard sell, but living in the UK provided them luxury to do as they pleased. Rasheed frowned. In the end, it still didn't last. His father had come home and married a woman of his status and religion.

"I'm fine, Mama. They've disrupted my business and for that I take offence. Other than that, I could care less."

Before his mother could respond, the driver brought the car to a halt in front of the Danjuma Group building. Before his death, Rasheed's father ran the company that had been in the Danjuma family for generations. The company was made up of two divisions—cement manufacturing and logistics. The group of companies was headquartered in Abuja, but also had a Lagos office. Their clients were spread across Nigeria and the continent of Africa.

The office was situated in the Garki district of the city. It took up the second, third and fourth floors of the ten-story building. The grounds were well manicured and had trees that provided shade for the lunch benches that were placed on the lawn in strategic positions. Rasheed got out of the car and helped his mother. Seconds later, his brothers pulled up in their mother's Jeep. The twins came to where they waited and Kamal drew his mother into an embrace, smiling down at her. Jabir took up space on her other side. At six feet two, the twins towered over their mother.

Rasheed lifted his sunshades to the top of his head and sized up the place. "This is it."

"My sons, come let's pray," their mother said.

"Prayer warrior Mama, we prayed at home, right?" Jabir looked at his watch. "That insurance should still cover us. It's only been an hour."

"Mama, we're good. Let's get this over with." Rasheed walked ahead, leading the way for his brothers and mother to follow.

***

Stepping into the building was like entering a whole new world. If Rasheed had seen a picture of the interior in a magazine, he wouldn't have believed it was located in Nigeria. The conference room they were directed to was huge. It was better than the conference room at Nylon Consults in London. It had a state-of-the-art communications system, a projector for presentations and was decorated in mahogany and beige colors. Rasheed and his family sat across from his father's wife, Aisha and her daughter, Halima. Halima was a carbon copy of her mother but she and Kamal shared the same dark, smoky eyes.

After brief greetings were exchanged, a man who looked like he was in his mid sixties with a receding hairline and bulging stomach spoke, "Good morning ladies and gents. At last with the presence of Mr. Danjuma's sons, we can proceed with the reading of the will."

Nobody spoke.

The lawyer cleared his throat. "This is the last will and testament of Zayd Fredrick Danjuma." He paused and looked around the room. When he was sure that he had everyone's attention, he continued. "If this will is being read, that means my sons are present. There is nothing I can say that will make up for the hurt, but know this—you were never far from my heart. To my wife Aisha, I leave my properties in Abuja and our home in South Africa. You'll also be entitled to an annual allowance of six million Naira. To Obiageli, once again, I'm sorry. I couldn't bring myself to tell you the truth. Thank you for my sons."

The lawyer paused again when there was a heavy sigh from Aisha. Halima gathered her mother in her arms and placed her head on her shoulder.

Rasheed's expression was blank. *Now it's their time to cry. We did it for all those years.*

"Rasheed."

When the lawyer called his name, his spine stiffened. Now he'd see why it was so important that he be present for the reading of this will.

"To you, my firstborn son, I leave the ownership of the entire Danjuma Group. I want you to continue my legacy. The family legacy. What I couldn't do while I was alive, I want to make amends for in death—"

"No! That's not going to happen," Rasheed barked. Anger propelled him to his feet. His mother's distressed look caused him to pause.

"Mr. Danjuma, please could we finish reading? We have some more ground to cover." The lawyer took off his reading glasses.

Rasheed looked around the room. All eyes were on him. He sat and fought hard to contain his heart rate. He felt as though he would explode. He didn't want anything from his father. He only came to get this charade over with. He did not and would not take on the responsibility of running a company and moving back home to please some man in death that could have cared less about him when he was alive.

"Rasheed, you came home for this. Let the man finish," his mother whispered.

Rasheed searched her eyes. They were weak and seemed weary. This whole thing was taking a toll on her. He and his brothers had tried over the years to make her forget the pain their father caused, but she never got back the spark she once had. A part of him knew that despite everything, she had never stopped loving his dad. For her, he would endure what he considered an insult to them, but he was already envisioning his return flight to England. There was no way.

Moving to Nigeria was in Rasheed's five-year plan, but it wouldn't be for his father or his company. It would be on his terms.

***

Rasheed stormed out of the conference room. His anger bubbled up burning his insides and he was ready to go off. He quickened his pace. He needed fresh air.

"Rasheed, wait up," Jabir called out.

"Man, not now." Rasheed waved his hand in the air and kept walking. He made a sharp turn around the corner and bumped into someone coming from the opposite direction. At once, his reflexes took over. He stretched out his hand and grabbed the lady in front of him to steady her from falling backward. He wasn't fast enough however to save the tray of assorted snacks she was carrying.

"I'm so sorry," Rasheed said when he found his voice. In an instant, his rage was replaced with frustration as he looked around at the mess he had caused.

"Oh no, oh no..." the lady cried out. She looked around at her baked finger foods lying across the hallway.

"I'm so sorry." Rasheed bent to help pick up the baked goods that were strewn all over the floor. He could feel her glare boring a hole in his back. He looked up to see the shock still written all over her face. Jabir came up to meet them.

"We are so sorry," Jabir said.

"Stop saying that. It won't produce new snacks that are due to a client in forty-five minutes. What on earth am I going to do?" She threw her hands up in the air.

"I apologize once again. I'm willing to pay for it," Rasheed said.

"Oh, you're the spend money and make it all better type? This is business for me. My name is on the line. What am I going to tell this client now?" She threw a glare at him.

"Look—I said I was sorry. What's done is done. So what can I do to make it better?" Rasheed's voice was laced with irritation. *Who was she to judge him?*

While she hesitated, Rasheed swept over her with his eyes. Although his schedule only allowed him to date on occasion and love was nowhere in his plan, he admired beauty when he saw it. He had seen a lot of pretty women in his life time and the woman that stood in front of him was no doubt in that number. She was gorgeous. Her hair was maintained in a low cut. Her flawless dark skin shone through the arm of her sleeveless, white wrap dress, which stopped right above her knees and accentuated her curves.

She looked up at him. Even in heels, he towered over her. Her brown eyes drew him in as her full lips began to move.

"You're right." She checked her wristwatch.

"Please, pardon my brother. Let us make it up to you," Jabir said.

Rasheed felt his jaw tighten as he watched his brother turn on the charm. He recognized Jabir prepare his "knight in shining amour, save the damsel in distress" routine.

"Tell me what I can do?" Rasheed made one more attempt to make amends.

She let out an exaggerated sigh. "I'll just go back to my bistro and see if the batch I left behind would be enough."

"I could drive you there if you'd like," Jabir walked toward the woman.

"Erm..." She hesitated.

Rasheed heard footsteps in the distance. He turned around to see his mother and Kamal headed his way. He could do without a lecture or an audience right now. He needed to get away.

Rasheed shoved his hands in his pockets. "Come on, I'll take you to your restaurant. It's the least I can do. You'll be back in no time."

She rolled her eyes. "Okay, let me make two calls."

Rasheed noticed the way her slender hips swayed as she took a few steps away from them. He observed her hand gestures as she spoke to what he assumed was a coworker. She hung up and then made a second call that lasted a few seconds.

Rasheed felt his mother's hand wrap around his arm. He looked down at her, drew her to his side and squeezed gently. They were not going to agree on the demands of his father's will. From the look she gave him, she'd want him to cave. But before they had their drawn out argument about it, he would give her the comfort she needed. Seeing his father's other wife and her daughter again couldn't have been easy.

"What happened here?" his mother asked.

"Stone Cold here was moving with the speed of lightening and knocked over this poor lady and her stuff," Jabir said.

"Bro *na wa o*. Hmmm... I wonder what you were running from," Kamal teased.

"Can we not talk about this here? I need you guys to take mama home while I take this lady to her restaurant to replace her damaged goods," Rasheed ordered.

"Good afternoon, Ma."

All three of them turned around to see the lady in a half-kneeling position in front of their mother.

"Afternoon, my dear. I'm so sorry for this mess."

"It's okay, Ma. Things happen." The woman smiled.

Rasheed couldn't believe there was a smile behind the frosted attitude she had given him. In her defense, he did knock down her items and his mother did have a soothing effect on people.

"You ready?" Rasheed asked.

"Yes." Her response was curt as she turned and walked away.

Rasheed followed.

As they headed toward the exit, Rasheed knew that the three people he left behind already had ideas forming in their heads. His mother saw a potential wife, Jabir saw a potential fling while he was here in Nigeria, and Kamal would be trying to figure out why his big brother would be willing to drive an unknown woman across town instead of just paying for the damages.

Rasheed was used to his family's vivid imaginations. But they were dead wrong. All he wanted to do was fix the mess he had caused. He repeated his motive to himself a couple more times so it could stick. His intent had nothing to do with the fact that upon impact, he felt a jolt not only in his body but his soul.

Chapter 5

The heat from the sun, now in full blast, hit Ibiso as she exited the cool interior of the building with the older lady and her three sons in tow. She waited while the man that had just ruined her afternoon exchanged cars with his family. His mother and brothers got into the car with the driver and sped off while he opened the door of a sleek looking Mercedes Benz Jeep. *These people must come from money.*

Once in the car, Ibiso glanced at the man who almost knocked her over. She concluded he must be the eldest son since he dished out orders like her brother, Sodienye. He, just like her brother, seemed to maintain a constant frown on his face. His attitude might need work but his outer appearance was downright unfair to other men. His chocolateness surpassed that of any man she knew. His well-groomed moustache linked perfectly with his low cut beard. His frame filled out his designer suit, revealing his well ripped body. His aura prickled her skin. With supreme effort, Ibiso forced her thoughts back in check and away from this dangerously handsome stranger with mesmerizing brown eyes.

When he held Ibiso to keep her from falling, the raw magnetic energy between them made her want to run in the opposite direction. Her truck that wouldn't start this morning was the only reason she was stuck riding with him. She needed to focus on the mission at hand – get back to her restaurant and her client.

"So, do you have a name?" The man's deep baritone interrupted her thoughts.

His rudeness crushed the fairytales forming in her head. She looked around the car. "Are you talking to me?"

He remained silent. His eyebrow furrowed even more. Whatever was on his mind didn't excuse his lack of manners and she wasn't going to take it. Not from someone who should be more than apologetic for the inconvenience he caused her.

"If so, show some manners. In case you don't remember, you knocked me over. What you should be doing is hoping I don't lose my client's business."

He didn't say anything. The tension grew thicker.

This man is not used to being challenged. Well, he got the wrong one because I've had enough of men like my brother thinking they rule everything.

"I'm sorry. That was rude of me."

"Now that's one thing we can agree on."

He turned to look at her. She lifted her eyebrow to meet his stare. She was not one of his younger brothers. He wasn't going to intimidate her.

He focused back on the road.

"Let's try this again. I'm Rasheed Danjuma. And you are?"

"Ibiso Jaja." She paused. "You're *the* Danjuma?"

She noticed a vein on his temple increase in size.

Okay so this one has issues.

"I'm related, but not *the* Danjuma."

She waited for a follow-up that never came so she laced her fingers together and gave him directions. She and Rasheed drove to the bistro in absolute silence. It was just as well because she had nothing to say to the arrogant man anyway. It was just a blessing that she listened to her inner spirit and kept enough of the meat pies, scotch eggs and kebabs behind. Before she got there, Amina had arranged everything for her. Ibiso gathered the treats and braced herself for the return fifteen-minute drive. She couldn't wait to be rid of the sullen man.

***

By the time Ibiso got back to her apartment later that day, a mixture of fatigue and relief took over her body.

In the end, she was able to make her delivery on time. Very important since the call she got to cater the Alaki Place open house three-day event had been god sent. The real estate company was based in a very influential office district so a good job could lead to more business. Today was just the first day and she couldn't afford to let anything happen. Their payment brought her closer to her goal.

Ibiso aimed the remote at the stereo and the opening chords of Ledisi's "Pieces of Me" filled the room. She stretched out on her chaise in the corner of the living room and closed her eyes. The events of the day flooded through her mind but somehow got stuck on one image she wanted to forget—Rasheed Danjuma.

The butterflies that fluttered in her belly at the sound of his voice betrayed her intention to be mad at him. He reminded her of Sodienye, so her attraction to him irked her. Despite his arrogance, he helped her carry her items up to the sixth floor of the building and stayed around until she had set up. She couldn't help but wonder what made him so upset earlier that afternoon. Her imagination was about to go wild with possibilities, but was interrupted when her phone rang.

"Don't tell me you were going to go to bed without telling me how things went with the new client." Boma asked when Ibiso answered the phone. "God is faithful. Just when we thought no new business was in sight, this gig dropped in your lap."

Ibiso turned off the stereo. "I just got in. I was resting for a moment. You won't believe the day I had."

"I'm all ears."

Ibiso suppressed her laugh. She wedged the phone between her shoulder and ear. She gathered up her shoes and handbag before heading towards her bedroom. She placed the phone on speaker and put it down on her bed as she recounted the day's event to her friend. Ibiso stepped out of the pool her dress made at her ankles and wrapped herself with her towel. When she was finished with the story, there was silence.

"Hello B, are you there?"

"Yes o. I'm still trying to understand how you casually ran over the fact that this man is a Danjuma."

"And so? He is rude and arrogant so his name means little to me," Ibiso said. When she uttered the words, she knew how untrue they were but no need to tell Boma that. Knowing her friend, she would hound her about whether she liked the man or not.

"You don't know what he was going through. He might not really be like that."

"Can we get back to my issues please? Like how my truck gave out on me today of all days."

"I've always told you that all things work together for the good. Didn't God come through? So stop complaining."

"Yeah, I guess so. You know I'm still learning this faith and trust stuff." Ibiso still considered herself a baby Christian, but was so sure she didn't want to go back to that place she once was. Sunday and mid-week service and being able to ask Boma about anything she still struggled with were a big help. She sealed the deal with daily communion with God, but still her past experiences plagued her even in this new era of her life. She had to keep reminding herself that her past was just that, her past. She would prove her family wrong. She was not a disgrace or a failure just because she hadn't danced to their tune. She would show her ex that even though she wasn't as driven as he was, she had enough determination to fulfill the purpose of her life.

"You still have about five months, so chill. What about the estimate you submitted to that Women's Summit? Have you heard back?"

Through Amina, Ibiso got wind that the wife of one of Nigeria's prominent senators would be hosting a women's leadership conference. It would be a huge opportunity if she were to cater the event. The exposure and the money could take her to heights unimaginable.

"I haven't heard anything back." She shrugged." Besides, the conference is in November. That's seven months away. How much good would that do me now?"

"I'm going to have to knock this negativity out of you. If they decide to go with you they will pay a down payment...duh," Boma said in an exasperated tone.

"I'm not negative, just realistic." Ibiso secured her towel and put on her shower cap.

"That's another name for doubt. In case you haven't heard, it doesn't go well with faith." Boma's tone had a hint of finality.

Her friend was right. *Nothing is impossible with God.* The Luke 1:37 verse came to mind.

"Anyways, for now, Dokubo gave me an extra 50,000. I'll send it to add to what you have," Boma said.

Ibiso's eyes widened. "Are you kidding me? B, you know I can't take that from you. Shouldn't it be going towards the big christening of my godchildren?"

"Soso, didn't you just hear me say extra? If it makes you feel better, you can pay me back later, but I'm not taking no for an answer. Bisso Bites has been your dream ever since I can remember. That degree you got in Marketing was just to please your brother. Now it's time to do something for you."

Ibiso beamed at her friend's use of her nickname. Sometimes she didn't know what she did to deserve a friend like Boma. She was in the throes of baby christening plans for her three month-old twins, but still remembered her dilemma.

"I'll pay you back, thank you. God bless your husband for giving you extra." Ibiso paused and did a mental calculation. "With this and my new client's payment, I'm just 600,000 shy of my goal. I know God will make a way. This is mid-April. I have 'til August."

"You see, there you go. God will make a way. I'll wire the money tomorrow."

They talked a little more. Boma brought her up to date on the christening plans and Ibiso told her of the progress she had started making with her brother. Sodienye was still mad at her—which was ridiculous after all these years—but at least now he answered the phone when she called. Although the conversation was strained, they were communicating.

When they hung up, Ibiso took a long shower and started her nighttime routine. She began humming the lyrics of an old school hymn when she remembered that she still didn't have a car. The money Boma sent would be used to get her 2008 Toyota RAV4 running again. Ibiso was grateful for that extra help since it would prevent her from going into her savings. There was no way she could get around Abuja paying for a rented car.

By the following afternoon, Ibiso's joy was short lived as she had underestimated her car troubles. She sat behind her desk looking at the invoice that had been handed to her. She needed a new transmission. The cost of which would take up the money Boma sent her and dig into the funds she had saved. The cushion she thought she had, disappeared. Now she needed to step up her efforts for additional income or she could watch her restaurant die a quick death.

She leaned her head back and closed her eyes. She began contemplating her next move when there was a knock on the door.

"Yes," she said.

Her sales girl entered. Ibiso wiped away the wayward tear that escaped the corner of her eye. She didn't need to worry her staff about their jobs.

"Madam, there's a man here to see you."

She didn't know who that could be and her brain was too tired to speculate. She stood and made the short trek to the front of the restaurant. She stopped for a moment when she saw the pink and white orchid arrangement in the man's hand.

"Yes, may I help you?" Her raised brows conveyed her curiosity.

"Good afternoon madam, my *oga*, told me to deliver this to you," the man dressed in simple khakis and a dress shirt said.

"Who is your *oga*?"

"Mr. Rasheed Danjuma."

Ibiso observed the man for a moment. She had a good mind to tell him to take the flowers back. But he was just the messenger. No need to take out the frustration with his *oga* or her present situation on him.

"Thank you." Ibiso took the silver container from him and walked back into her office. She looked for a note. There was none, but his phone number was typed on a card.

Just typical of these rich people. He didn't even take the time to write a simple message. She looked for a place for the flowers, and then decided on the corner of the office. If Rasheed didn't think it important enough to write a note, then it didn't deserve prime space. She couldn't believe he left her a number to call. She tore the card and tossed the pieces in the trash.

Ibiso reeled in her thoughts when she realized she was about to spend precious time fuming over Rasheed's conceit. She had bigger problems. She needed additional income. With that thought, she picked up her purse, opened the door and left to find some clients.

Chapter 6

There was no denying his mother's mood as Rasheed opened the door of her home for her to enter. It had been a week since the reading of his father's will and the tension in the Danjuma household hadn't seemed to dissipate. His mother made her stand pretty clear. Despite that way his father treated her—treated them—it was all in the past and they should let the anger and pain go and move on. She couldn't understand why he didn't want anything to do with the man or his money. It was his inheritance, she insisted. At the end of the day, his father had done right by them.

His mother took off her head wrap, exposing her salt and peppered colored hair, and plopped down on her favorite recliner in the corner of the living room. Rasheed swallowed and placed his keys on the center table. If there was one thing he knew about his mom, it was the guilt she carried around. She blamed herself for not shielding her sons enough from the pain she went through. And as a result, she felt responsible for he and his brothers' unwillingness to forgive their father.

He settled his long frame into the chair at the corner of the room. The space was huge compared to his flat in London. But it felt warm and cozy. The light crème and red curtains that shielded the sunlight from entering the room must be new because he hadn't seen them the last time he was here.

Rasheed took in a deep breath. The aroma of her *onugbu* soup filled the room. His stomach roared for attention, but it would have to wait. This discussion needed to be had now.

After her routine doctor visit this morning, the doctor was concerned about her blood pressure and had recommended low stress and a change in diet.

"Mama, you heard what the doctor said. You have to change

your cooking and eating habits."

"I'm fine."

Her reply rattled him. Her health was paramount and it displeased him that she seemed so nonchalant about it. She must have seen the worried looked on his face.

"Stop frowning. I'm not dead yet—"

He stood up and walked into the kitchen to get a bottle of water. The humidity was higher than usual today.

When he returned his mother continued, "Stop worrying. I have no intention of leaving you and your brothers now. Especially since none of you have given me grandchildren yet." She paused. "You worry about me too much and I understand that, but I'm okay. I have made peace a long time ago. Right now, I need to talk to you. And don't dismiss me."

"Mama, whatever it is can wait until we get this squared away."

"I'm not deaf. I was there and heard what the doctor said."

"Okay, but—"

"But nothing. What I have to tell you is important." His mother fidgeted with her chair, returning it to the upright position.

"What is it, Mama?"

She paused, looked up to the ceiling as though asking God for help, then continued, "*Nna*, I don't have to tell you the story of my life, the good, the bad and the ugly. The one regret I have is exposing you to the ugly for so long."

"Mama, what are you talking about? Why are you sounding like this?" Rasheed didn't know where she was going with this speech, but he didn't like it. It wasn't like she deliberately put herself in misery, but it happened. So why was she acting as if she wasn't the victim in all this?

"I'm saying this because I don't like where your life is headed."

"What's wrong with my life? I have a good job, a house in London, and I can afford to give you the best."

"That's just it. I've watched you over the years focus on only material things."

He clenched his jaw. This was a topic he didn't like discussing, but he knew his mother wouldn't let up 'til they did.

He remained silent and she continued, "I'm not telling you not to go after your dreams and desires, but don't allow the need to prove something to yourself deprive you of living. It's been years. Stop letting it consume you. Have you given more thought to your father's will?"

Before Rasheed stormed out of the conference room, the lawyer had made it clear that his dad had stipulated that Rasheed had a month to agree to the conditions of the will after it had been read. If he didn't, his dad's brother would take over Danjuma Group.

"I don't care what happens to that man's company." He shrugged.

"You told me yourself you wanted to move back home sometime soon. That company is your right." She paused. "Your dad came back to ask for your forgiveness when you were twenty, but you didn't want to have anything to do with him. A stance that you've maintained. Your father realized his mistake, but you never forgave him and the twins followed your example. But you don't have to ruin your chance of taking what is yours by right. You are his first son."

Rasheed bolted up from his chair. "It was too late. He wasn't there when I needed him. When I needed a father, or when I had to tell the twins it wasn't their fault he left. Or when you had shut us out. Don't you understand? He wasn't there. He made his choice, so I made mine."

"It's a long time to still hold on to anger. Please, my son, let it go. Fulfill the conditions of the will for me," his mother pleaded.

Rasheed saw the appeal in her eyes. She looked weak. He didn't want her talking about this issue any more. His dad had come back all right, but only because his socially acceptable wife hadn't been able to give him a son and he needed to claim him and his brothers. What Zayd didn't achieve in life, Rasheed for sure wasn't going to allow him to achieve in death.

"You have to find time to live. Find time to enjoy all the things that you have amassed over the years. I know you don't like to hear this, but you need to also find someone to share your life with. Trust me; doing it alone is a very lonely existence. It means nothing if there's no one to share it with."

"I'm not lonely. I have friends." His mind drifted to Ibsio. Since he had bumped into her, he couldn't get her out of his head. Their meeting was brief, but much to his surprise, the impact was lasting.

"It's not the same thing and you know it. Look at that nice Ebele girl that you disappointed."

"Mama, don't start. Ebele wanted what I couldn't give."

"I want to see my grandchildren," she said with a faint smile on her face.

"These children you keep talking about—" It amazed him how she always skipped the wife and jumped straight into him having children. That was the least of his worries right now.

"Rasheed you're thirty-six. Do you want to be walking with a cane before your first child is born?

"Please, let's drop this," Rasheed said. He didn't have time to regret things that had happened. He and Ebele weren't in the same place, but no matter how much he told his mother that, she never understood it.

The door opened and Rasheed had never been so happy to see his brothers. He needed to take a drive. The conversation had drained him.

"Mama, I can smell that *onugbu* soup, oh." Kamal headed towards the kitchen.

Jabir took their mother's hand and navigated towards the kitchen. They paused at the entrance. "Stone Cold, are you not coming?" Jabir asked.

"No, you guys go ahead." Rasheed picked up his keys and headed out. "I'll be back.

***

Rasheed leaned his head back as the driver navigated through traffic. Memories of childhood came flooding back along with the feeling of insecurity he felt when his dad left. He was grateful for Mr. Bready, an Englishman that had entered his life through the Turning Destinies camp. The man took a special interest in him and a couple of others. He went the extra mile to teach and nurture them. Rasheed loved their once a month fishing trips.

How dare his dad now want to come and reap where he didn't sow? The initial years had been hard. But with willpower, he had studied hard and made sure his brothers did too. He got a scholarship and that took a load off his mother, which was all he wanted to do. Make sure she didn't worry about anything.

His thoughts shifted to their doctor visit and his recommendation that his mother change her eating habits. She needed to minimize her meat intake and bake more than she fried.

"Madu," Rasheed called to the driver. Madu served as his mother's grounds keeper and driver. He had been with her for a while and was very dependable.

"Yes *sah*."

"I've told you to stop calling me, sir."

"*No vex oga* Rasheed."

Rasheed shook his head at the roundabout way Madu had just called him the same thing.

"Where can I find fresh fish in Abuja?" On their way back from the doctor's office, his mother had hinted to getting some fish the next day. Since he was out, he could do it for her and save her a trip.

"Ah yes, my brother's *oga* opened this new Point and Kill fish market. Rich, rich people go there. Smells very nice – you wouldn't know they sell fish there." The excitement in Madu's voice was evident.

Rasheed couldn't reconcile the words, 'fish market' and 'smells nice' in the same sentence.

"If it's near here, let's go."

"It's not too far. But *Oga*, the place can be rowdy, so when we get there, let me go in."

Rasheed nodded. There was no need to reiterate for the umpteenth time that living in London didn't make him fragile or handicapped.

About twenty minutes later, they pulled up to the fish market and if the exterior was anything to go by, Madu was right. It was rowdy.

Madu parked and got out of the car. Despite the warning, curiosity got the better part of Rasheed and he also got out. He wanted to see what this place that Madu had raved about looked like.

Rasheed walked into the well air-conditioned facility and just as he thought, the smell of fish overwhelmed him. The porters wore plastic boots and toted around baskets of the day's catch. There were different kinds of fresh seafood in the glass showcases. Madu showed him the point and kill section. There were people gathered around the glass where the large, live catfish were held. Rasheed watched for a few moments as customers pointed to the fish they wanted and in one swift motion the attendant grabbed the fish and went to the back to kill it. Hence the name, point and kill.

"*Oga* come *dis* side, so you can see well." Madu directed him to a less crowded area.

Rasheed followed and immediately spotted the fish he wanted. He could already envision it swimming in a pot of pepper soup.

"This one," he shouted.

But so did someone else. He turned around to see who the other voice belonged to. Their eyes held for a few moments. It was the mystery lady. She had become a regular visitor in his dreams. She wasn't a mystery since he knew her name and where she worked, but he wanted so much more. He thought the flowers would do that but he never heard from her. He had asked Madu so many times what she had said and his reply was the same every time.

"*Oga*, she didn't give me any message for you."

"*Make una talk now. Who want this fish?*" The attendant's voice interrupted their moment. He was irritated that they were wasting his time.

"I do," Rasheed and Ibiso said in unison.

He walked closer to where she stood. "Hello again."

"Hello to you, too. I would never have imagined seeing you here," Ibiso said.

"*Una no go talk?*" The attendant's voice halted the next thing he was about to say.

"I'll let you have the fish on one condition."

"Let me?" She laughed. "Mr., I pointed at the fish first. I have an important banquet to cook for, so no can do."

"*I go give the fish to anoda pesin oh,*" the attendant shouted.

Rasheed stepped back and stretched out his hand, ushering her forward. He surrendered now, but he wasn't done with Ms. Jaja.

Ibiso smiled and wheeled her cart closer to the attendant. She pointed out two more fish of the same size. Rasheed pointed out his and the attendant took them to the back to prepare.

"Such a gentleman," Ibiso said, as they waited for the attendant to return.

Rasheed detected a hint of sarcasm in her voice, but wasn't bothered. "Did you think I wasn't?"

She shrugged, refusing to meet his eye. "Hmm, I don't know. I barely know you."

"We have to fix that." Rasheed raised his hand to his face and gently stroked his moustache.

"And how do you suppose we do that?"

"Well, since I just let you have *my* fish and you're a caterer..."

"If you want to taste my cooking, you could always come to the restaurant."

"I could, couldn't I? But I was thinking something more personal. Seeing as I sacrificed my fish for you." He lifted his hand to his chest and frowned in feigned pain.

Ibiso broke off her giggle when the attendant came back. He handed them their parcels and they proceeded to the cash register. After they paid, Rasheed walked Ibiso to her car and helped her put her things in the trunk. Satisfied that the trunk was secured, he leaned against the car and crossed his legs at the ankles. The sun hit her from the perfect angle causing her skin to glow. The capris and oversized t-shirt she wore did little to hide the curves that were beneath.

"So?" His eyebrow shot up.

"You're actually going to guilt me into cooking for you?" She wrapped her hands around her waist.

Rasheed shrugged. "You call it guilt. I call it reward for my sacrifice."

"If I say yes, would you let me go? I've got a lot of cooking to do for tomorrow."

"Yes is the magic word."

"Okay, yes. But I'll call you." She pointed to him. "I'm booked this week and next." She handed him her cellphone. He put in his number and dialed, immediately disconnecting when he felt his phone vibrate.

"You do that. I don't want a repeat of the last time," he said.

"What last time?"

"I sent you flowers and my number. But I didn't hear from you. Not even a thank you text." His accusatory tone was playful.

Ibiso chuckled. "I did say thank you... to the man that brought them to me." She stretched out her hand for her phone.

"As for your number, there was no note to say what to do with it, so I trashed it."

Rasheed wanted to defend himself, but hearing her retell it made him sound like a jerk. He handed the phone back to her.

"Ugh...when you put it that way, it sounds terrible." He winced, took her keys from her hand and unlocked the door. When she got in, he leaned over to secure her seat belt. The whiff from her light perfume almost made him lose his balance. Her words challenged him, but her scent weakened him.

"It was."

"How about I make it up to you, by *allowing* you to cook for me." He closed the door.

"You're too much. Too much." She smirked and shook her head. She started the car and she drove away.

Once inside his car, Rasheed pulled out his phone and saved her name and number in his contacts. If she didn't call him, he was going to call her. Either way, they would be seeing each other again pretty soon.

Chapter 7

A week later, Ibiso settled down on the couch in her office with her laptop on her lap. She took the pencil she had lodged in her hair and jotted a note in the notebook beside her. She was making last minute memos on some new variations to her existing recipes. For her new spaghetti sauce, she was going to make the base with vegetables in addition to ground beef. Although she didn't serve breakfast, earlier while commenting on another food blog, she ran across pan fried akara that looked like pancakes. She was going to try those. Replacing the pencil, she took a sip of her fruit punch and continued to scroll down the page.

Every other week on Fridays, she and Amina stayed late and prepared baked goodies as a donation to various less privileged homes. Tonight it was for her favorite center, Hopes & Dreams. It was a boys and girls club that kids went to after school and on the weekends to keep them occupied. Business had been good this week so they didn't have much left over. That meant they would have to bake for a hundred kids from scratch.

The door of her office opened and Amina entered with a worried look on her face. She wiped her hand on her apron.

Ibiso furrowed her brows. "What's up?"

"I'm so sorry to leave you in a bind like this but I have an emergency and need to leave now," Amina said.

Ibiso listened as Amina told her about her son being sick in school. With her husband out of town, she had to go get him.

"Did they say what happened?"

"According to the school, he fell from the swing set this morning and hasn't been himself since then. Now he has a slightly elevated temperature."

"Okay, go. I'll manage. Keep me posted." Ibiso walked toward Amina and hugged her.

When she left, Ibiso began to contemplate what to do. She had given the center her word, so she had to deliver. It was one hour to closing and she couldn't ask the other girls to stay so late on such short notice. She had a little relief in the fact that she had done most of the prep work. All she needed was to develop a strategy to have fifty meat pies and fifty scotch eggs done by 11 a.m. the next day. This required caffeine.

The ringing of her cell phone stopped her stride to the kitchen. She glanced at the name on the screen—Rasheed.

Ibiso ran the days of the week through her mind again. She hadn't called him as promised but she did tell him she would be busy last week and this week. She nodded absently, sure that she wasn't missing something and answered the phone.

"This is Ibiso."

"What's wrong?"

"Huh?"

"You sound different. I'm almost tempted to say worried. What is it?"

Rasheed's smooth baritone settled her nerves. She hadn't meant to sound melancholic but that was her present state.

"I'm sorry. Hey, how are you?"

"Nice try. Are you going to share what's wrong? I might be able to help."

"A little setback, that's all. Nothing I can't handle."

"But you shouldn't handle it alone. So I ask again, what's wrong?"

"You're a bossy one, aren't you?"

"Your stubbornness brings it out of me," He quipped.

Ibiso heard the smile in his voice. She narrated her problem as she headed towards the kitchen.

"I'll help," Rasheed blurted out.

Ibiso rolled her eyes as though he could see her. She didn't need anyone slowing her down. "Err... never mind."

"What? Are you sexist now? Because I'm not a woman, I can't help?"

That wasn't the problem at all. She couldn't be in close proximity to him alone. Both times she had been with him, she had had to will her mind to focus on what he was saying, rather than his rippled muscles and ultra-fine face. She knew she only succeeded in not falling all over herself because of her new relationship with Jesus and the fact that they were around others. So, she and him alone? Bad, bad idea.

"No it's not that. I'm fine really." She began filling the coffee maker with water while the girls locked up.

"Then what is it?" He paused. "Running?"

"I have no idea what you're talking about. I don't want to be rude but I really have to go. I have a lot to do."

"Hold on, Ibiso. You obviously need help. Let me help you. It's not rocket science to roll up some eggs and stuff meat into some dough. I'll be on my best behavior."

His sweetness was tearing down her defenses. Ibiso weighed her options. Cancel on one hundred kids or plead the blood of Jesus and get through some hours of baking and packaging with Rasheed. The second option seemed like the more viable one. She could do this.

"Okay, meet me in my bistro in two hours."

"A'ight mate. See you soon," he said in his best British drawl and disconnected the call.

She leaned against the counter. This would be the first time she'd be in close company of a man since her ex. With her focus on her business alone, it shouldn't mean anything but Rasheed wasn't just any other man. The mere thought of him made her stomach clench and electricity pass through her. She questioned how she could be attracted to a man she didn't even know.

53

Give me clarity Lord. Order my steps and instill your wisdom in me. She took in a breath as she meditated on the James 1:5 verse, trying to restore sanity in her head. If she veered down this road this early, she knew she'd be in trouble.

***

One of the sales girls let Rasheed into the restaurant on her way out. The minute he entered Bisso Bites, he was bombarded with a barrage of aromas. The whiff of flour, eggs and butter transported him to a happier time. His heart enlarged with joy. He remembered how his mother used to bake cupcakes every Saturday morning. He and his brothers would take turns licking the spoon.

He was dressed in lounging slacks and a t- shirt. If he was going to be around flour, he didn't want his clothes to be covered in it.

He looked around the place. There was a food bar toward the far corner which was protected by a glass barrier. At the end of the bar was the cash register and to the right of that a soda machine. There were speakers placed at the four corners of the bistro. When he entered, the music had changed from gospel to rhythm and blues. The décor had a casual feel to it with its red, black and white theme. Considering the location and setting, he concluded that she served mainly expatriates and returnees who were used to light meals. The tables were covered in red and white checkered cloths. In the middle of each table was a slender vase that held a single fresh flower.

"Rasheed, is that you?" Ibiso called out.

"Yeah, it's me."

"I'm in the back, please lock the door and turn the sign to 'Closed'," Ibiso called out.

He did as she requested. "You're putting me to work already."

"Hey, you offered and you're half an hour late."

"Stubborn and bossy." Rasheed walked toward the sound of her voice.

He was late and had his brothers to blame. Just as he was about to leave, Jabir and Kamal picked that time to inquire about his decision concerning the will. To be honest, he hadn't made one. He hadn't given it much thought. His mind had been occupied with Ibiso since they last met. For him, it was strange ignoring his troubles – the responsibility that plagued him and the pressure to step into his father's shoes.

He still had some time to make a decision. His mother's pleas rang through his mind and he tried to shake them off with no success. This had been the story of his life—carrying the weight of his family on his shoulders and neglecting his own. He wanted to start his own consulting company, not run a group of companies. Once again, he found himself tilting towards fulfilling the family's needs.

He walked into the huge industrial kitchen. At first he couldn't find Ibiso, but then he followed the noise coming from the pantry. He walked in and saw her on a step stool reaching for something on the top shelves. He knew he should help her out but his eyes needed to admire the view in front of him.

She stood on her tip toes, stretching out her well-shaped, toned legs. Her stance hiked up her shirt and bared her mid riff. Rasheed felt a surge of desire. He had been so busy with work in the last few years that he didn't have time to enjoy the company of a woman. If memory served him correctly, he hadn't been intimate in a year. After the first couple of dates the women always wanted more. With the way things had ended with Ebele, he didn't want to risk hurting any other woman, so he just focused on work.

But nevertheless, his reaction to Ibiso couldn't be normal. From the first day they bumped into each other, he couldn't get her out of his mind. If they hadn't crossed paths in the fish market, he would have made his way to her soon.

He cleared his throat to alert her of his presence but it turned out to be a bad idea. The sound startled her and she lost her balance. But before she hit the floor he caught her. They held the embrace for some moments. He was able to look into her eyes and noticed the color wasn't brown as he thought before but dark hazel. Their bodies were so close that a sensuous shiver raced through him. She jerked herself from his grasp.

Ibiso nervously adjusted her denim shirt, and ran her hand

over her hair. Rasheed could only guess she must have felt the heat, too.

"I didn't hear you come in here." She hurried out of the pantry and he followed.

"My bad." He rubbed his palms together. "So what are we doing?" Rasheed knew that she was already very uncomfortable and he didn't want to increase the tension.

It took all the will-power he had not to think about the dark chocolate smoothness of the exposed skin he caught a glimpse of earlier. If he was going to get to know her better, he had to make her feel comfortable around him. He snickered at the cockiness of his thoughts. Of course he was going to get to know her. There was an attraction between them that he wanted to explore. But he was going to let her know up front—he didn't do the love thing. He had seen the damage that reckless emotion could cause. His work came first. Always.

"Here." Ibiso tossed an apron to him. "Wash your hands and start peeling the eggs."

He hung the apron on his neck and secured the sash behind. Then he turned and looked at the extra-large bowl she pointed to.

"All this?" There must have been about fifty eggs in there.

She looked up from the dough she was kneading and laughed at the surprised look on his face. "Yes, silly. I'll help. But first I have to knead this and allow it to rise."

Over the next three hours, they worked in light chatter. Their conversation centered on topics like politics, the weather, and the pros and cons of living abroad versus Nigeria.

Ibiso rolled and stuffed the meat pies while Rasheed worked on the eggs that were wrapped in sausage, coated with bread crumbs, and fried.

He loved the feel of her body next to his when she came over to teach him exactly how to coat the eggs and show him how long they should remain in the fryer. She was a patient teacher considering she was on a tight schedule. Rasheed observed as she carried herself with grace and poise when other women he knew would have been freaking out.

While the last batch of meat pies began baking, Ibiso escorted him to her office at the back. It was small and simple, but looked quite cozy. It contained a cherry desk just large enough for a laptop and some writing supplies. The red and white colors from the restaurant were carried on in here as well.

"Have a seat." She pointed him to the crème colored sofa in the corner of the office.

Rasheed was about to walk to the direction of her finger when he noticed the picture of her and a man on her desk. He moved closer to pick it up. His jaw set.

I assumed she wasn't seeing anybody. She wouldn't have agreed to dinner otherwise.

He must have stared at the picture too long because she looked up from her purse and saw him.

"Are you okay?"

He replaced the photo and walked to the sofa and slumped down. "Yes." Even to his ears his response was lackluster. She looked at the photo and looked at him again.

"Who is that?" he asked.

"My brother, why?"

"Nothing," he replied. The tightness in his chest eased. What was wrong with him? He had no claim over this woman, so why would he be feeling this type of emotion seeing her with someone else? Rasheed hoped she didn't notice his reaction, but the minute she walked over and stood next to him, he knew she did.

"Is that green I see?"

"What are you talking about?

"Don't tell me you're jealous, because you don't even know me. We've met like what—two times?"

He drew her down to sit beside him. "And yet you agreed to my offer to bake with you late into the night. It's almost 11 p.m.

"And…"

"If you're going to be like that, then fine. We'll revisit this discussion later. Trust me."

"You're just like Sodienye. Always thinking he can push me around and get his way."

"Your brother?"

"Yes. I'm yet to figure out whether it's a man thing or a big brother thing."

"I *do not* want to be your brother, but I always get what I want." He paused, making sure she had no doubt about his mission. "Tell me about Sodienye."

Over the next couple of minutes, Ibiso told him about her family and what led her to this point in her life. He did, however, get this feeling she was leaving a huge chunk of information out. She never mentioned a man. Past or Present. Rasheed could tell that it wasn't easy for her to talk about, although he was happy she could be vulnerable with him.

From her talking about her family, he realized the absence of a father affected them both, but in very different ways. He also found himself relating to Sodienye, a man he had never met. He understood the feeling of responsibility for a sibling when you're still a child yourself. The difference was that unlike Ibiso's dad, his father had of his own free will walked out on them.

There was a long silence between them. Talking about her dad caused her to visibly tremble. He drew her close and wrapped his arms around her.

"A penny for your thoughts," Rasheed said.

"They're worth much more than that." She smiled at him. "But my immediate thought is sleeping. I'm so tired."

The timer in the kitchen went off and she stood. He stood with her.

"No you sit here, Let me get you something cold to drink."

Rasheed could tell that in instant she had laid her burdens down on him, something had changed. Ibiso had changed from the confident, sassy woman he was talking to some minutes ago to this shy, reserved person before him.

"Ibiso, look at me," he said. Yet she refused to make eye contact. He used his index finger to lift her head. She raised her eyes to him.

"Please don't do this. Don't go into the shell I see you retreating into. Don't tell me to explain it, but I like you. I'm glad you shared your family story with me. Someday I'll share mine."

She smiled. It wasn't a full smile but Rasheed figured it was all he was going to get tonight.

"I didn't mean to offload all my family drama on you. I honestly thought that I was over trying to gain the acceptance of my brother. She wiped her eyes. "I'm sorry for letting go like that. You must think I have a lot of baggage."

"We all have baggage and it's okay. We are friends right? Friends share their burdens."

The timer went off a second time and she scurried from the room. Rasheed ran his hand over his face. He had no idea what this feeling inside of him was. He hadn't experienced it before.

It's just an attraction. Yes, that's what it was, an attraction. Only an attraction could happen that fast. Whatever it was, he needed to get a grip because it was throwing a monkey wrench in his plans.

He was in Nigeria for one purpose—to attend the will reading. He never expected to even have an iota of doubt about that plan. But his family and now Ibiso had derailed that agenda. He couldn't possibly go back to London now without establishing what this was. He had a little over eight days to make a decision and he planned to spend as much of it with her. He had to find out where this was going.

Chapter 8

Ibiso was too wired to sleep. Despite not getting to bed until 2 a.m., she was up earlier than usual. It was sanitation Saturday—a day mandated by the government that all citizens clean their environs for a couple of hours—so she knew the center wouldn't open till noon. Her plan was to get there by 11 a.m., drop off the snacks, and head back home to get some rest.

She sat up in her bed and turned on the side lamp. She opened up her iPad and looked for the YouVersion Bible app. Although she preferred using her Bible for devotion so she could mark through it, she didn't feel like getting out of bed just yet.

She scrolled through her reading plan. Isaiah 40 vs. 28 and 29 *Do you not know? Have you not heard? The Lord is the everlasting God, the Creator of the ends of the earth. He will not grow tired or weary, and his understanding no one can fathom. He gives strength to the weary and increases the power of the weak.*

Ibiso read the verses a couple more times. She wasn't sure of what God wanted her to learn from this verse. Then she read verse 29 again, *He gives strength to the weary and increases the power of the weak.* She began to reflect on the state of her life. She was so grateful to God for how far she had come. It hadn't been easy, but by His grace.

The Lord indeed increased the power of the weary because three years ago she was at a loss for how or where to start picking up the pieces of her life. After she had begun to depend on Him for everything, and trust more, her life began to change. Her life wasn't stress free but she had rest knowing that Jesus was by her side.

Those thoughts led to visions of Rasheed. She couldn't figure out how they got to where they were. They seemed to have crossed the friendship line the day before, but there was still a lot she didn't know about him. She didn't want to make another mistake, no matter the physical attraction that existed between them.

"Dear Father in heaven, thank you for the dawning of a new day. Thank you for sending a helper to me yesterday. But while we are on this helper thing, I know without a doubt that there is a reason Rasheed and I crossed paths. Please reveal it to me. Lead me so I do not go astray. Let me be the vessel of whatever message You have for him. Please bless his family and mine. Also You know I'm still down with this rent matter. Please increase my territory so I can make up the balance. In you dear Lord, I place my trust. And thank you for answered prayers. In Jesus' name, amen."

Ibiso closed her iPad and lay still in bed trying to hear the voice of God. Boma had taught her that in walking with God, prayer was a two-way street. You talked, He talked. After a couple of minutes, she drifted back to sleep. She hadn't heard from God, but she was at peace.

Ibiso woke up to the buzzing of her phone. It was her voicemail. She fumbled for it on the night stand. It was 10 a.m and the missed call was from her mother. She flung the cover off her. She couldn't believe she had slept an additional three hours. She remembered the verse that says the Lord does give his people sound sleep and after talking to Him a couple of hours ago, she was at peace.

Ibiso contemplated calling her mother back, but didn't know if she had to energy to deal with her this morning. They had a cordial relationship, but she always sided with Sodienye on everything. Then she heard the whisper, *I will give strength to the weary.* She dialed her mother back. After a couple of rings, her mother answered the phone. Ibiso inhaled and exhaled quietly.

"Good morning, mother." Ibiso walked to her closet to bring out what to wear.

"Ibiso good morning, oh," her mother said.

With the drawn out "oh" at the end of her mother's greeting, Ibiso braced herself for what lay ahead.

"So if I don't call you, you can't call to check on your mother?"

"I called you two weeks ago."

"Does that sound good in your ear? You aren't living abroad. We're in the same Nigeria and I only get to hear from you once in a couple of weeks. Your brother was—"

"Mother, it's too early for the Sodienye 101 lecture. I don't need a reminder of how I let you both down."

"Ibiso, your brother and I only want what is best for you. And you're not a failure. It's just that you make your life too hard when it can be simple."

"And how is that?"

"Well, for starters if you hadn't run off with that man, by now—"

"What's done is done. If God can forgive me, and you and Sodienye can't, then I can't kill myself about that now can I?"

There was a long pause.

"You're my only daughter. All I want for you is happiness."

Ibiso rolled her eyes. She wanted to reply but decided against it. Silence would ensure her mom wrapped this talk up right away.

"When are you coming home?" her mother asked. Like most parents, Ibiso knew that her mother would never acknowledge her hurt nor say she was sorry, but asking her to come home was her roundabout way of saying I miss you and want to see you.

"I'll come for Boma's twins' christening in a couple of months. Did you know she made me godmother?"

"Yes, she told me. I'm glad to know you're okay and despite what you think, I love you and I know your brother does, too."

They chatted a little bit more, then said their good-byes and hung up. Ibiso needed a little pick me up. This call was not going to ruin her day. No more tears. She turned on her radio and the cool beats of Mary Mary's *Shackles* filled the room. The song was so appropriate now. She needed the shackles to come off. Ibiso danced around the room as she made the bed and laid out her clothes. She decided on blue skinny jeans and a denim shirt with her flat strap sandals to finish off the look.

A few minutes later Ibiso was out of the shower and dressed. She was about to put on her make-up when her phone rang again. This time she knew it was Boma because of the distinctive ring tone she had assigned her best friend. She put the phone on speaker and placed it on the dresser and proceeded to apply her eyeliner.

"Hey B, what's up?"

"How now?"

"*I dey...*"

"No time to waste. I know you're getting ready to go to the center, so fast, how did it go last night?"

"We baked, he went to his house, and I went to mine."

"You're joking right? If you don't want me to reach through this phone and strangle the gist out of you, better stop playing. So..."

Ibiso laughed. They had been best friends since nursery school and it still amazed her that through the disagreements and distance, they were still close. Closer than most sisters and Ibiso was grateful for it. "What do you want to know?"

"Soso, you're playing with me? You know my time will come. You can't tell me that you guys just baked and that was it. Girl, please...," Boma said.

Ibiso used her hand to muffle her giggle. Boma always retaliated, so she couldn't let her know she was stalling on purpose.

She went on to give her friend a blow-by-blow replay of the previous evening with Rasheed.

"So? After the timer went off, what happened?"

"Nothing. It was kinda awkward after that. We packed up the stuff and left." A beat of silence passed between them, then Ibiso grinned. "He insisted on driving behind me until I got home, and then promised to come help me out this morning."

"Awww, that is so sweet."

"Yeah, he was sweet..." Ibiso's thoughts travelled back to his displays of chivalry. He opened doors for her, insisted on carrying out everything, and mostly how he listened to her.

"*Kai*! I'm so happy for you. But before we go any further, I have to ask is he a Christian?"

"Yes..." Ibiso contemplated. She really didn't know. He hadn't talked about his family. Danjuma was Muslim, but the day she ran into him, his mother had a cross around her neck.

"Okay, good. Not trying to sound like Mother Jessica, but you know it's really important."

Ibiso laughed at the inference to one of the ushers of the church they had grown up in. People always joked that with the way she carried herself and scared the living daylights out of them with stories of hell in Sunday school, she was probably next to Jesus in lineage.

"But he's so guarded. I get the sense he has a lot of things to work out."

"Don't we all? If your heart is leaning towards him, take a chance. Just don't take on a crusade to be his savior. Only God can do that. Through your walk in Christ, you'll break through any barriers or resistances that are there."

Ibiso looked at her wristwatch. She loved how Boma helped her with clarity. However if she didn't hurry, she'd be late. "I love you, B, but I gotta go."

"Love you, too. Dokubo and I are going to the golf course today. He needs to schmooze some new clients. After the center, what are your plans?"

"Nothing – straight home to sleep."

"Alright, text me a picture of our guy."

"I don't have a picture." *Our guy? He isn't my or our guy, but no need to argue with Boma once she gets an idea in her mind.*

"Then get one. I need to see whom I'm praying for. And also who I'll come after if he makes one wrong move..." Boma let the remainder of her sentence trail off.

"You're something else."

"And you love me for it."

"Bye."

Ibiso picked up her purse and made her way to the kitchen to brew some tea. The yawn she had been trying hard to suppress escaped. With any luck, she'd be home in three hours max. If she didn't rest, she was going to be sick. Her heart skipped a beat as the anticipation of seeing Rasheed grew. She just hoped he'd make it. When he got home, he had sent her a text and it was almost three in the morning.

Strength Lord, strength, I can't mess up this time around.

***

Later that morning, Ibiso had taken the last items out of her truck. She was set up in the center's kitchen as normal. The kitchen contained only the barest of essentials. In the months she had been coming here, she had noticed there wasn't any cooking being done, although there was an industrial cooker.

The kids were occupied with various activities and would soon be out for their snacks. After that, all she had to do was clean up and be on her way. She loved volunteering here but today, she felt the aches and pains from sleep deprivation.

She put on the oven mittens she always brought with her, then bent over to check the batch of meat pies she had heating in the oven.

"*Kyau*, I see you're already hard at work."

Ibiso heard the voice that had now invaded her thoughts whether she was awake or asleep. She carefully closed the oven door and turned around.

"You made it. Erm...what did you call me?" She placed one hand on her hip and the other on the table. This chocolate decadence that stood in front of her was too lethal to be left roaming the streets. He looked tired, but flashed a smile that almost made her lose her balance.

"I told you I'd be here to help you. *Kyau* is Hausa for beautiful." He walked forward and kissed her cheek.

Ibiso was ashamed to say it, but even though she had lived in Abuja for two years now, she never picked up the Hausa language. Except the common phrases like *"sannu"* and *"na gode"* which meant "hello" and "thank you."

"You didn't have to. I'm almost done. Besides I'm sure you have other things to attend to." She began laying out the napkins and disposable cups.

"Do you always refuse help or just my help? The right thing to do is say thank you," he said. "However, I didn't just come for you. I had to handle some other business here. I'll tell you about it later."

"And here I was thinking I was important."

Rasheed chuckled and joined her in setting out the disposables. After a few moments he said, "You are, but if I told you, you'd just object again." He winked.

She was distracted by the noise coming from the common area. The kids must have been let out and were gathering for lunch. For the next hour, Rasheed helped her serve the snacks to the kids with fruit cups she had bought on her way over, accompanied with a choice of juice or water.

Soon after, everyone was fed and assembled back for the last activities before the center closed. Ibiso watched in admiration as Rasheed helped her tidy up and put things back into her truck. His behavior was so uncharacteristic of someone who came from money. He was so down to earth. At the fish market, her restaurant and here today, he was really handy. She was sure that since he and his brothers never lived in Nigeria, their father must have ensured they had servants to their left, right and center. But there was something about him. He was so unlike any of the rich men she had met.

Rasheed closed the trunk of her car and walked around to the driver's door. She had the door opened but hadn't gotten in yet. He opened it wider and trapped her in between the car door and his body.

"Thank you so much. I'm indebted to you for helping me out last night and today," Ibiso said. She had put on her sunglasses in an attempt to avoid direct eye contact.

"Be careful lady, you already owe me for the fish. Now this. It's soon gonna be time to collect." He moved closer.

If this man comes any closer, he'd hear my heart beating at twice the normal rate.

Even with all the people around them and how busy they had been earlier, she couldn't deny the effect his presence had on her. He looked suave in his casual, caramel colored kaftan over blue jeans with leather slippers.

"I know how you can thank me..." He removed her sunglasses from her face and slid them on top of her head. He caressed her cheek with the back of his hand. "Let's start with breakfast tomorrow morning, then you show me the sights of Abuja."

"No, buddy. Tomorrow is Sunday. The only place you'll find me in the morning is church." She put her glasses back over her eyes and patted his face. "So if you wanna hang out, that's where I'll be."

Rasheed hesitated. "Are you sure I can't change your mind?"

"Nope." She got into the car and started the engine. "I'll call you some time to pay my debt. Thanks for everything."

Ibiso didn't want to push him to come with her, but she wasn't going to compromise on that part of her life either. More than a good looking man, she wanted a God fearing one.

Chapter 9

Church. Rasheed couldn't remember the last time he had entered a church. He wasn't keen about a God that stood by and let bad things happen to people that served Him. He couldn't remember how many times he had heard his mother pray about their situation when they were growing up. Times were really hard on them, before his maternal grandfather decided he had punished his daughter enough and began to send them money to supplement his mother's income.

His mother had dragged him and his brothers to church when they were younger, but as he grew older he decided to walk his own path. Nowhere along that path was a church. Rasheed decided he would create his own destiny through hard work and determination. His thoughts revisited the events of the past weeks. A lot had happened – the will reading, the talk with his mom, and the pressure that followed.

That was all until he ran into Ibiso at the fish market. She, through no knowledge of her own, had calmed his troubled mind. Her beauty was unlike any other he had known. Her smooth skin, her flirty haircut that shaped her oval face, and those eyes – those unforgettable eyes that haunted him day and night.

Ibiso was kind, compassionate, and sassy. The previous day, she had transformed from the no-nonsense businesswoman to a compassionate down-to-earth person that helped the kids. Her ability to put her own need for rest on the backburner until she had fulfilled her obligation was so admirable. It fueled his desire to want to know her more.

He was on a tight deadline to make a decision about the Danjuma Group, so time was of the essence. If he decided to return to London, he wanted to get things solidified between them. That thought brought him full circle to his current dilemma.

Church. If he didn't go to church, there was no telling when he'd see her again. The church invitation might be a test. Since that was where she was going to be and he wanted to spend time with her, that's where he needed to be.

Rasheed rifled through the bedside dresser 'til he found his cell phone. He checked the time and it was exactly two hours before her church started. Before he could change his mind, he typed a text asking her for the location of the church. Within minutes, she responded along with a smiley face. He swung his legs over the edge of the bed.

The things I do for the company of an intriguing woman.

An hour later, dressed in his native pink and white embroidered *gbamu* that stopped at his knees, matching white pants and slick black Moccasins, Rasheed knew what to expect as he made his way into the living room. It was a little bit after 9 a.m. His mother was should be back from early morning mass while his brothers would be lounged out in front of the television watching soccer.

His mother lifted her eyes from the tray of beans balanced on her lap when he entered the room. She was picking out the tiny stones that could sometimes get missed by the farmers. Rasheed's stomach leaped for joy because that meant she was going to cook some *moi moi*, a moist bean cake that went so well with any kind of rice. She smiled but said nothing when she saw him. Jabir, who was stretched out on the sofa, was the first to speak.

"O boy, where are you going?"

Before Rasheed could respond, Kamal asked, "Stone Cold, you're decked up to the tilt. Did somebody die?"

"I've told you to stop calling me that." Rasheed warned. He turned to the dining table to look for the keys.

"Leave your brother alone," his mother said. "*Nna* you look handsome, but I'm curious just like your brothers. Where are you going?"

"*Haba*, is today not Sunday? Mama didn't you go to church? I'm going to church."

69

His brothers busted out in mocking laughter that made Rasheed's temper rise.

"Since when? Okay, who is she and where did you meet her?" Jabir asked. "How can you be slicker than me in your old age? We just got to Abuja three weeks ago and already some chick has gotten to you."

Rasheed remained silent.

"Hold on, let me do this investigation." Kamal brought his recliner to an upright position. "Okay, yesterday and the day before, he was gone all day. Then he came back smelling like a bakery." He paused and Jabir nodded.

"Food...food. Who could it be?" Jabir rubbed his chin in contemplation.

"*Ejima*, leave your brother alone," his mother said. She called Jabir and Kamal *ejima*, which meant twins in her native language, Igbo, when she wanted to sound serious. Normally it would have worked, but this time it didn't. His brothers spent the next couple of minutes coming up with different guesses on who could be luring him to church.

Rasheed looked at the time. He needed to get a move on it.

"Alright, you guys should keep guessing." Rasheed walked over and kissed his mother on her cheek. "I'll see you all later."

Rasheed walked out of the door, but not before he heard Kamal yell, "Let's not hear on the news that this church burnt down or collapsed once you entered it." His brother's laughter got on his nerves, but he couldn't blame them. He wondered if God would even recognize him because he hadn't been to church in years. But then again, it wasn't his fault. God knew the reason – it was His fault.

***

Rasheed had underestimated Garki traffic on a Sunday. He didn't like dealing with the hassle of driving in Abuja, but Madu, their driver, always had the weekends off when he and the twins visited. Besides Rasheed knew that unlike the church he grew up in, this one might last more than three hours. He had been raised

Catholic but over the years had also attended Pentecostal churches on invitations from his friends, so he wasn't a total novice on how they conducted service.

He pulled into the parking lot of Overcomers Chapel with just a few minutes to spare before the beginning of the service. He spotted Ibiso waiting outside the chapel for him. She hadn't seen him yet so he had the pleasure of getting lost in her beauty. She had on a green and black *Ankara* dress with a matching thin, red belt that made her waist look small. She was stunning. Rasheed willed his heart rate to slow down. This reaction was not normal for him. He knew he needed to slow things down, but his body and mind hadn't gotten that memo.

Ibiso saw him and waved. She then began to walk toward him. When she got to him, he kissed her on the cheek, a move he could tell she was uncomfortable with.

Well she's just gonna have to get used to it.

"You're late."

"My brothers. Long story, but I'm here now. I should get points for that."

"Let's see how well you behave."

He smiled down at her. "You look stunning by the way."

"Thank you. I'm glad I decided to dress up with you looking like you just fell out of *GQ*. I love the traditional attire by the way. Looks dapper on you."

He wasn't sure his chuckle disguised the reaction of his body to the way she looked at him.

"Let's go." She led him inside.

The church was medium-sized. The burgundy and crème walls gave the space a warm feel. There were potted plants by every corner, and on top of the podium.

The choir was singing praises in native languages. Everyone seemed happy as they swayed to the beat. Ibiso led him to a pew in the middle of the church. They eased in amidst glaring eyes. Once she was satisfied that he was settled in, Ibiso stood and started

71

clapping and moving her feet to the beat. Rasheed, not wanting to look like the oddball, stood and clapped along.

Moments later, after a couple of announcements, they were all seated. A man stepped up to the podium.

Ibiso whispered in his ear, "Did you bring a Bible? If not, we can share mine."

The pastor greeted the congregation and told them to turn in their Bibles to Romans chapter 12. "Today I want us to revisit Christian living. The whole chapter tells us of the things we are to do in order to live the life that is pleasing to God. In particular, I'll like to draw our attention to verse 2. It admonishes us not to be conformed to the things of this world. We are to be the example. By the way you represent Christ on earth, people would want to know what He is all about. You can quote scripture all day long, but to win souls you have to be about action. To effectively do this, we have to allow God to transform us inwardly. Only then will you be able to do His will and what is pleasing and good."

The pastor took a sip of water from the bottle placed next to him. He paused and looked out into the congregation, then continued. "Create in us a new heart Lord. You have to surrender to Him for this transformation to take place. Let go of the need to have our way. In tribulations, remain steadfast in prayer, enduring with hope and walking in love. Then watch the God you serve fight your battles."

The pastor continued for a couple more minutes with the congregation responding with shouts of praise and applause.

Rasheed looked over at Ibiso. She had her head bowed in prayer. He looked around. People were actually buying this stuff. That was all well and good for them, but he wasn't biting. He had memorized this "fight your battle" line. His mother had hammered it into his ear so many times in the last decade. But where was God when it was time to fight her own battles? Where was He on those days that she was too depressed to even get up and take care of him and his brothers? The responsibility fell on Rasheed to feed them, so he had to make sandwiches and do things that an eleven year-old boy shouldn't have to. Where was this God when his mother prayed for his dad to come back morning and night?

Granted, he had provided for her generously in his will, but that couldn't make up for his absence all those years ago.

Rasheed was forced out of his reverie when Ibiso nudged his shoulders. It was time for prayer and offering. Rasheed realized he had been so lost in his thoughts that he didn't realize the pastor had finished preaching. He followed the motions as they danced out to put their offering in the baskets. Once everyone was done, they gave a couple more announcements and the benediction. Rasheed looked at the time. Three hours had passed.

This better be worth it. He stood to the side as Ibiso greeted a couple of members. Soon after, they left the sanctuary.

"Did you enjoy the service?"

"It was okay..."

"Just okay?"

"What more can I say?"

"Well you came. That's a first step. The rest can be worked out because I see some heathen spirits lingering around you." She laughed.

That sound was like music to his ears. "So, are you going to keep your end of the bargain?"

"What bargain?"

"To show me around..."

"I agreed to no such thing." She smiled. "Besides, this stomach needs to eat. So if you agree to feed me, then maybe we can talk about me being your sight-seeing escort."

"Woman, you already owe me a cooked meal."

"And I'll deliver. Just not today. However, if you're feeding me, then I'm all yours."

He raised his brows and she hid her eyes.

"That didn't come out right."

"Okay, deal. Come on, I have the perfect place in mind." He grabbed her hand and headed towards his car. "Will your car be safe here? We'll come back for it later."

She nodded. "Where are we going?"

He unlocked his car. "Trust me." He caressed her cheek with the back of his hand. She rushed into the car.

He whispered in her ear, "*Kyau*, why do you run from me?"

She remained silent. He wasn't expecting an answer but wanted her to know he was aware of how she lowered her eyes or shrank away from him when he came close. She was cautious at first, he understood, but after the last two days, he felt they should be farther along.

His initial thought was a restaurant he heard just opened in the city. But once they hit the highway, Rasheed headed towards his house. Why? He couldn't explain, especially since he knew that his brothers would have a field day with teasing him. But there was something about Ibiso that made him act irrational.

Chapter 10

It didn't take long for Ibiso to realize they weren't going to a restaurant but the Danjuma home. They pulled into the gated house. Ibiso had never seen anything so large.

These rich people know how to waste money, sha. *How can just one woman live in this type of mansion?* Her family was not poor, but their house would be a hut compared to this. The brown and white, three-story house was surrounded by a perfectly manicured lawn and well maintained garden. Rasheed parked under the covered parking and walked around to help her out.

"We're at your house," she said leaning against the door of the car.

"Beauty, as well as brains."

"Very funny. I'm serious. You didn't tell me we were coming here. I don't want to intrude."

He placed his hand at the small of her back, nudging her forward, "It'll be fine. Don't tell me you're shy. I happen to know for a fact that isn't true. My family won't bite." His eyes reassured her.

She hesitated. He stretched out his hand. She took it and he led her towards the house. Ibiso's breath caught at the magnificence of the foyer. She wondered what the rest of the house looked like. The walls were decorated with expensive African art as well as a black and white picture of his mom. She was seated with Rasheed and his brothers standing behind her. She wondered why his father wasn't in the picture.

Rasheed didn't let her hand go as he led her down the hallway into the formal living room. The space was so well put together, just like those model living rooms in magazines. From the gleaming wood floors covered in Persian throw rugs to the gold and black curtains that hung on the tall ceiling windows, everything looked so luxurious. The furnishings were sleek and modern. It didn't feel like anyone lived there. He dropped his keys and escorted her to the family room.

Rasheed squeezed her hand as they made their entrance. Ibiso relaxed a little. This room was more like what she was used to. She smiled nervously as the twins' attention shifted from the television to her. She had met them once before, but no formal introductions were made. Their shorts and t-shirts were a huge contrast to the suits they had on when she first met them.

"I knew it! I knew it!" the brother who tried the pickup line on her that day said.

Ibiso looked to Rasheed for an explanation.

"Jabir, shut it. Don't pay him any attention," Rasheed said to her.

The other twin turned around. With his sunshades off, she recognized him immediately. He was *the* Kammy Danjuma who was just transferred from his soccer league in Spain to the Lions League in the United States.

Both brothers walked over to her as Rasheed made the introductions. "Jabir, Kamal this is Ibiso Jaja. Ibiso, these are my brothers."

"Nice to meet you." They said in unison.

"Likewise." She paused and nudged Rasheed with her elbow.

"What?"

"You didn't tell me that Kamal is *the* Kammy Danjuma."

He grunted.

"My chosen career is not something he brags about," Kamal said.

Something about the way he said it made Ibiso's heart sink. She knew what it felt like to have a big brother who believed they knew what was better for you than you knew for yourself.

The side eye she gave Rasheed was met with a shrug.

"Someone is in trouble," Jabir said noticing the exchange between her and his older brother.

"Behave like gentlemen." Rasheed ordered his brothers. "Let me go get mama."

"Aren't we always?" Kamal said.

Rasheed turned to leave, then paused and picked up a throw pillow which he flung in Kamal's direction.

The twins offered her a seat and tried to catch her up on the game on television. She was half listening as her mind wandered about the story behind these three brothers. The twins' resemblance to each other was uncanny, but she caught on soon enough how very different they were.

She could tell they were surprised that she knew so much about soccer. She had Sodienye to thank for that. Those were the good old days – the days when they were inseparable. She willed her mind from the place of sadness it was trying to enter.

A couple of minutes later, Rasheed re-emerged with his mother. Now that Ibiso was calmer, unlike when they first met, she noticed the woman's striking beauty. The older woman who Ibiso figured was about 5 feet, 4 inches had low black hair that contained patches of gray. She smiled at Ibiso, displaying her high dimples. As the older woman came closer, Ibiso noticed her unblemished, dark chocolate skin. Dressed in a stylish yellow and purple print Ankara *boubou*, she waded barefoot through the plush carpet. Ibiso stood and waited for them to approach her.

"Good afternoon, ma." Ibiso bowed her head slightly.

When she looked up, she gave Rasheed an I'm-going-to-kill-you look. He got the message because he winked at her. There was a lot of mental preparation that had to be done when being introduced to a man's family, even if it was just as friends. She had been robbed of that preparation.

"Good afternoon, my daughter. How are you?" Mrs. Danjuma patted her on her back and sat in the recliner in the corner of the room.

Ibiso could tell the chair was reserved for her. Its

surroundings mirrored her mother's chair back home. There was a small stool to one side of the chair which held prayer books and a Bible.

"Fine, Ma." Ibiso hoped the nervousness in her voice wasn't obvious.

They all chatted for a while in the living room. Rasheed's mother asked her the normal things parents did. Like where she was from, about her parents and what she did for a living. Then the conversation shifted to more general topics like the top news stories, politics and sports.

Half an hour later, the kitchen staff announced lunch. They all made their way to the dining table. Rasheed and his mother sat at both ends of the table while she and the twins sat on either side of them. Conversation was light, but dwindled when everyone concentrated on the fried rice, moi-moi, plantains and goat meat.

Ibiso got to see a different Rasheed. The interaction with his brothers bordered between big brotherly and fatherly. He was extra attentive towards his mother without letting Ibiso feel left out. He sent glances her way very often while squeezing her hand with his free hand. At a point, she tried to remove her hand but the warning in his eyes was loud and clear.

The doorbell broke their conversation.

"Nkechi, Nkechi," Rasheed's mother called out. The woman who just served lunch appeared after the second call.

"Yes, madam."

"Please, see who's at the door," Mrs. Danjuma instructed.

Ibiso was constantly amazed at the matriarch of the Danjuma household. Her kind and polite nature was not a common trait among people of her monetary status.

"You mean you got my brother to bake?" Jabir asked, continuing the conversation. They were all having so much fun hearing of Rasheed's escapade in the kitchen.

"Yes. He was hilarious at first, but caught on pretty quickly." Ibiso turned her attention to Rasheed. She could tell that his ear was tuned to the slight noises coming from the front door.

"Well, I guess a man would do anything for a woman he likes," Kamal said.

Rasheed grunted and they all laughed.

Their laughter was short lived when Nkechi returned with a somber look on her face. "Madam, it's those people that came the other day."

"What people?" Rasheed asked. He stood and placed his napkin in his chair. He headed towards the door when the visitors, who apparently had gotten tired of waiting, let themselves in.

There, in the middle of the living room stood two very beautiful women. Their facial features resembled that of Fulani women—high cheekbones and pointed noses. The part of their body that was visible despite their hijab showed their fair complexion. The hair on their head wasn't completely covered so Ibiso could see their flowing auburn colored manes underneath. The women were exact replicas of each other, except it was clear that one was the mother and the other the daughter. At a closer glance, Ibiso recognized the older woman as *the* Mrs. Danjuma she had seen in the papers.

"What the heck are you doing here?" Rasheed barked.

Ibiso forced herself not to stare. A puzzled look took over her face as the man she had become fond of transformed into someone else right before her eyes.

What have I gotten myself in the middle of?

Chapter 11

Rasheed's mother took her time in getting up. He saw the look she gave him and knew that she was angry at his outburst. Right now, he couldn't care less. He would pacify his mother later, but first he wanted to know what these people were doing here.

"I ask again what are..."

"Rasheed, that's enough." His mother stepped down the step that elevated the dining area. She walked toward the visitors.

Rasheed shoved his hands in his pockets. His jaw set in anger but he remained quiet in respect of his mother. He stood by as Halima—his half-sister and his father's other wife greeted his mother.

"Hello Aisha, what are you doing here?" his mother asked calmly.

"I didn't mean to intrude, but I need to talk to you and Rasheed," Aisha said.

"Nkechi, please get us drinks. We'll be in the other living room," Rasheed's mother instructed. She ushered the ladies out of the dining room.

"Bro, don't allow these people to make you so angry." Kamal dug into his second helping of moi-moi.

"I agree. Besides you're scaring our guest," Jabir nodded in Ibiso's direction.

Rasheed opened his mouth to speak when his focus shifted to his mother who walked back into the room.

"I hope you've found your manners?" she asked him.

Rasheed paused for a moment. "I apologize. I just don't want them here."

"The last I checked, this was my house. Now act like you have some good home training and come join us. They want to talk to you," she said and retreated back the way she came.

A beat of silence passed.

"I should go. I can get a taxi back to my car," Ibiso said.

Rasheed turned around. "No. Stay here, I'll be right back." He then nodded towards his brothers. "Keep her company."

"Sure thing," Jabir said.

Kamal nodded.

Rasheed turned around. "Please stay, this shouldn't take long." He kissed her on her forehead and disappeared the way his mother had.

She had lost her appetite and so had Jabir. They both walked into the family room. Kamal followed with his half empty plate in his hand.

***

The tension was so thick that Ibiso wished she could transport herself away right into her bedroom. Rasheed was just as mad if not madder than the first day she met him. Or rather the day he knocked her over.

"Come have a seat, he'll be right back." Jabir patted the cushion next to him.

Kamal must have noticed her unease because he said, "Don't let Rasheed's bark scare you. He's harmless and he likes you, so you're safe."

Ibiso was not comfortable having this conversation. Not after what she had just witnessed. She changed the subject. "So tell me what you like most about playing soccer. I didn't think it was that huge in the USA."

Ibiso saw Kamal eyes light up. His look alone told her how passionate he was about his sport. She recognized it because she was the same way with Bisso Bites.

"It's not as big as it is in Europe and Africa, but it's catching

81

on," Kamal said.

"What do you care? You're getting paid a hefty sum to play in front of a half-filled arena. I wonder why they bother. Just like that club that signed Beckham in the US. They paid all that money, but I wonder if they got any of it back," Jabir said.

"Won't you mind ya business. Who called you into this discussion?" Kamal tossed one of the throw pillows towards his brother who ducked to avoid its impact. Throwing pillows seemed to be their thing.

Ibiso was about to respond when Kamal's phone rang. He looked at the caller ID.

"Excuse me, I've got to get this." He stood and walked towards her. He extended his hand and Ibiso placed hers in it. "It was nice meeting you. Hope this won't be the last time." He smiled at her, put his phone to his ear and left the room.

Ibiso extended her neck toward the doorway Rasheed had gone through. She could hear his raised voice. She didn't know what was going on but wished she could be there for him. Although she knew it was crazy considering they just met, she had this pressing need to comfort him.

"You hurt my feelings. Am I not good enough company?" Jabir voice brought her thoughts back to him.

"Excuse me?"

"I promised my brother I'd keep you company, so don't let him come in here and see you moping."

Ibiso smiled. From the first day she met Jabir, she knew he was a ladies' man. He even tried to hit on her then.

"That's better. A smile. I'm glad I finally get to meet the woman behind Stone Cold's recent strange smiles and laughter."

"Stone Cold?" Ibiso asked puzzled.

"Yeah, that's what we call him when he starts to exhibit that sided of him that is best kept hidden."

"The part I just witnessed?"

"Yep," Jabir confirmed.

"And what do they call you?" Ibiso laughed.

"Me? I'm a lover not a fighter." Jabir popped his collar.

Ibiso laughed. "Has anyone told you that you're just too much?"

"All the time."

They laughed. And she relaxed. Jabir was so easy going. He and Rasheed were like night and day.

"Rasheed tells me you're a doctor."

"He told you right. I'm a surgeon," Jabir said sitting up in the chair.

There was an undeniable spark in Jabir eyes as he began telling her about his practice and how he volunteered twice a year for a program called Doctors in the Skies.

"So you get to go around the world helping people. That's amazing," Ibiso said.

"I'm not a saint or anything. I just do my part."

Modesty was not a trait Ibiso would have guessed Jabir possessed.

Rasheed stormed into the room, his mother close behind. "Mama, I don't want to talk about this anymore."

Ibiso looked from mother to son. She clutched her purse tighter. Rasheed walked over to her and grabbed her hand. "Let's go." He then headed towards the door.

Ibiso snatched her hand away. "I have to say good-bye properly."

Rasheed's eyes challenged her, but she didn't budge.

"Fine. I'll be in the car." He opened the door and walked out.

Whatever was going on with him was not about to make her rude. She said her goodbyes and headed out the door.

Chapter 12

Ibiso glanced at the man in the driver's seat. He looked like Rasheed, but was not behaving like him. This couldn't be the person she had gotten to know. They had been driving for five minutes and he had not so much as offered her an explanation. His anger was taken out on the accelerator as she was sure they were doing twice the speed limit. The good thing however was that the roads were next to empty.

"Rasheed, are you going to talk to me?" Ibiso reached over and put her hand on his shoulder. He was as tense as a pack of rocks.

He remained silent.

"I am a good listener, you know. I shared my drama with you."

"Don't joke. I'm not in the mood." He turned and looked at her.

Ibiso could feel his glare burning a hole through her. He honked the horn at a pedestrian who wasn't even in his way.

Ibiso's nostrils flared. Her hands closed into fists. Whatever was his problem, he also seemed to have lost his mind.

"Rasheed, you must be kidding me." She turned in her seat to face him. "You bring me out here to meet your family. Then behave like a madman and I ask about it and you tell me you are not in the mood?"

He exhaled loudly. "This has nothing to do with you—"

"Of course it doesn't. I'm trying to be a friend and offer you some comfort for what is wrong with *you*."

He shook his head and turned into the church parking lot. He parked near her car and turned off the engine.

"Look, I'm sorry you had to witness that. But I don't want to talk about it." His fingers tightened around the steering wheel. "I just need to be alone right now."

Ibiso searched through her purse for her keys. She then turned to him. "You know what Rasheed, I'm the one who's sorry. You don't have to worry about me asking you anything again." She opened the car door and got out without a backward glance.

***

Wednesday morning, Ibiso placed an oversized tuber of yam on the prep table with more force than necessary. She sliced it down the middle and began chopping it up into huge slices. The lunch special today was fried yam and pepper sauce. She turned around but couldn't find the colander. She rummaged through the cupboard for a few seconds then shouted, "Amina, have you seen the colander? I need to drain these vegetables."

Ibiso watched as Amina in silence walked over to the other counter, picked up the colander and handed it to her. She took it and muttered her gratitude. Ibiso was running behind again, which seemed to be the case the last couple of mornings.

"Is there anything wrong? You've been in this mood for two days. Let me do this." Amina tried to take the knife from her hand.

"Nothing's wrong. It's my restaurant. I got it," she snapped, and then immediately felt remorse. Amina had always been good to her. There was no need to offload her personal drama on her.

"I'm sorry." Ibiso took off her apron. "I didn't mean to snap. I'll go and get some paperwork done. I've got the fryer going...remember to pat off all the excess oil. The base of the pepper sauce is already done."

With a smile on her face, Amina ushered Ibiso out of the kitchen. "Go on. I got it."

Moments later, Ibiso sat behind her desk and leaned into her chair. She couldn't believe she was letting someone she should consider a stranger affect her this much. How dare Rasheed not call or explain himself? She was so mad at him she wanted to curse. He had literally dragged her out of his mom's house, drove in complete silence, scolded her when she tried to help and hasn't called her since. Despite his attitude, she had called and left him a message on Monday evening. Still, he hadn't bothered to return her call. She was done.

Ibiso logged on to her computer and signed into her back account. She had more pressing problems—her rent. She was still short and time was running out. She rubbed the nape of her neck as her eyes traveled to the wall calendar. She had four months. She checked her bookings. Three corporate luncheons, a kid's birthday party and a baby shower. That, in addition to her earnings here, should bring her pretty close, but not there. What was she going to do? "Jesus, please make a way. You don't do anything halfway. Your promises are sure. This dream of mine can't fall by the wayside. It just can't."

Trust God. She could hear Boma's voice in her head. Ibiso knew she owed her friend a call, but she wasn't ready to be badgered about Rasheed when she couldn't explain what was going on herself.

Over the next hour, Ibiso busied herself with running her business. She updated social media fan pages, wrote a blog post with some recipes and entered her expenses into QuickBooks. As she sorted through her neglected receipts, she chided herself for doing it again – letting a man's issues take over what she needed to get done for herself. The restaurant would open soon and so she needed to get back to the kitchen and make sure that everything was ready. She sighed, stood, and walked toward the door. She couldn't wait to get home and relax. She hadn't been sleeping too well but that was about to end. She couldn't worry about someone who was not worrying about her.

***

Later that morning, Rasheed stood in the study of his mother's home with a cup of coffee in one hand and the cordless phone in the other. He had just gotten off a call with his best friends—Kene Odili and Jide Adegoke. The three of them attended the same private school in London until his mother could no longer afford it. Despite that fact that he and his family moved, the three boys had remained close. It was a friendship they still maintained. Rasheed never felt comfortable sharing his feelings and vulnerabilities with his brothers. His job was to shield them and not unload his problems on them.

Kene relocated back to the Nigeria a while ago and opened his own law firm based in Lagos. Jide, who was a chartered accountant, still lived in the UK, but shuttled back and forth in hopes of starting his own firm.

They convinced him that his mother was right. He owed it to himself to agree to the conditions of the will. The day before, Rasheed had begun to entertain the idea. At least the one-year trial. It might not be so bad after all. However, the thought that his father would have his way stopped him.

There was a quick knock on the door and it opened without him giving an answer. His brothers walked in.

"Thanks, man. I'll call you soon," Rasheed disconnected the call. He studied his brothers. Their demeanor told him they had something on their mind.

"What's up?" Jabir asked. He walked to the couch in the corner and sat down.

Kamal leaned against the desk and folded his legs at the ankles and crossed his arms. "So what are you going to do?"

Rasheed looked at his brothers as he contemplated his answer. He knew that he was kind of holding everybody up with his indecision. His brothers had accompanied him here but they had jobs and lives to get back to. He paced back and forth.

"You're hesitant which means you're at least considering it. So what's it going to be?" Jabir leaned forward in the chair. "You know I would've stayed with you, but I have to get back to the hospital. But I also don't want to leave you here in limbo."

"Okay, let's look at this sensibly. Let's see if we can help you decide," Kamal said. Rasheed could feel the intensity of both sets of eyes on him. He was about to speak when Kamal continued. "You always wanted to move back to Nigeria in the future. Well the future is now. It will also save you the hassle of starting from the scratch. You can just pick up from where the old man stopped."

"And why would I want to do that?" Rasheed spat.

"Because the only person you hate more than the old man is

his brother, Musa. And according to our father's wife, she overheard Musa planning to sell half of the business to foreign investors because he knows you won't have the guts to run the company," Jabir explained.

Rasheed's jaw tightened in annoyance at the mention of the name Musa Danjuma. When his father grew a conscience and came looking for Rasheed in London, they had a long talk. Zayd told him that his dad and his brother Musa had threatened his inheritance for years if he didn't get his act together and come home. Zayd's final decision to leave came when his father threatened to "take care of" his wife and sons. Since, in his opinion, they were the reason Zayd was bringing disgrace to the family. The explanation did little to dissipate the dislike Rasheed had for his dad or the Danjuma family.

"The mention of that man's name boils my blood," Jabir said.

"Mine too, but the ultimate decision to abandon us rested on our dad." Rasheed pulled out the chair behind the desk and sat.

"Yeah. At least he grew a conscience and came looking for us almost a decade later." Kamal sighed.

Rasheed waved off Kamal's comment. "Don't be fooled. The only reason that man came looking for us was because his second wife didn't have a male child." In the end, Zayd had succeeded in making two women miserable because of his inability to follow his heart.

"I know, right!" Jabir stood up and put his hands in his pockets. "So bro, what's it gonna be?"

"You know that you can't allow that Musa to win. Not after all we've been through." Kamal said calmly.

Rasheed rubbed his hand over his head. His brothers were right. He knew that, but he didn't have to like it.

"Besides, wouldn't you like to explore that hot number you brought home the other day? If you go back to London...you'd miss out." Jabir grinned.

Rasheed knew that with Jabir, women were always the end result. He had messed up big time with Ibiso, so he was apprehensive about calling her.

Kamal walked over to sit next to his twin. "Yes, the babe was indeed hot. It's been a while since I've seen dark chocolate skin, and her short cut was on point. But you know Stone Cold here won't be moved by that. You have to talk to him in business language."

Rasheed knew his brothers were just fishing for information. He wasn't going to give them the satisfaction of an answer. Truthfully, he had no answers when it came to Ibiso.

"Big bro, if you're confused let me know, oh. I bet when God made her, He gave Himself a pat on the back," Jabir said.

"Don't even think about it," Rasheed said, walking around to the front of the desk. His voice barely audible, but he was sure the seriousness of his tone was not lost.

"Think about what??" Their mother walked in. They maintained a straight face as she fished for an answer but wasn't provided one. "Silence, *okwa ya?*"

"Mama, it's nothing. We were talking about the demands of the will," Kamal said, walking up to her and draping his arm over her shoulder.

Their mother turned to Rasheed. "*Nna*, what have you decided? Don't let these people win everything at the end of the day."

"Mama, we are comfortable without the Danjuma's money. Why should I turn my life around because of this?"

"It is your right. Your inheritance. I pray that someday, you get to a place where you can forgive your father. But please, let this be your motivation to prove the Danjumas wrong. Despite what they thought, *they need you.*"

Rasheed saw the distress on her face. His brothers also looked at him with anticipation in their eyes.

"I don't know. The thought of doing anything for a man who couldn't stand up for himself just rubs me the wrong way."

"Rasheed, you know better than to speak ill of the dead," his mother chided him. "It's time to let it go. God will heal your heart, my son."

"Mama, leave God out of it. All those times you cried at night, God should have answered you then. I'll make the decision." Rasheed walked behind the desk and stretched out in the chair.

"Please do it sooner rather than later. The time requirement will soon be up." His mother walked to the door and opened it slightly.

She paused and then turned around. "As for God, we do not question Him. What you don't know is that, my comfort in suffering was that His promises preserve my life. When I look at you and your brothers, and how well you all are doing, I know that His promises are sure. One day soon, God will touch your heart. Until then, I'll keep praying for you." She walked out of the room.

"What?" Rasheed barked at his brothers. They had been silent the whole time, but he could read disappointment in their eyes.

"You've mastered the art of pissing off the women in your life. Good luck, brother." Jabir patted his brother on his back and walked out.

"You know he's just joking. Whatever you decide, you've got our support," Kamal said. "By the way, if Jabir was right and you've messed things up with Ibiso, you might wanna fix it. That chick digs you." Kamal walked out leaving Rasheed to his thoughts.

Rasheed sighed. *Jabir has a big mouth. I should've known better than to tell him that I hadn't spoken to Ibiso since Sunday.*

He indeed missed her. Her laughter and the way her eyes sparkled. He owed Ibiso an explanation and had to do it in person. His behavior had been awful and it was time to make amends.

The sudden sharp pain in his stomach reminded him that it lacked food. His eyes darted towards the timer on his laptop. It was a little after noon. The solution to both his problems lay in one place—Bisso Bites.

Chapter 13

Ibiso came out of the kitchen with another hot pan of food and did a double take. She had no idea where all these people came from. God was showing out. For the second day in a row, the line of customers was almost at the door. The busyness of the restaurant served a dual purpose— the added money which she was in dire need of and the distraction from thoughts of Rasheed. Although she welcomed the business, her feet were killing her, making her grateful that the weekend was in sight.

Amina and the sales girls found it difficult to cope with the crowd, so Ibiso joined to assist. The extra help hadn't made a difference since a majority of the customers decided to dine in, thereby stretching the girls even further as they now also served as waiters. The boiled/fried yam with ata, red pepper sauce, was a huge hit. Ibiso also kept an eye on the checkout queue to ensure the cashier wasn't overwhelmed or too slow. She wanted to make sure her customers enjoyed their meal and also had time to relax before going back to work. On days like this she toyed with the idea of hiring more people but knew she wouldn't be able to afford it. She made a mental note to look into hiring a contract worker who'd come in as needed.

"May I help you?" Ibiso asked without looking up, adjusting the hot pan in its place.

"I'll have your lunch special."

Ibiso paused, then lifted her eyes in slow motion. She'd recognize that voice in her sleep. But this wasn't a dream. Rasheed was standing before her. Their eyes met, and an immediate rush of excitement came over her.

He wore his signature kaftan and matching pants. It was the first time she was seeing him in red and it accentuated the darkness of his skin. His smile brought a frown to her face. She was angry and she wouldn't let his good looks and charm make her forget that.

She forced her frown into a phony smile and asked, "Here or take out?"

"Here." Then he leaned closer. "Dine with me?" His eyes pleaded with her.

Rasheed had a way of making her heart melt and blood boil at the same time. She leaned forward. "Do you see the line behind you? I can't dine with you."

"I'll wait," he whispered. He must have figured she had a comeback, because before she could reply, he said, "I won't leave this line 'til you say yes."

She hesitated until she saw the lady behind him check her watch. "Okay, now move."

It wasn't until two hours later that the crowd died down. She smiled when she saw Rasheed in the corner seat he had chosen with a disgruntled look on his face. She was sure he was very hungry by now. She smirked. Served him right for trying to strong arm her in front of everybody. She took off her apron and walked to him, greeting some customers who were still dining along the way.

Her eyes connected with Rasheed's and his spine straightened. She could feel his nervous energy which was probably mixed with hunger. She walked toward him and tried hard to suppress the urge to giggle. When she got to his table, she lost the battle.

"You think this is funny, right?"

"What?"

"Don't act coy woman. You think I can't tell you decided to take your sweet time and starve me?"

"Stop being dramatic. You could have eaten and left a long time ago." She put her hand on her hip.

"I can't argue with you now. I'm weak." He bent over and rubbed his stomach. Ibiso knew he was exaggerating, but she wasn't ready for someone to faint on her premises.

She picked up the tray. "Let me go heat this up."

Minutes later she returned with a hot plate of the boiled yam for Rasheed while she settled for the fried yam. She placed the tray down and Rasheed proceeded to combine both plates of sauces into one plate. Her eyes questioned him and he just winked.

"Give me your hands?" Ibiso asked, inviting him to put his hands in hers in prayer. After she blessed the food they started to eat.

Ibiso stole glances at him. He was devouring the meal with gusto. The chef in her was glad, but his silence irritated her.

"So? I'm waiting," Ibiso said. "I called you. You should have called me back or sent me a text."

"I'm sorry."

"That's not going to do. Explain." Ibiso dabbed the side of her mouth with her napkin.

Rasheed swallowed the food in his mouth, drank some water and leaned back in his chair. "My dad *is* the late Zayd Danjuma. He and my mother met in England and fell in love. Foolishly, they depended on love to conquer the cultural and religious differences between them."

Ibiso sat upright and rested her chin on her hand. "Like?"

"For one, he was Muslim, she is Christian. Then there was the language and economic differences between them. But as with people in love, they thought it didn't matter." He paused and looked away. "But it did. A couple of years after the twins were born my dad started travelling to Nigeria very often. My mom told us it was business. I'm sure that's what he told her. But the truth was he had a secret family here that was approved by the Danjumas. When I was ten, he left and never came back."

Ibiso's heart began to hurt for him. She could feel the pain and bitterness in his voice. His behavior the other day began to make sense and why he detested the Sunday visitors so much. She thought about her father. Some days she'd be angry at him for dying and leaving her to the mercy of her brother. But at least he didn't die on purpose. He'd fought to stay alive, but it wasn't meant to be.

She listened in awe as Rasheed told her about how he and his mother discovered the truth about his dad. How horrible for a boy who had once adored his father to find out that way. He told her about how he took on the role of father to his brothers. She saw so many similarities between him and her brother. Sitting across from Rasheed hearing him recount his story stirred a strong urge in her to reach out to her brother. She understood him so much better now.

"After his trophy wife couldn't give him a son, he came looking for me. I was twenty and didn't need him anymore." Rasheed's nose flared.

Ibiso saw what looked like a tear at the corner of his eye. She placed her hand on his and squeezed. "Rasheed, I'm so sorry you went through that. Look at it as his loss." She paused. His expression was blank. "But, you have to find a way to let go. That's the only way you can heal. The person I saw on Sunday was scary. Your father is resting in peace and you're still tormented by his actions. Don't let him do that to you."

He remained silent and pushed his plate away.

She furrowed her brows. Something still didn't make sense. "Your dad's burial was about six months ago. What are you and your brothers doing here now?"

"The old man insisted his will shouldn't be read until my brothers and I were present. I guess he thought he could make up for all those years. The coward wants me to run the company or it goes to my uncle."

"You mean..."

"Yes, he wants me to leave my life in London and run Danjuma Group here in Nigeria."

Ibiso felt a slight chill run through her. She rubbed her palms up and down her upper arms. Running a group of companies was not an easy feat and all of a sudden she began to question what she thought was growing between them. She had dated a workaholic before and there was no way she was doing it again, especially not with one who had unresolved issues. She wanted to be there for him. Her heart ached for him, but her heart was incapable of making the right decisions. It had been broken.

"How long do you have to decide or have you decided?" she asked quietly.

"No and soon," he whispered.

There was an uncomfortable silence between them. After a few seconds, she asked. "So what are you going to do?"

"Everyone, including my father's second wife and my step-sister want me to do it. Each for different reasons. Aisha and Halima think that somehow they are guaranteed their monthly upkeep if I'm in charge. My mom and brothers say it's my inheritance so I need to do it."

"What do you want? You've lived all your life for your mother and brothers. What do you want?" She asked.

"I honestly don't know."

"Sounds like you do. You're leaning towards being a martyr for your family again." She paused. His tortured eyes lowered. "That in and of itself is not a bad thing. It is your inheritance, but if you do it, make sure it's because you want to."

"My mother and brothers deserve this. They've been denied for years."

"I know, but what do you want?"

He tilted his head. "I want you to forgive me. I can't explain it, but I feel something happening between us and I know you feel it too. I can see it in your eyes when you're not mad at me."

Ibiso raised one of her brows. "Are you for real? We're talking about a serious issue here and you're goofing around."

He stretched his hand across the table and stroked her cheek. "I am serious..." His eyes were intense.

Ibiso looked around. The restaurant was almost bare but still, this was her business place. She couldn't set this kind of example for her staff. She removed his hand and placed it back on the table. "That's sweet but you have too much going on now. Let's not complicate things."

He leaned closer. "There's nothing complicated about it."

"Rasheed, stop. You still haven't told me what you're going to do."

He raised his hands in surrender. "Truth is, I never wanted anything to do with that man or his wealth. I've worked hard to give my family everything he didn't. Funny how, years later I find myself bonded to him through the request of that same family."

"I'm sorry." She scrunched her eyebrows together. He sounded trapped.

"The will states that I have to agree to a year's trial at first to keep the company."

"Hmm...again, if you're going to agree to the terms, be sure. Life is too short to be a body sitting in an office waiting out a one year sentence."

They spent the next few minutes talking about the businesses that made up the company. His enthusiasm grew with every word. By the end of their conversation, it was apparent that his decision was made.

Ibiso had a bittersweet feeling. She was developing feelings for Rasheed and there was the possibility his stay in Nigeria would be a temporary thing. She needed to think, but right now she was so tired that it was hard for her to process.

She yawned. "Excuse me."

"If I didn't see how hard you worked today, I'd have taken that personally."

She placed her hand over her mouth.

"Thank you," he said.

"For what?"

His eyes were so penetrating that Ibiso had to turn away. He used his index finger to move her face back towards him.

"For helping me make a decision. Ibiso, I meant it when I told you I'd like to explore this thing between us," he said. "Forgive me. Give me another chance, remember you still owe me dinner."

"I do owe you dinner," she muttered under her breath. She branded a faint smile. Things just got more complicated than she bargained for. There was no denying that she did feel something for him. But with building and maintaining her business, a man who had issues of his own was the last thing she needed.

***

Later that night, as tired as she was, Ibiso couldn't relax. Her cup of tea had done little to help. She decided to cook and call Boma. She wedged her phone between her ear and shoulder while she stirred the *moi moi* mixture. Ibiso already knew what her best friend's reaction would be, but she still needed to talk. She liked Rasheed, a lot, but what he told her earlier had her head and heart at war.

"So you mean you didn't give him an answer?" Boma asked, after listening to Ibiso's narration of the day's events.

Ibiso lifted one of the folded banana leaves and scooped some of the mixture in it. "I do owe him dinner but other than that, I didn't say anything. What should I have said? I'm not ready for another man's *wahala*."

"What problem? You do know you're being unreasonable. It's been three years since your ex. Will you keep punishing every man because of that knucklehead?"

"First of all, I'm over Tokoni. But the point here is that Tokoni and Rasheed have one terrible thing in common. Their need to succeed is driven by the wrong reasons. In Rasheed's case its worse, because he already has everything, but the demons of his childhood keep pushing him to want more." Ibiso placed the wrapped leaf on the counter and secured its contents with a small string before placing it at the bottom of the pot.

"What are you cooking this late anyway?" Boma asked.

Ibiso could tell her friend was trying to hold back her frustration. She knew that Boma felt bad about being the one to introduce her to Tokoni, so she took the blame for the way things ended. No matter how many times Ibiso tried to convince her it wasn't true, it never seemed to stick. Boma's guilt trip worsened when she got married. From the depths of her heart, Ibiso was happy for her friend and wished she could see that and stop feeling so remorseful.

"I'm making *moi-moi*. I called to talk, not to be harassed."

"You sure didn't expect me to tell you what you wanted to hear. If so, you dialed the wrong number. Give Rasheed a shot. Who knows, you might be the exact thing he needs to heal."

"I'm not Jesus o—"

Boma exhaled deeply. "You liked this guy before he unburdened his heart. Now you know he comes with baggage, you want to run. Do unto others as…"

Ibiso cut her friend off with a loud laugh. "Don't even go there. You forgot I'm not a heathen anymore. I know the Bible too and it also says I should guard my heart above all else because the source of my life flows from it. I finally got my life together, and can't afford to jeopardize it."

A beat of silence passed between them.

Boma chuckled.

"Don't try me o. I'll match you Bible verse for Bible verse." Ibiso covered the pot, picked up her mug and headed to the living room.

She turned on the television, sat on the couch and folded her legs underneath her. The ladies talked for a couple more minutes about the preparations for her Port Harcourt trip. Ibiso was nervous, but she was going to be there for her friend even if it meant having to deal with her judgmental family.

Ibiso caught Boma up on the progress she had made towards her rent issue. The caretaker hadn't come around in a while but she knew it wouldn't be long. Her deadline would be here soon. There were a couple of jobs she had lined up which, barring no unexpected expenses, would create a sizable dent in the deficit. Enough to plead for more time.

"Alright girl, I have to go. Give that man a chance. If your intuition says go for it, then go for it. Don't trust your heart, it's been broken. Despite what you say, I don't think it's completely healed."

"Hmmm...Okay, goodnight. Kiss my godbabies for me." Ibiso disconnected the call and stretched out on the sofa. As she stared at the ceiling she wondered whether Boma was right. Was her heart still so broken that she didn't want to give Rasheed a chance? Or was she right to be weary of his baggage?

Chapter 14

The next morning, Rasheed gathered with his family in the living room. The air was so thick as he could feel their anticipation, but he decided to let them stew for a minute. He had thought long and hard and he was going to do this. For how long, he had no idea, but he never hid from a challenge.

He walked over to the window and stared out to the large expanse of well-manicured land. He loved this house, but if he was going to work for Danjuma Group, he needed something closer to town. It would help with the commute and ease his mother of her worry when he had to keep late nights in the office.

"How long are you going to keep us waiting? If I'm gonna fly to Lagos and back today, I need to get a move on it," Jabir said.

"Lagos? *Maka gini?*" their mother asked.

Rasheed chuckled on hearing their mother ask Jabir why he was going to Lagos. He always found it amusing when she acted like they were kids any time they came home. There was only one reason Jabir would be going to Lagos—Damisi Ndungu. She was the half Nigerian, half Kenyan television anchor that had eluded Jabir since they were in college. Six years was a long time to keep chasing after one lady. She wouldn't give him the time of day and Rasheed knew that it was the thrill of the kill or something more than he wanted to admit that kept his brother going after her every time he came home.

"Mama, business is taking me there," Jabir said, winking at Kamal.

Their mother opened her mouth to speak when Rasheed interjected.

"Okay, before we get off track, the reason I called this meeting is to tell you of my decision concerning our father's company."

His mother straightened her back and his brothers scooted forward in their seats.

"And...," Kamal said.

"I've decided to agree to the one year trial run. Like you all said, I never want to have a reason to regret anything," Rasheed said.

His mother stood up and began shaking her waist from side to side while lifting her hands up to the heavens.

Kamal shook his head. "Mama, calm down, oh. He said for just one year."

Rasheed and Jabir laughed when they saw their mother give their kid brother the side eye. She turned and walked toward Rasheed. "*Nna*, that's all I ask, that you at least give it a try. It's your inheritance. Don't let anger deprive you of what is yours, no matter the circumstance."

Their mother danced out of the room, rubbing her hands together in supplication. Rasheed knew that she'd be relieved. That thought alone played a big part in his decision. Well that and a certain young lady that he needed to talk to right after he made some urgent calls.

Kamal let out a sigh of relief. "Big bro, I'm really proud of you for doing this. I know we don't say it much, but thank you for all you've sacrificed for us."

"Let me get outta here before you guys start crying," Jabir said.

Rasheed balled up a piece of paper and threw it at Jabir. "If you can't say anything nice, zip it."

Jabir paused, and then a smirk appeared on his face. "Come on, Stone Cold, you know we're really proud of you." Jabir checked his watch. "I'll see you guys later. Lagos is calling."

Kamal snickered, crossed his legs at the ankles and stretched them out on the ottoman. "Stone Cold *haba*? We're going to have to change that name. Haven't you seen the way he's been smiling lately?" He covered his ears with his Beats headphones.

Rasheed would've argued, but then again, it wasn't far from the truth. Was it really that obvious? There was an undeniable chemistry between him and Ibiso, and he wasn't letting her run away from him. However, he needed to remind himself to keep his heart in check. Love was not his thing. His mother had smiled a lot all those years too before her world came crashing down.

***

By the next Friday evening, every muscle in Ibiso's body ached. She knew she had overdone it, but she had to keep going. She was experiencing an Ephesians 3:20 season and wasn't about to complain. Over the last two days God had really done exceedingly more than she had imagined. She got two emergency corporate jobs. The caterer they previously hired cancelled, she was told. She had no complaints, because at this moment, she was just 200,000 Naira short on the rent. So pain or not, she was pushing forward.

Ibiso lifted the empty cooler off the floor and placed it on the bottom of the trolley. She had sent Amina back to the shop, so was left to pack up alone. The board members of Xanter LLC seemed to be pleased with her spread. For lunch they had a choice of coconut friend rice and prawns or diced fried plantains mixed with gizzards. She packaged them in moderate sized containers and was surprised when the executive assistant came to ask her if she had some left over. Luckily she did. Ibiso was really pleased as success like this often meant that she would be remembered the next time they had an event to cater. She worked with speed gathering up her trays and serving spoons, taking one last look around to make sure she didn't forget anything.

Ibiso stepped outside and shivered when the cool breeze brought on by the previous day's rain hit her skin. She longed for some painkillers, a cup of tea and a cool bath. It would help bring down the temperature of her now warm body. She had a bad headache.

Oh no, I can't afford to be sick. At times like this she really wished she had someone to dote over her. Some days, as strong as she was, she still wanted a man whom she could lean on. One with whom she'd share her bad or good days. As she let down the trunk, her thoughts shifted to the man whom had taken residence in her mind, morning, noon and night.

She longed for Rasheed, but he was decadence too costly to indulge in. Her missed calls log was evidence of the number of times he had called in the last couple of days. Calls she hadn't returned, partly due to her schedule but mainly because she was still conflicted on what to say to him.

Rasheed didn't strike her as the kind of man that would let up so easy but she was determined to put him off as long as she could. Ibiso had learned the hard way and never again would she deliberately place herself or her needs second to a man whose quest for success was skewed. Rasheed was not only that man but he was also a man that was driven by revenge and anger— a dangerous mix.

***

Anger racked his body as Rasheed sped down the highway. He had been trying to reach Ibiso for days with no luck. And she didn't even deem it fit to call him back. Each time he tried to make it to her restaurant, he was delayed by some endless meeting with the Danjuma lawyers. He hadn't started work yet but with his announcement, they had wasted no time getting all the preliminary stuff out of the way.

Her flawless, dark chocolate faced haunted him anytime he tried to close his eyes. Her laughter constantly rang in his ears. She was avoiding him but that ended in a few hours. He couldn't understand what she was so afraid of. As far as he knew there was no other person in the picture and no harrowing break up story. Or was there? These were things he intended to find out when he saw her.

He turned his car into the parking space closest to the entrance of the center. Ibiso was supposed to be here this Saturday. One thing he was sure of was that her commitment to the kids would bring her out of hiding. There would be nowhere to run.

As the hours passed, his irritation grew. His well thought out plan had failed miserably. Ibiso was a no-show. The fact that she deliberately allowed the kids to go without the normal snacks because she was hiding annoyed him. At the last minute when it was apparent Ibiso wasn't coming, neither was she answering her phone, he and the kitchen manager had gone to a nearby supermarket and gotten what was needed. At the very least, Rasheed thought Ibiso had enough character to keep her commitment. If she didn't want to be associated with him, she was going to have to say it to his face.

Twenty minutes later, Rasheed knocked again for the second time on Ibiso's front door. There was still no answer. His anger gradually gave way to worry. She still was not answering her phone. He knocked again and there was no answer. He decided to go to her restaurant. Rasheed knew that might be a futile journey as the last Saturdays of the month, she closed to allow them take stock. It was four o'clock in the afternoon so he knew she would be done by now. He knocked again and turned to leave when he heard the locks turning. The door slowly opened. Rasheed was not prepared for what he saw or his reaction to it.

The sight of a frail looking Ibiso pulled at his heartstrings. She had on a pair of flannel pajamas with a blanket draped over her shoulders. Her head was covered with a scarf. She stepped aside and he entered the apartment.

"Rasheed, what are you doing here?" Ibiso asked, on her way to the sofa. She sat and covered herself with the blanket.

After securing the door, he followed her into the living room. The bright colored theme of the apartment was just as he had imagined it. The yellows, greens, oranges and white were just like Ibiso, bold. She had good taste. Different comingled aromas tickled his nostrils – precisely what he expected the home of a chef to smell like.

He approached the sofa and sat next to her. "I didn't see you at the center today so I came to check on you." He raised his hand to her forehead. It was hot. "What's wrong with you?"

"I'm not feeling well," she said.

"I can see that. What is it? Malaria? A cold? What's wrong?" Rasheed stood, lifted her legs off the floor, and stretched them out on the sofa. He then unfolded the blanket more and covered her. He looked down at her. She looked beautiful and fragile. His main goal became to care for her and nurse her back to health. He couldn't take her looking like this. He longed for his sharp tongued, witty Ibiso. That person he could handle.

"I don't think it's malaria," she whispered. "I guess it's just exhaustion and a cold."

"You guess? Why are you guessing? Haven't you seen a doctor?" Rasheed asked. He saw her wince in pain and his heart constricted.

"No I haven't seen one, and I don't think I need to. All I need is a little rest. I've been working pretty hard. I'll be fine."

"Ibiso, get up. I'm taking you to our family doctor. Or do you have one?" Rasheed picked up the empty tea mug from the side stool and took it to the kitchen.

"I'll be fine. Don't worry about me."

Her stubbornness drove him crazy. "Either you get up and get dressed or I'll carry you out like this. One way or another, you're going to see a doctor." He raised his brows challenging her to dare him.

***

Ibiso slowly opened her eyes, allowing them to adjust to the sunlight peering through the cobalt curtains in her bedroom. She looked at the digital clock seated on her bedside dresser. It was 9 a.m. She couldn't believe that she had slept so late. The aroma of her special brand of coffee and eggs tickled her nostrils. She sat up in the bed in a panic. Was Rasheed still here?

The events of the previous day came flooding back. Rasheed had shown up expectedly and blatantly refused to leave. Although she wasn't thrilled that he had seen her at her worst, she was glad that he didn't listen to her because she indeed needed him. Ibiso remembered him driving her to their family doctor. The elderly man had diagnosed her with malaria. This wasn't good at all. She had things to do.

Some minutes later, she emerged from the bedroom. The cool shower was just what she needed. After minutes of trying to decide on what to wear, she settled for a simple Ankara black and green jumpsuit. She slipped her burgundy polished toes into her flip flops and made her way to the kitchen. The butterflies in her stomach went into frenzy when she saw Rasheed setting the dinette in her kitchen. He looked up at her and winked.

"Hey, you. Feel any better? Hope you're hungry?" He said filling a small glass with orange juice.

Her eyes roamed the table. "Good morning. No, I don't think I can eat."

"Well too bad, you have to." He had prepared oatmeal, eggs, sausages and toast.

"Are you going to force me?" She picked up the glass of juice and drank a little.

"If I have to. You have to eat and take your medicine. Malaria is nothing to joke with."

"Are you always this bossy?"

"Are you always this stubborn? Now put your pretty self in the chair and eat." He returned the juice to the fridge and joined her at the table.

Ibiso took a look at the spread in front of her and furrowed her eyebrows. Her stomach was queasy and couldn't take anything. She looked up and saw Rasheed watching her. After a few seconds, he took the spoon from her, stirred the oatmeal and scooped some of it. Smiling at her, he lifted the spoon to her lips. She opened her mouth and he fed her.

After a few more spoonfuls, she asked, "Umm...did you sleep here?"

He stared at her with a sparkle in his eyes. That look always made her question herself. "No, I didn't. Giving me a spare key was the only way you could get me to leave. Remember?"

"Vaguely."

"After this you need to rest. Why are you working yourself so hard? I understand the restaurant is hard work, but all these extra jobs without help are bound to take their toll."

Ibiso nodded. He was right. She must have exposed herself unnecessarily with those late nights and the mosquitoes had a field day. However, the reason she was doing the extra without help was not up for discussion. From what she knew of Rasheed, he'd want to come to her rescue. She needed to do this on her own.

"You didn't need to worry. I told you I'd be fine."

"When someone I care about looks as lousy as you did, I do worry." He shrugged.

"Geez, thanks for the compliment." She put a piece of sausage in her mouth and chewed slowly.

Rasheed lifted his coffee to his lips and emptied it down his throat. "I call it like I see it." He stood up and started to clear the table.

Ibiso tried to stop him, but he banished her to the living room. After a few minutes of trying to negotiate with him, she gave up. She found herself comparing him to her ex. Tokoni had never been around when she was ill. He always had to travel or was attending to one business engagement or the other. He often scowled when she mentioned even a headache. He saw it as a sign of weakness.

But here was Rasheed whom she knew had a million and one things he was dealing with, actually taking time to take care of her. Despite her resistance, he was slowly breaking down her walls of defense, but her head reminded her of what was at stake. He had a lot of healing to do and she couldn't let another man take her down.

***

Rasheed entered the living room and stared at the television. "What are you watching?" Ibiso sat up to make room for him to sit. He waved her back down, sat next to her and placed her legs across his lap. He then covered her with a light cloth. "No lie down, you need your rest."

"I'm not handicapped."

"You could have fooled me. I was actually angry at you for ditching the center to avoid me. When I saw you, all my anger flew out of the window."

"Humph...is that what you think? I'd neglect my commitment, because of something that silly?" She shook her head slightly.

Rasheed didn't like that his words where the reason for the hurt he saw in her eyes. He had misjudged her. He had learned long ago not to take anybody at face value, but he had ignored the knowing feeling that Ibiso was different.

"So what are you watching?" He decided it was best to ignore her question and change the subject.

"Since I couldn't go to church, I'm watching one of my favorite televangelists."

Rasheed nodded but remained silent. He really wasn't up to listening to any pastor preach. He wanted to talk about the reason he came here in the first place yesterday - why she had been avoiding him. He turned to look at her in hopes that he could read her mood. He opened his mouth to speak, but the sound of her voice stopped him.

"I receive it in Jesus name."

"Huh?"

"Aren't you listening? The pastor just said something about old things passing away and we're made new." She looked at him intently. "I can change the channel if you want."

This wasn't his cup of tea. He had come to believe that there are certain people God helped and there were those that had to help themselves. God had abandoned them and left the work for Rasheed. However, he didn't want to appear like he was the devil's first son so he governed himself accordingly.

The pastor strutted from one end of the church to the other, sometimes out of breath. He was constantly being interrupted by shouts of, "preach pastor" and, "the Lord is good." Rasheed watched but barely listened to what the man was shouting about love. His focus was on Ibiso. He sat in amazement at how she was eating this stuff up. Of course the man had references from the Bible but everyone interpreted that book the way they liked.

After an excruciating thirty minutes, the program was over. Ibiso bowed her head for a bit and then whispered "Amen." She then picked up the remote and lowered the television and turned to him.

Rasheed raised his eyebrows with a feigned look of hurt in his eyes. "Oh, so you have time for me now."

"Oh honey, God always comes first in my life. At least I try very hard for Him to."

"I like the sound of that..."

"Of what?"

"You calling me honey."

Her dark skin couldn't hide her blush. She had just given him the perfect segue into the reason he was here. Rasheed waited for her to take the bait but she didn't bite. Instead she ignored him and asked, "So what did you think of the sermon?"

Was this a trap?

"Err, I don't know. If he believes what he's saying, and those he's preaching to believe it too, then I guess it's all good." He shrugged.

If she didn't look like she was about to pass out, he would have laughed.

"You're joking, right?" she asked.

"Ibiso, I'm not the devil, you know. Love God and love your neighbor – isn't that what the good book commands? He and I might not be cool right now but it doesn't mean I hate Him. And I love my neighbor by giving to charity and volunteering my time. I think I'm good."

"We'll come back to the reason you and God are not cool later. If you think that all those things you listed equate love, then you're wrong. Those things are nice, but don't mean a thing without love. And I mean true love like the one Christ showed when He died," Ibiso said.

He watched as she took a sip of her juice. Then she did the unexpected and picked up her Bible.

Rasheed raised his hands up in surrender and laughed. "Woman, I didn't come here for a Bible lesson. I'll take your word for it."

"You like me, right? A big part of me is my faith. Okay, I won't preach, just read this later." She scribbled something on a sheet of paper and handed it to him.

Rasheed opened the folded note.

1 Corinthians 12vs.31 and 1 Corinthians 13 vs.1 & 2

"Promise me."

Rasheed saw the pleading in her eyes. This was important to her, so he'd at least try. Just the way he tried when he sat through church with her a couple of weeks ago. "Okay, don't look at me with those sad eyes. I just don't understand a God that will make the people that serve Him faithfully go through so much."

"Have you considered the fact that He gave you the ability to persevere what you had to go through? God is never the cause of bad things happening to us, but be sure that He will sustain you to go through it," Ibiso said.

He had never heard her speak with such emotion and passion. Except for the time she talked about her family.

"I'll read it."

He didn't think it would change anything but to amuse her, he would. The silence in the room produced tension. He needed to change the topic.

"The twins leave to go back to the US tonight."

"I'm so sorry I didn't have the opportunity to see them again."

"You would have if you weren't so busy running from me."

"I wasn't running. I was working."

Rasheed watched her tug on her lower lip with her teeth. He noticed she did this each time her brain was about to go into overdrive.

"I must have worn my sign today." He wiped his forehead.

With a puzzled look on her face she asked, "What sign?"

"The one that says, "tell me anything and I'll believe."" He paused. "The minute I told you how I felt, you suddenly became busy."

He searched her face for some kind of reaction. Ibiso's expression was unreadable, but she lowered her eyes. He could almost hear the wheels in her head churning.

"After the way you took care of me, I do owe you some kind of explanation."

There was something about her tone that made him uncomfortable. But he wanted to hear this.

Chapter 15

Ibiso pulled in a deep breath. It was time to lay her cards on the table. Well, not all of them, but just enough. She no longer had time for games. It was either she was in or she was out. There was no longer any denying what was happening between them. Her caution was birthed out of the quickness with which things were developing between them. It was eerily similar to the swiftness of her romance with Tokoni, but it was time to move on. She should at least try. It had been three years.

Ibiso felt the power from Rasheed's stare, his eyebrow arched up waiting for her response. She felt the emotion rise in her as she closed her eyes to hold back any stray tears. She didn't want to be this close to him as she bared her heart, but she was too weak to stand. She shifted to an upright position, tucked her legs underneath her, and turned to him.

"Everyone I knew was against it, but I did it anyway."

"What?"

Ibiso bit her lower lip. "My marketing degree was for my family, but ever since I could remember, I wanted to cook. After expressing his disappointment, Sodienye assisted in paying for me to go to culinary school in Europe."

She paused but Rasheed's expression was blank. Ibiso guessed it was probably because he shared the same views when it came to Kamal, who played soccer instead of being an architect.

She shook her head and continued, "On my return, I was ready and set to start up my business in Port Harcourt. I had the plan all laid out. I would use my savings and what my late father left me. One day, we were scouting locations – my friend Boma and I – when she introduced me to my ex, Tokoni." Ibiso sighed. "He was very handsome. So…"

A frown came over his face and Rasheed shook his head, "Spare me the details, please."

"Umph…anyways, long story short we had a whirlwind romance that…"

"Everyone disapproved off."

"Yes. Even though she introduced us, I couldn't get Boma to be on my side when I relocated with him a year later to Lagos."

"So how did you end up here? In Abuja?"

"I finally became aware of what everyone saw when he decided that a relationship was slowing him down. He was driven by success for all the wrong reasons. His was more egotistical."

"As opposed to me, right?

"I didn't say that, you did. But yes, I'm scared Rasheed."

He lifted his hand and caressed her check. "Don't be. My issues have nothing to do with you."

Ibiso held on to his hand. "How can you say that?"

He remained quiet for a moment, and then asked. "You didn't answer my question."

"Which one?"

"How did you end up in Abuja?"

"I needed a change. I couldn't go back to my family. I had disgraced them enough. Lagos reminded me of my mistake, so Abuja was a fresh start. Here I came to the realization of God's love and that He is a God of second chances. I picked myself up and got my restaurant started. *By myself.* No man. No family."

Rasheed stood, stared at her for a moment and then he began to pace the length of the room. After a few seconds, he stopped and leaned against the bookcase.

"You're right. Since my father left, I've been driven by the need to prove I can be a better man without him. Achieve on my own what he did with the help of his family. But those I cared about never suffered as a result of my ambition." He sat back down next to her. "Ibiso, I care about you. There is something here

113

and I know you feel it too." He grinned.

"Your cockiness is refreshing."

"I'm not cocky, just confident." He cupped her face in both his palms. "Sweetheart, I haven't done this in a while but if I must, I want it to be with you. We'll take it a day at a time."

His self-confident, take charge attitude was irresistible. His eyes dimmed as his lips connected with hers. Ibiso closed her eyes. The kiss was tender and sensual. She knew it was his way of telling her to trust him.

Rasheed broke the connection, but continued to hold her face. His eyes sought hers. "I have to go but think about it." He kissed her forehead and stood.

Rasheed made sure she was back in a horizontal position on the sofa and fluffed the pillows so she'd be comfortable. He handed her the remote, and refilled her juice glass. Then he left, but not before reminding her to take the next dose of her medication.

***

A week later on Monday morning, Ibiso was ready to get back at it.

Don't punish the one in front of you for the mistakes of the one behind you. As she dressed, she couldn't get those words out of her head. The words Boma had stressed during their thirty minute conversation last Sunday when Rasheed left. Since then, Rasheed had called to check on her every day and had visited once. She had become used to hearing from him at a particular time the first couple of days, but those calls became irregular as each day passed. She missed them, but understood that he had a lot to handle since he had started in his new role.

Ibiso sat on the chair in her bedroom to fasten her sandals. She was having a hard time aligning her heart with her head. Her heart seemed to be walking down the road to love all by itself. *Love.* She couldn't be in love that quick. But Rasheed had crept into her heart and taken residence since that night. There was no use fighting it anymore, but that didn't stop her from being terrified.

She exhaled and walked to her dresser. She put on her wristwatch and a dash of lipstick and left the bedroom. Stopping by the kitchen, she picked up her travel mug and made her way out. As she pulled out of her complex, her lips curled up in a smile as the classic Whitney Houston's *I Look To You* played on the radio. She would trust God and embrace this second chance at love He was giving her.

Rasheed had made many strides towards a connection between them. Now was it her turn to so the same, by doing what she did best—cooking. She'd surprise him with lunch. That was sure to bring a smile to his face.

***

It was the middle of May and the second Monday Rasheed had walked into the Danjuma Group building as the CEO. The meetings and introductions didn't seem to be easing up. He glanced at his watch as he entered his new office. It was 2 p.m. He had been in meetings since a little after ten.

Rasheed placed his tablet on the mahogany desk and plopped down into the large leather chair. He leaned in and swiveled it around to face the expansive windows behind him. He liked the way the office had turned out. It gave him a small sense of normalcy with its new modern and minimalistic, yet sleek look. The beige browns and fabrics had made way for black, silver and leather.

The scenery was spectacular as it covered a large expanse of the city. He could easily get lost in the view. He already had the feeling that working here, he would need to get lost once in a while. From his tour earlier he could tell his dad ran a well-oiled machine, but most of the processes were manual. He turned around and studied the files arranged in a neat stack at the right corner of the desk. He rubbed the back of his neck; he hadn't seen physical files in a while. His mind wandered as he pondered adding eliminating them and adopting a computerized system to the first changes he would make. He picked up a file labeled 'Real Estate.' Nothing in the documents given to him earlier indicated that Danjuma Group dealt in real estate.

Rasheed pressed the intercom to his left. A few seconds later, his secretary, Ireti, entered. According to her file, Ireti, who was probably in her late forties had joined the company in the last decade. Word was that Madame Ireti, as she was fondly called, had been his father's right hand and helped him keep things on track. The light complexioned, plump woman couldn't be taller than 5 feet 3 inches but everyone in the office revered her. Rasheed had no desire to start with anyone new, so he kept her.

"Yes sir," she said.

Rasheed looked up from the paper in front of him just in time to see the pen in her hand tremble. She followed the trail of his gaze and quickly put her hands behind her back.

"Please call me Rasheed or Mr. Danjuma. No sir, please."

Ireti nodded.

Rasheed pointed to one of the chairs in front of the desk. "Sit."

She hesitated for a moment then sat. He could tell that this wasn't the kind of employer/employee relationship she was used to.

"I need you to set up a meeting with the IT and HR heads. Probably next week." His first project was brainstorming on how to get things more automated and what would be required to retrain the staff.

"Yes sir.....I mean Mr. Danjuma." She scribbled in her notebook.

"Also on your way out, tell the managing director I want to see him." He placed the real estate file in front of her. "I wasn't aware this company dealt in real estate."

"Oh, sir, that was just a property your father decided to buy to help one of his friends out. We don't deal in it."

"That explains it. Don't worry about it then."

As Ireti got up to leave, Rasheed perused the file. They weren't making a profit. Why keep something that wasn't turning a profit? "On a second thought, set up a meeting with the managing director for tomorrow as well. In the meantime, set up a Skype session later this evening with the general manager of the cement plant in Lokoja."

"Yes, sir...err I mean..."

"Call me whatever makes you feel comfortable." He smiled to ease her tension. "That would be all for now."

"Okay, sir," she said.

His stomach growled, reminding him that it lacked food. He had been so busy all day that it completely escaped his mind that all he had was coffee and a breakfast pastry.

"Is there anywhere close by to eat?" He thought of Ibiso, but her restaurant was about forty-five minutes away. A journey he could make, but didn't for one reason. He didn't want to be too desperate. He had shown her his hand, now it was time for her to show hers.

"Yes, sir. Hold on let me get you the menu." Ireti opened the door to exit the office and paused. "Madam, you can't just come in here like that, "she said, causing Rasheed to look up.

A smile danced in his eyes when he saw Ibiso. "It's okay Ireti, let her in."

Ireti stepped aside. Her irritation was clear as Ibiso walked into the office. "I'm sorry. I had been waiting for a while and your cell was off. I didn't want to leave without at least seeing if you were in."

Rasheed removed his cell phone from the clip on his belt. It was indeed off. It must have powered off by mistake. She waited – that thought made him happy.

"I'm glad you didn't leave." Rasheed walked from behind his desk. He brushed his lips against Ibiso's cheeks. "Ireti, this is Ibiso Jaja. Interrupt me whenever she comes by or calls."

Ireti nodded and exited the room.

"I think I may have pissed off your secretary. She seems a little protective over you."

"Ireti will be alright. She takes her job too seriously." He glanced at her hand and took the basket she was holding, placing it on the center table in the sitting area of the office.

"I brought you lunch. Hope you haven't eaten? "Ibiso began to unpack the contents of the basket.

"No I haven't, and your timing couldn't be better." Rasheed watched with admiration as Ibiso set up the light meal of white rice and stew, baked hen, plantains and steamed vegetables. "A woman after my own heart."

"Food will make a starving man say anything." She rolled her eyes then smiled.

Ibiso stretched out her hands. Rasheed placed his in them and she blessed the food.

"*Oya,* eat so I can go. Ireti will get me if I stay here past your lunch time."

They both shared lighthearted laughs as he ate and fed her some pieces of plantain off his plate.

"How was your first day back?" Rasheed asked.

"Busy. Amina did a great job holding down the place."

"I knew she would."

"So how has it been here? You've filled me in over the phone, but I can't believe I'm here." Ibiso placed her hands on her cheeks and looked around. "Love the décor. It's so you."

 Rasheed updated her on what has been going on and the immediate things he wanted to tackle. She gave him some ideas on rebranding, which he welcomed.

"You see why I need you beside me."

"For free food and marketing advice?" She lifted an eyebrow.

Rasheed grinned. "Sweetheart, I see your sharp tongue is back." He reached for her hand and caressed it delicately. "Have you given us any thought?"

"Rasheed, what you have on your plate and a relationship is a lot. It scares me, but, I *sha* like you. So hey…"

His looped his arm around her neck and drew her to him. His

eyes danced with excitement. "I *sha* like you too." *She kinda likes me. Okay that's a start.* He sought her forehead and placed a lingering kiss on it.

Half an hour later, Ibiso was packing up when Rasheed came up behind her and turned her around, keeping her in place with his hands on her waist. "I could get used to this."

"Oh really now?" She dabbed the corners of his lips with a napkin. The atmosphere was charged with the electricity between them. Rasheed bent down to kiss her, but was surprised and pleased when Ibiso raised herself on the tip of her toes and placed a brief kiss on his lips.

He was about to speak when she placed her index finger over his lips. "If you're willing to be brave, then so will I." She kissed him again, picked up the food basket and walked to the door. "Don't make me regret it." She smiled, opened the door and left.

Chapter 16

Over the next two months, Ibiso and Rasheed spent every moment they could together. They fell into a comfortable routine. Early morning prayer sessions, and check-ins once or twice during the day. Wednesdays and Fridays were reserved for date night, Saturday morning they met in the gym and they ended the week with church service and lunch on Sundays. Life was great. She was in love.

Ibiso stretched out and rolled over in bed. She let out a faint sigh. The uneasy feeling that had plagued her for a while washed over her. This was the last week in July and the deadline by which she had to have her rent or be kicked out of her restaurant. She had just a week left. Unexpected repairs to the freezer and the gas cooker caused her to still be short by 80,000 Naira. Money which she had no idea how she was going to come up with by weeks end. Ibiso had been tempted to call home so many times, but the reason she didn't was the same reason she hadn't told Rasheed. She wanted to do this on her own. Pulling this off would restore her confidence in herself, and maybe have her family trust her again.

She walked into the living room and turned on the television to the news channel. She entered the kitchen to put on the kettle. She leaned against the sink while she waited on the water to come to a boil. In the distance, the news anchor was talking about the opening of new business in the area and the change in leadership at Danjuma Group.

After all this time, it was still news. That probably had more to do with the fact that Rasheed was Danjuma's "long lost heir" than actual interest in the company. The mere mention of the name however sent her heart racing and sinking at the same time. Days of pretending she didn't know what was going on were over. Of recent, she had become restless about the thing that gave her the most joy—her relationship with Rasheed. Things were going so great that she was having a hard time enjoying it and being present because she was waiting for the other shoe to drop. Ibiso shook her head to rid herself of the thought.

She set a small fry pan on the stove, swiftly diced one tomato, half a pepper and some onion and placed it in the pan. The vegetables cooked in some peanut oil while she cracked two eggs, added salt and red pepper, and whisked them together. "Lord, Rasheed makes me so happy but what I desire most is that he comes to the knowledge of you. Help me to be a witness for him to see your goodness." She prayed as she buttered her toast and poured the eggs into the vegetables tomato, pepper and onion mixture.

Rasheed already had her heart. She didn't intend for it to happen so soon but it did. She knew she loved him. Was he as serious about her as she was about him? She could not afford another Tokoni fiasco. After her ex and coming to Christ, she had promised God she'd never date again just for the sake of it. Very soon she would have to have a discussion with him. At that time, she hoped he wouldn't make her choose because although she loved him, her love for God and her soul was greater.

***

Rasheed looked up from the file again. After learning he owned the building that housed Bisso Bites, he also found out that Ibiso was having difficulty making the rent payments. He had given Ibiso enough prompts for her to tell him what was going on with her business herself but she remained evasive. He had let this play on for too long and it was time to put an end to the pretense. He tossed the file to the side and pressed the intercom.

"Yes, sir," Ireti answered.

"Please, tell Alhaji Hassan I want to see him."

"Yes sir, right away."

Rasheed leaned back in his chair. One thing he had learned about Ibiso was that she was one of the most strong-headed people he'd ever met. If only she would tell him what was going on, he could help her. But now he was just going to have to do what needed to be done and deal with the consequences later.

Alhaji Hassan entered after a brief knock. "Good morning, sir."

"Morning, have a seat." Rasheed stood and walked over to the window. He shoved his hands in his pockets and turned to face Alhaji. Rasheed could tell he was nervous from the way he tapped his feet.

"Friday, August 1st is the deadline for the occupants of that property. How is it going?" Rasheed asked.

"Sir everything is fine, o. Except one *yeye* woman *wey* always need more time. But don't worry. By Friday, if she doesn't pay, *I go* lock her restaurant." The man made the gesture of locking a door with his hands.

Rasheed's jaw tightened when Alhaji Hassan referred to Ibiso in the pidgin adjective that meant useless.

Rasheed walked over to his desk drawer, opened it and pulled the check he'd been mulling over for days. He tossed it on the table.

"Here – take this and pay it into the bank on behalf of Bisso Bites." Rasheed observed the man's questioning look. "Listen to me, a word of this to anyone and you might as well consider your contract as caretaker for that building over."

"Ah, yes *sah. Abeg*, I need this job *sah*. I won't say a word." Alhaji rubbed his hands together in a pleading gesture.

"I'm glad we understand each other." Rasheed paused. "On Friday when you make your rounds, skip over her restaurant." Rasheed banked on the fact that she'd be so busy that she wouldn't notice. "Are we clear?" Rasheed asked, as he sat back down in his chair.

The man opposite him stood and nodded, "Yes *sah*."

"Good, you can go now." Rasheed picked up his pen and twirled it between his fingers. When the door cracked open, he looked up and said, "Alhaji thanks, by the way, for all your hard work."

***

Ibiso squeezed her fingers as she paced the length of her office. The clanging of pots in the restaurant's kitchen offered no distraction from her thoughts. Amina had banished her from the kitchen after she almost poured sugar in the *Banga* soup instead of salt. The soup that was made out of the liquid from palm kernels was one of her customers' favorites. Growing up, she remembered how she had to gently pound the boiled kernels in a mortar to extract the liquid that was used for the soup. Now things had changed as there were factories that specialized in extracting and storing the liquid for sale in stores. This made the process simpler for restaurateurs.

It was Friday morning and she was supposed to be preparing for the lunch crowd. Instead she was in here rehearsing the lines she would tell Alhaji when he came by at five p.m. In the last couple of days, she had only succeeded in cutting her 80,000 Naira deficit by 30,000. This was made possible by a baby shower she catered two days before.

Rasheed had been upset when she cancelled their date, but she had to do what she must. Only a promise to make it up had pacified him. Despite the promise, he started to question her on the reason she agreed to take a job with such short notice, but she changed the subject.

Ibiso walked behind her desk and shook the mouse pad gently with her finger to exit the screensaver. She refreshed the screen. Her account balance hadn't changed since the last time she looked at it.

"Father, please help me soften this man's mind when he comes by today. Let him show me some kind of mercy," she prayed.

Then she opened the side drawer, pulled out her check book and wrote one that was 50,000 short. She had done all she can, now she just had to trust God to help her out. She placed the check in her apron pocket and went back into the kitchen. She had cast her worries onto Jesus, now it was time to get back to running her business and wait for five p.m.

Hours later, Ibiso sat at the back of the restaurant with a cool glass of *Zobo* to quench her thirst. The crowd had died down and she was thankful because it had been a great day. She looked at the

Cartier watch that adorned her wrist. It was a quarter to five. Feeling antsy, she stood and walked outside. A few moments later she spotted Alhaji Hassan as he exited the bookstore three doors down. He was talking to the owner with a smile on his face. Ibiso wondered for a few seconds why he hadn't stopped by her place first, but dismissed the thought. She might as well take advantage of his good mood.

Ibiso rushed back in and made a bee line for her office. Taking off her apron, she clutched the check in her hand and rushed back out. After a quick scan of the parking lot, she saw Alhaji headed to his car.

What is this man's plan? Is he trying to find a way to shut me down? He didn't even come to ask me about the money. Ibiso scurried across the open space to the crème colored Peugeot 504.

Almost out of breath, Ibiso tapped on the car. Alhaji wound down the window. The expression on his face was blank. She immediately got the vibe that she was wasting his time, and she hadn't even said anything yet.

"Miss Jaja, how may I help you?" he asked.

"Good evening Alhaji," Ibiso greeted the older man and waited for a response. She got none. So she continued, "Err, today is the deadline and I wanted to give you the check for the rent. I saw you at Mr. Okon's bookstore, but you didn't stop by my restaurant."

Alhaji Hassan stretched out his hand and took the check from her. Ibiso could swear she saw disgust written on his face. *Oh Jesus, help me not to curse this man out. How can he turn his nose up at my hard earned money?*

"It's short fifty thousand. I promise to have that by next weekend," she pleaded.

His eyes left the check and met her eyes. Then he looked back at the check, then back at her. What happened next left her stunned. He handed the check back to her.

"Here, take. Don't worry about it. It's not even complete."

"Huh? I don't understand. Alhaji, please *abeg*, I've worked so hard to get this place together. Don't shut me down. Look at me like your daughter. I'm just trying to make it."

The comparison to his daughter must have hit a nerve because he removed the *fula*, embroidered cap, from his head and tossed it to the passenger seat, exposing his bald head. "Look young lady, stop wasting my time. And don't ever compare yourself to my daughter."

"I didn't mean any harm. I was just trying to say, I could be your daughter so please just give me some more time."

"My daughter is living in her husband's house with two children, expecting a third. Never one day did she have a man that wasn't her husband pay her bills. She went straight from my house to her husband's house."

Her blood boiled. Ibiso scrunched her eyebrows together. "Excuse me. What are you talking about? You're holding a check that is short by just fifty thousand. That is *my* money."

"I would have respected you more if you had come out to speak the truth, instead of this cock and bull story. You know that your boyfriend has taken care of it." He shook his head and returned his cap to his head. "You these single girls are very fast...*kai*! That man just got into Nigeria a few months ago. Already you have your claws in him."

Ibiso jaw tightened and sweat dripped from her armpits. Her eyes stung from the angry tears that escaped them. *Who in the world did this man think he was talking to?* Her hands trembled in desire to connect with his face.

"I have no idea what you're talking about. If you were not old enough to be my father, I would have slapped the taste out of your mouth." She snatched the check out of his hand. "In fact give me my money. I'll look for who owns this building and go to him or her myself."

His laughter was mocking. "Young lady, why are you pretending you don't know the Danjumas own this place?" He wound up his glass and backed out of the parking space.

Ibiso stood in shock at Alhaji's Hassan's revelation. Her mind was racing but her body seemed to temporarily lose its motor skills.

If what Alhaji had implied was true, Rasheed was about to see another side of her. And it wouldn't be pretty.

Chapter 17

Rasheed looked at the phone in his hand. His eyes darkened with frustration. He was just about to shut down for the day when Ibiso's call came through a few minutes ago. She was so angry that she was inaudible. She hung up before he could ask for clarification, but the words Hassan and restaurant painted a pretty clear picture of the trouble he had gotten himself into. He did expect her to be upset but her anger was unexpected. It couldn't be the money alone that left her enraged. But since she was no longer answering his calls, there was one way to find out.

Adrenaline from his curiosity propelled him from his seat. He headed towards Ireti's desk. After asking her to get Hassan on the line, he shoved his hands in his pockets to wait.

"Sir, I can't get Alhaji on the phone," Ireti said after two tries.

"Okay thank you. I want him in my office first thing Monday morning." Rasheed stormed back into his office, shoved his laptop in its case and headed back out. "Have a good weekend."

Traffic was terrible and Ibiso hadn't returned or answered one of his numerous calls. An hour and a half later, Rasheed turned his car into her apartment complex. He walked up to her flat on the first floor and rang the bell. He waited a few minutes, but there was no answer. He knew she was at home because he saw her car outside. He rang the bell again, and then he thumped on the door.

"Go away, Rasheed. I don't want to see you." Ibiso's harsh voice came from the other side of the door.

"That's not going to happen, so open the door," Rasheed said.

"I've said all I wanted to say over the phone. Go away."

"I didn't. So it's either you let me in so we can talk in private or I can start talking here. Your choice, but you are going to hear me out."

He knew she was a private person and wouldn't want the neighbors hearing her business, but with her anger, she just might call his bluff. She didn't. The door swung open a few moments later.

"What." Her eyes narrowed. The daggers in them aimed for his heart.

Rasheed stepped inside with caution. He looked around as though he hadn't been in her apartment before. He was stalling to gauge her next move. From the thick tension in the room, it was safe to conclude that nothing much had changed since she hung up on him. He turned around to face her once he heard the door slam. Clad in an ankle length dress that hugged her hips, she looked so sexy, that his hands itched to reach out and pull her close. Common sense, however, told him to keep his hands to himself. The situation was near volatile and this was not the time. Her arms were folded across her chest. Her left eyebrow rose demanding an explanation.

Rasheed decided to take his chances and reached out to touch her. Ibiso dodged his touch and walked to the other end of the room. "Rasheed, it's late and I want to get some rest. Say what you have to say and go."

"I was only trying to help..."

"Help? Is that what you call it? You deliberately kept the truth from me and allowed that crazy old man to think I was after your money."

"What did he say to you?" His nostrils flared. If it was anything degrading, Alhaji was a goner.

"No you don't...pass this off like you have no blame in it. Why didn't you tell me that you were my landlord? How long have you known and kept it from me?"

"I should have told you..."

"You think?"

"But when I found out, I tried asking you about your restaurant's state so many times, but you dismissed it."

"For a reason. I wanted to do this on my own. I want my family to believe in me again. I wanted to believe in myself. I told you this."

Rasheed sighed. "Sweetheart, I understand that, but you were in trouble. All I did was help... a little." He used his thumb and index finger to demonstrate.

"By making me look so cheap in the process. That man fell short of calling me an *ashawo*."

Rasheed winced at the pidgin word for whore. That's it. He was going to kill him. Not only did he not follow his directives for discretion, but he voiced his opinion where it wasn't needed.

"I apologize. That wasn't my intention. I didn't want him harassing you and paying the rent outright would've raised unnecessary attention."

"Hmph...which you managed to do anyway." Ibiso walked into the kitchen and got herself a bottle of water.

"None for me?"

"No...I'm so mad at you right now."

"Some of this is your fault, too."

"My fault? How?"

"You should have told me. Part of being in a relationship is sharing, right?"

"Yes, but this money thing..."

His shook his head. "What are you talking about?" he asked with a puzzled look on his face.

"Your money. The first day we met, you thought money could fix everything. Same thing here...it's not about the money but the satisfaction I get from knowing that despite the mistakes of my past, I did this by myself." She paused. "I'm not with you because of your money."

Where did that come from? Rasheed moved towards her. In her state, she looked so unsure. He wrapped his arms around her waist, bent his head and brushed his lips against hers. She didn't withdraw

129

and he was glad. He had been dying to do that all evening and it felt so good. He was tired of fighting with her and from the way she melted in his arms, so was she.

Seconds later he lifted her head. "I never thought you were with me because of money. I apologize for putting you in that situation."

She poked his chest with her finger. "I'm still going to pay you back, every dime." She gestured her head toward the center table where a check laid. "That's everything I owe short fifty thousand. And you'll have that by month's end."

"I agree to anything you say, but only because I'm desperate to get back on your good side." Rasheed smiled. "But I have a better idea. Pay me back in kind."

Ibiso swatted him on his shoulder. "Be careful mister, you're treading on dangerous ground."

He rubbed his shoulder. "Ouch woman! Get your mind out of the gutter. What I mean is, I have a proposition for you."

***

"Have you eaten?"

"No. Why?"

"Let me get you something to eat while you tell me about this proposition of yours," Ibiso said. "I owe you two dinners and now a lot of money. Before I met you, I owed no one." She picked up the remote and tossed it to him. "I might as well get one meal out of the way."

Rasheed laughed. "Well, that's not entirely true."

Ibiso knew he was referring to the numerous times she had asked for an extension. She knew the crazy Alhaji probably gave him the run down. That man angered her so much. "Honey, being granted an extension on the rent is not the same thing as owing the rent."

Ibiso walked into the kitchen and turned on the burner. Her stainless steel gas stove was built into the island that was in the center of the kitchen. It was perfect for being able to cook and entertain company at the same time. She didn't have a lot of friends, but the ones she did have loved to eat anytime they came over.

She poured some oil in a large skillet and placed it on the burner. Next she took out three ripe plantains, peeled and cut them into diagonal slices.

Replaying the last few minutes in her head made her lips curve into a smile. Even after his explanation, Ibiso still thought Rasheed should have told her, but it was also the sweetest thing anyone had ever done for her. Her ex, on the other hand, just took and took from her. She had kept hidden the fact that she had given Tokoni almost half of her savings for one of the numerous business ideas he had. An investment he "guilted" her into the minute they got to Lagos. After she obliged, things changed and she never saw a return.

She diced up an onion and red peppers then added oil to a smaller pan. As she began to stir fry the vegetables and chopped spinach, she heard footsteps.

"I couldn't take it any longer, I had to follow the aroma." Rasheed pulled out one of the bar stools on the other side of the island.

Ibiso beamed, acknowledging him for a split second before she used the spatula to flip over the plantains. "Have a seat. We can talk while I cook."

"Didn't tell you before, but I like your apartment. Your kitchen is very chef like."

She giggled. "You are making up words now? I like it - Chef Ibiso of Bisso Bites."

It was his turn to chuckle. "Suits you. I never asked, what does Ibiso mean?"

"My full name is Ibisowari and it means good fortune." Her dad always told her she was his good fortune. "And so the story goes, I was conceived at the wrong time. When my mother was pregnant with me, things were really rough financially. My dad just lost his job and they contemplated abortion. One day, they had a change of heart. They stopped fretting about having a new mouth to feed but believed that and began to confess that the baby…me, would be their good fortune."

"Did you? Bring them good fortune."

"Yes, I did."

"So you're now *my* good fortune."

She grunted. "Your turn. What does Rasheed mean?"

Ibiso removed the brown plantains and placed them on a paper towel to drain the oil. She always did this before plating them. She then added some red sauce and a few large prawns to the vegetables and moved them around the pan to cook. She lowered the burner and looked up.

"It's Muslim as you know and it means 'rightly guided,'" he said, then remained silent.

Ibiso waited as she could sense he had more to say.

"We never went to church in the UK. I guess my parents couldn't agree on which one. But when my dad left, my mom raised us as Christians. I wonder why she didn't start calling us by the Ibo names she had for us."

"That's a deep name. I always believed that our names sometimes mold us. No wonder you carry the weight of the world on your shoulders, trying to live up to that name. What's your Ibo name?"

He smiled. "Naetochi – keep praising God."

She could tell he loved the name, but she decided to change the topic. "Nice…so you want something to drink?"

Rasheed flashed that smile that made her weak in the knees. "Just water. Thanks."

She handed him a glass of water and began serving their dinner. Rasheed took their plates to the dinette while she moved dirty pans to the sink.

Once they said grace, Ibiso watched Rasheed as he closed his eyes and savored the taste of the vegetable stir-fry.

"This is fantastic."

"Thanks." She took a couple more bites. "So, spill it. What do I have to do to pay off my debt?"

Rasheed swallowed. "I need your help with the center and finding an apartment."

"Excuse me? The center?"

He snickered at her alarmed response. "I would love to do more for that center and I need your help in the catering department."

"What else can I do? I already contribute there. And how would this repay what I owe?"

"I need your to help equip it, and hire and train new staff for the new state-of-the-art kitchen I want to donate," he said, pushing his empty plate away.

Ibiso's heart swelled with admiration. She leaned to the side and pouted her lips. He met them with a light kiss. She stretched her hand and caressed his cheek. "Honey, that is fantastic. I know how much centers like that mean to you, but isn't that a lot?"

He shrugged, but remained silent.

"But how can I do that with my schedule? I still have a restaurant to run."

"There's no rush. Moreover the longer it takes, the longer you owe me. It's a win-win." He teased her, raising his eyebrows up and down. You're stuck with me."

Ibiso stood and Rasheed did the same. She stopped with their dishes in her hand. "Oh, I forgot there are two parts to this. What are you doing with an apartment? Don't you have a house?"

He placed their glasses on the counter. "If you are referring to my mom's house, it's too far from the office and it's really a family home. I need a place to myself."

"Understood, but last I checked, I was a caterer and not a real estate agent. And FYI, everything you're asking is way more than 50,000 Naira," she said.

"I was thinking that the fact you like me would make you want to give me a bonus. To alleviate your fear, my realtor has some places to show me. I need your help decorating whatever I decide on."

"Hmmm, I gotta think about this." With her palms opened, she moved them up and down like they were a scale. "I'm weighing my options. Being your personal work horse or going to beg for your 50,000 to pay you off. Right now, the latter is looking very appealing."

He laughed. "You got jokes. Come on, please."

"The way you beg is cute. Now let's clean up."

Later that night, Ibiso knelt by the side of her bead, said her prayers, then slipped between her sheets. Rasheed had left right after the kitchen had been restored to its normal state. Doing something extra for the center was so appealing. It would also give her a chance to use some of her knowledge to help others. She would have jumped when he offered it, but she didn't want to seem too eager. So she promised to give him an answer if he attended church with her Sunday. She should feel bad about making him wait, but she found herself looking forward to him stewing about her answer. Moreover, anything to get Rasheed to church was worth it.

Chapter 18

Saturday went by in a haze. Ibiso took off and spent the day cleaning her apartment from top to bottom. She did her laundry and watched a chick flick then ended the evening with a call to her mother. The conversation was going on well until she heard her brother in the background. Just as quick, her mother's tone became distant. Ibiso, not wanting to ruin the memory, rushed off the phone, promising to call back during the week.

Feeling lonely, she longed to hear Rasheed's voice, but he had told her earlier he was spending the day with his mom since he rarely saw her during the week. He had been working crazy hours recently, so she could imagine. To brighten up the rest of the evening, she did the one thing she loved doing the most apart from cooking—working on her cooking video log to upload to her YouTube channel. She set up the camera, pulled out the pots and pans then began her 'how to' video on making Basmati coconut rice with baked turkey. She wasn't done until way past midnight. She uploaded the video and scheduled the post to appear on her social media platforms on Monday.

Her late night was the reason she was now waking up an hour later than her normal time. If she didn't hurry, Rasheed would get to the church before her. It wasn't until he got home from his mother's house that he confirmed by text that he was looking forward to going to church with her.

When Ibiso arrived at Overcomers Chapel forty minutes later, the praise team was deep in the throes of their own rendition of Tye Tribbet's hit, "Same God." She located Rasheed and slid into the pew, careful not to draw attention to herself. When he called her a few minutes ago asking where she was seated, she knew that her fears had come true. He did make it to the church before her. After telling him she was around the corner, he told her where he was seated. He smiled down at her, but didn't miss a beat, nodding his head to the music.

Ibiso tried to keep focused on worship, but her heartstrings played to their own music at the mere presence of the man standing next to her praising God. How sexy. Rasheed's light intoxicating scent of what she had come to know as Giorgio Armani's Aqua for Life caused her to steal glances at him. The dark green Kaftan with orange embroidery fitted him perfectly. He finished off his look with matching moccasins. The edging of his facial hair told her he visited the barber shop the day before. The inner man might be broken but the outer one was perfect. She needed Jesus' help to stay focused.

The praise team lowered the tempo of the music. As the soloist performed Shekinah Glory Ministry's "Yes", Ibiso knelt in prayer. *"Lord help me. I love him. If You brought us together for a reason, give me the wisdom to fulfill it. I know that for whatever temptation comes my way, You have already given me provision to overcome, in Jesus' name. Amen. Oh, thank You again for sending that helper for my restaurant to me. I would never have imagined it would be Rasheed. Thank You, again. "*

A heart that forgives and your destiny was the topic of Pastor Okiri's sermon. Ibiso heart skipped a beat. She glanced up at Rasheed. His jaw was set. Ninety five percent of the time when she came to church, it was as though God Himself was talking to her. This time, judging from the stiffness of Rasheed's body, she could tell that God was going to speak to him through this sermon. Rasheed had too much class to walk out now, so Ibiso knew he would listen, but something told her that he wasn't going to like it.

***

"In order to walk into your destiny you have to let go," Pastor Okiri told the congregation after initial pleasantries. "In Hebrews 12: 15 the Bible tells us to, *'Look after each other so that not one of you will fail to find God's best blessings. Watch out that no bitterness takes root among you, for as it springs up it causes deep trouble, hurting many in their spiritual lives.*

"Your destiny is that God-given assignment you have been called to do. Sometimes we remained stagnated in our human will and we are unable to fulfill our destiny… Why?
Because we haven't crossed over to His divine will and the reason

is rooted in our insistence on holding on to past hurt. The only way to avoid this is to let go."

Rasheed adjusted in his seat. He hated the way the word forgiveness was thrown around like it was that easy. Whatever happened to just shutting out the foolishness? If his mother wasn't preaching forgiveness, Ibiso was. Why couldn't they see that it was not that easy? He had sacrificed his dreams by fulfilling his father's wish of running Danjuma Group. Something the family had looked up to him to do. What else did they want from him?

He felt Ibiso's hand cover his gently. He looked down to meet her faint smile. He interlocked his fingers in hers and held on tight. Their eyes remained on each other for a few seconds before the pastor's shout of, "Fix us, Jesus" caught their attention. Over the next few minutes, he illustrated his point with the story of Joseph in the Bible. He was wronged, but had later shown mercy to the very people that perpetuated the crime—his brothers.

Rasheed was about to convince himself that he had done the same – after all, he was showing mercy by running the business he didn't have intentions of getting involved with at first. That was until he heard a voice in his spirit. One he hadn't heard before.

Blessed are the pure in heart, for they will see God. Rasheed shook his head, and then turned to Ibiso. He was about to ask if she heard the voice too when he was interrupted by the Pastor. "If you are struggling with this, as we all are sometimes, just like David did in Psalm 51:10, let's ask God to 'create in us a pure heart, and renew a steadfast spirit within us'."

***

It wasn't until the following Friday evening that Ibiso and Rasheed had the opportunity to see each other again. After church, he made an excuse of being tired and went home. Ibiso noticed his pensive mood, so wasn't buying his story but decided to let it slide. Before she let him go however, she told him of her decision to help him with his proposal. The smile on his face was worth making him wait. During the week, they both had been so busy that they only managed to check in with each other for a brief period during the day.

Ibiso bound her braids in a neat up-do and freshened up her

lip gloss. She reached for her keys when the doorbell rang. She studied herself in the mirror then twirled around, satisfied with the impeccable way her tailor had put her fuschia and blue Ankara jumpsuit together. The off-the-shoulder ensemble made her feel sexy.

Rasheed had refused to discuss the details of the proposal over the phone, so tonight he was taking her out for dinner and a movie. Ibiso was excited when she found out he was taking her to Abuja's newest ultra-modern theatre. The theatre didn't serve regular movie snacks, but high-end appetizers and full entrees. Each theatre in the complex seated fifty people and had waiters assigned to each room to cater to the needs of its customers. The only other place Ibiso had seen a movie theatre set up like this was overseas.

She opened the door just as the bell rang a second time. Her stomach went into knots at the sight of the man who stood in front of her. Her breath caught in her throat, silencing her greeting. Rasheed entered and kissed her on the cheek

"You look beautiful," he said.

Finding her voice, she replied. "Thank you, so do you."

"Ready to go?"

She nodded and he ushered her out of the apartment.

A couple of hours later, Ibiso and Rasheed exited the theatre after enjoying a romantic comedy. Walking hand in hand, they made their way to the car. The breeze was light and fresh. It brought with it a stillness that Ibiso welcomed, but at the same time dreaded.

They didn't have any particular movie in mind that they wanted to see, so when they got to the theatre, both of them opted for the next movie that was playing. It was *The Other Woman*. Ibiso was hesitant having seen the commercial. The movie was about a cheating man and the women seeking revenge. It was sure to remind him of his real life, but Rasheed had been insistent. She didn't want anything to spoil this evening. But judging by Rasheed's mood, it already had.

"So did you enjoy the movie?" Ibiso asked.

"It was okay. Not my thing, but I'm glad you enjoyed it."

Ibiso wanted to do something to salvage the evening, and she remembered the perfect thing. "Do you still have that blanket I saw in your car the other day?"

"Yes, why?" He unlocked the car and opened the door for her.

"I know you love music. There's a music festival going on in the park not too far from here." Ibiso watched his expression lighten.

"I'd love that. You sure you're up to it?"

"Are you calling me old?"

He got into the car and turned to her. "If the shoe fits..." He shrugged and laughed.

Ibiso gave him a playful punch on his shoulder. "Even if I were, it's just 9 pm. Let's go."

Half an hour later, Ibiso sat with her legs folded beside her on the blanket with Rasheed's arms around her shoulders. The park looked different. The organizers had done some major cleaning and decorating to make this a great experience for those in attendance. She took in a deep breath and exhaled slowly as she savored the moment, enjoying the jazz musician who was now on stage. The hairs on Ibiso's neck stood as she felt Rasheed nuzzle her neck. She turned her head. The look on his face was tender, and their eyes locked in a moment filled with intensity. The pull between them caused his lips to land on hers in a sensual but brief kiss.

"That was unexpected. Nice, but unexpected. Are you okay now?" She asked.

He looked at her with a puzzled look on his face. "Why wouldn't I be?"

"Err, I don't know. Since Sunday, you've been kinda distant and the movie tonight..."

"Oh so you think because another person talked about forgiveness and I watched a movie about a cheating man that all of a sudden, I'm fragile?"

"Rasheed, that's not what I mean—"

"Let's just drop it."

"No."

"No?"

"I won't drop it. You just snapped at me. That confirms my fears that despite what you say, this thing with your dad still has a hold on you. " She sat up straight and faced him.

"You have no idea what you're talking about."

She took his hand in hers. "Look, I won't pretend to know what it feels like, but I do know what pain is and you gotta forgive him. He's dead."

Ibiso felt Rasheed flinch as he removed his hand from hers. "Are you ready to go?"

"Are you dismissing me?"

"I'm kind of tired. Let's call it a night."

"Fine." Ibiso felt her blood rise. She remembered her conversation with Boma several weeks ago. She was not going to be caught up being Rasheed's savior.

I tried to do it for Tokoni and failed in a terrible way. She forced on her shoes and stalked off, leaving Rasheed to fold up the blanket.

Ibiso was leaned against the car with her hand on her hip as Rasheed approached. *The anger of a man doesn't produce the virtue of God.* The words came through a tiny whisper in the air. She relaxed, as God's word resonated in her spirit. Rasheed unlocked the car and she got in.

"I'm sorry." He gripped the steering wheel.

She remained silent.

"I seem to be saying that a lot lately." He turned her face towards him. "Sweetheart, I didn't mean to take any of this out on you. I'm not good at talking about my father or what he did to destroy our family. Then the fact that he had the nerve to have me clean up his mess now that he's gone makes me so angry sometimes."

Ibiso placed her hand over his. "I'm so sorry. I'm trying to help. That's what people in relationships do."

"That's the problem. You can't. Left to my mom, you and the pastor, you all want me to forget my past, but it has become part of my future."

"I'm not saying forget, but forgive." She raised her hand to stroke his face. "Forgiveness doesn't mean amnesia."

"Are they not the same thing? How do you do one without the other?" He paused. "I refuse to absolve him of his wrong."

Ibiso's heart clenched at the pain and anger she saw in his eyes. "Honey, you won't be absolving him. You'll be freeing yourself from bondage. Don't you see, everything you've ever done revolves around him and trying to prove something based on what he did?"

He turned away. "So you've analyzed me in a few short months?"

"Rasheed, don't shut me out, please. You've made me care for you and I don't want to see you in pain."

His mocking laughter filled the car. "Pain? Look who's talking. Isn't everything you've done in the past couple of years to prove something to your family because of what Tokoni did to you?"

His words cut her, but she wasn't going to cower. That's what she would have done with Tokoni.

The tension was thick. "Doesn't the Bible say something about removing the log from your eyes before you remove the one in another's?" he asked.

"For your information, you and I are different. I do *not* walk around angry and bitter. I learnt from the wrong done to me and moved on. My success is the best revenge I could have. I could say the same for you, but you can't enjoy your success because you're still holding on to the past." She paused and tugged on the seat belt then fastened it. "And since we're talking about the Bible – newsflash – all the charity you do to means nothing in the sight of God when you are failing in His one command."

"Which is?"

"Love. Your swag is great, but your love walk sucks. You can't even begin to love if you can't forgive."

Rasheed sighed. "Ibiso—"

"No, Rasheed. I'm done for the night and tired. I know you are, too. Just take me home."

Rasheed started the car and Ibiso leaned her head back and closed her eyes. Both of them were angry and frustrated. She knew he was lashing out, but it was hurtful to hear what he had to say about her. They needed space before things got out of hand.

Neither of them spoke, each deep in their thoughts. In trying to help Rasheed heal his brokenness, Ibiso was beginning to think she had just been putting a Band-Aid over hers. She shook her head to rid herself of the thought.

I have forgiven Tokoni. That chapter in my life is a done deal. I have moved on. As she reflected on the thought, her inner spirit convicted her. *You might have forgiven, but have you been able to let go?*

Chapter 19

Rasheed stood by as the movers placed the last piece of furniture in its place. His mother came out of the kitchen with her hands behind her back. Her expression told him she was impressed.

"*Nna*, I'll miss having you around the house. But, I'm happy for two reasons," she said.

"Which are?"

His mother walked over to him and rubbed his back. "One, you'll be closer to the office so driving that distance late at night will be over. Two, at least you aren't thousands of miles away in London."

He put his arm around her shoulders and pulled her close. "You have your late husband to thank for number two, but I'm glad you're happy."

She nudged him with her elbow. "Who are you deceiving? Your family isn't the only reason you decided to stay in Nigeria. I have Ms. Jaja to thank for that, too. I see she makes you happy and you're now relaxing. Not as much as I'd like, but I'm grateful for baby steps." She paused and looked around. "Where is she, by the way? I haven't seen her lately and thought I would see her here."

"She had an event to cater today," Rasheed replied. He hated lying to his mother, since she had already started naming her imaginary grandchildren. But Ibiso was grating his nerves. However, if he was truthful, he'd admit that he missed her like crazy.

It had been some days since their disastrous date in the park. He sent her flowers the next day to apologize. In return, he got a polite, "Apology accepted. Thank You for the flowers." via text message. Things hadn't quite been the same.

She did fulfill her end of the deal and help him decide on the house, but had to get back to the restaurant immediately after. He knew she had a business to run and so did he, so he couldn't question her on it. But of late, something always came up or she had some pressing matter with the restaurant. Rasheed knew he had taken their relationship a few steps back, but hoped to redeem himself later in the evening when they would meet at the appliance store to look at the kitchen appliances and fixtures for the center. Rasheed was thankful that at least she was still willing to do that. He kind of knew she would. Nothing gave her joy and put her in a good mood like talking about her passion—cooking.

"Hmm, okay. Tell her she has an open invitation to lunch any time she's free," his mother said.

He nodded. "I'm glad you like the new place. The fact that it's close to the office is a huge plus."

"So how are things at work?"

Rasheed observed his mother. She seemed happy. He didn't want to bother her with the happenings at Danjuma Group. There were a lot of people trying to frustrate his efforts for change and bringing the company into the new century, but there were others that were very supportive. The close association between his half-sister Halima and Uncle Musa had begun to worry him. Something was just not right with them.

"What's that look on your face? Is anything wrong?" she asked.

"I'm sure it's nothing, but I was just wondering about how close Halima and Uncle Musa are becoming."

"That man is after everything your dad ever built. Please be careful. As for your sister..."

"Half-sister..."

Rasheed was not moved by his mother's extended stare at him. Jabir and Kamal might consider her their sister, but she was his half-sister. Plain and simple.

"How long?"
"Huh?"

"How long will you carry this anger around? That girl is just as much a victim in all of this as you and your brothers are. Put yourself in her shoes. After worshipping her father and wanting to follow in his footsteps, he opted to have the son he abandoned fill his shoes when he died."

"Since when are you her advocate?"

"I'm not, but I'm a Christian and you're not behaving like the son I raised. I taught you better than that. At least I thought I did. Learn to forgive or you *will* end up destroying yourself."

Rasheed sighed. Truth is, he wished he could but he didn't have it in him. This was supposed to be a happy day for him and his mom. He had taken her out to breakfast and now she was at his new house. He seemed to turning all his dates into disasters these days and he didn't like hurting the people he cared about.

"Mama, I'm sorry. Pray for me." He smiled at her, "You swear it works right?"

"Yes, it does and I will, but you have to make up your mind to let it go. As for your sister, I think she's just looking for an ally since you made it pretty clear you didn't want anything to do with her. My advice would be to draw her close. She could help you. Those people have known her much longer. Besides, she is your blood."

***

Ibiso turned her car into the parking spot closest to the entrance of the appliance store. She turned off the engine and leaned her seat back. She had chosen to meet Rasheed here instead of having him picking her up. In the last few days, they had seen each other once. He did send her flowers to apologize, but she was still conflicted on how she could help his brokenness when it was pretty obvious she was not completely whole.

At first, she was in denial of the truth he had pointed out. She told herself that she was still mad at him. To some extent she was, but she was in fact mad at herself. She hadn't come as far as she thought she had. If that was the case, she had no business trying to help someone else with their drama.

This relationship was moving too fast anyway. She was ready to work on herself, but it was clear that Rasheed had no intention of doing the same. She couldn't spend time trying to save a man who didn't want to save himself. The only person that could heal Rasheed's hurt was Jesus. But he had to make the first move and surrender. As much as she knew she loved him, she couldn't do it for him.

Her mind flashed back to the verse in her devotional that morning, from the book of Proverbs. It was the same thing Boma drummed into her head when she was a new babe in Christ. *"Make no friendships with a man given to anger, and with a wrathful man do not associate, lest you learn his ways and get yourself into a snare."* Considering how fast she had fallen for Rasheed, and the time they spent together, she would end up being influenced by him sooner or later.

The buzzing in her purse interrupted her thoughts. She reached in and saw the caller ID display 'Boma.'

"Hey B, you finally called me back."

"Sorry *jare*. I've been so busy with getting a nanny. I told you, I go back to work after the twin's dedication. I wish you were here so we could do this together... *godmother*," Boma said.

Ibiso felt a pang of guilt. This was her friend's happy time. Her own issues could wait. "Don't mean to be so insensitive with my needs. My BFF is dedicating her twins...twins! I'm excited for you, really I am."

"I know you are, but I could use the break. So what's going on?" Boma asked. "Oh real quick before I forget, have you found shoes to go with the *aso-ebi*?"

"Yes, you'd die for the navy and silver shoes I got. They match the *gele* perfectly. In fact I have a picture in my phone. I'll send it to you."

Ibiso spent the next few minutes reassuring her friend that her seamstress would have her silver toned lace *aso-ebi* ready by next week. As the godmother to the twins, Ibiso's attire had to be on point.

"Okay my bad, so what has Rasheed done now? How many days have you given him the cold shoulder?" Boma asked.

"How do you know that's what happened?"

"Because I know my friend. Spill."

Ibiso narrated Alhaji Hassan's incident, Rasheed's apology, his plan for her to pay him back, the church service and then ended with the disastrous park date.

"Hello?" Ibiso asked when she didn't hear anything at the other end of the phone.

"I'm here. Just trying to wrap my head around the soap opera that has become your life. My husband and I need to move to Abuja. A lot more seems to happen there." Her friend began to laugh.

"I'm happy to be your afternoon entertainment, but my problem is not funny."

"What problem? You don't have any except the one you're creating. You're so upset about nothing that you can't see the blessing God just handed you."

"What blessing?"

"You've been working day and night to get this money. The women's summit you were counting on didn't happen, and God sends you a helper, case closed."

Both friends were quiet for a long moment.

Then Boma continued, "So what? Shoot the man for wanting to free his woman from stress by helping out financially. He could have gone about it better, but it's the thought that counts. Secondly, remember when I was telling you about Christ? You shot me down every chance you got. Did I stop being your friend? No, I kept at it, witnessing with words and actions. You can't keep shouting Christ to him in words and when he does something you think is wrong, you stop talking or avoid him. What message are you sending? Remember you can be angry, but do not sin. Let it go."

Ibiso shifted in her seat. She looked out of the window to see if Rasheed had arrived. He hadn't.

"I'm not saying that you should forfeit your soul to be with

147

him, but if you care about him, you'd want him to experience the freedom in Jesus. Just like we do. The only way you can do that is with action and not words. Be kind, loving, and forgiving and he will follow you to Jesus faster than you think."

"But B, I think he might have been right. What qualifies me to help him? I don't even think I'm healed myself."

"Then heal. Love is a risk…you know that."

"Yes, I do and look what happened."

"Hey, it wasn't meant to be. Quit letting your past continue to make you cautious about everything."

"I thought I had, honestly," Ibiso said.

"Listen to me. You *are* qualified and I believe called. Stop trying to do it on your own. Lean to the Holy Spirit."

Ibiso sighed. She felt bad for her childishness. "Have I told you I love you?"

"Love you back. Lately, I hear so much joy and laughter in your voice, so Rasheed is good for you. Your process to forgiveness is different from his. Respect his process and help him through it. Love is supposed to cover all."

Ibiso was speechless. She hadn't looked at it that way. As she was about to respond, there was a tap on her window—Rasheed. She wound down the window and gave him a faint smile. Signaling that she was on the phone, she returned to Boma. "I have to go now. Thank you and I'll call you later tonight."

"Is that Rasheed?" Boma asked.

Ibiso hesitated and responded slowly, "Yes. Why?" She knew her friend was about to embarrass her.

"Give him the phone."

"Huh?"

"Give him the phone."

Ibiso got out of the car and with a sideways glance, she handed the phone to Rasheed.

She locked the car and stood by as Rasheed nodded a few time and laughed before handing the phone back to her. Ibiso put the phone to her ear but got a dial tone. *I'm gonna kill Boma.*

"You look nice. Ready to do this?"

"Ummm...aren't you going to tell me what you discussed with Boma?"

"Let me think about it." He looked up to the sky in feigned contemplation. "I thought about it...no." He grabbed her hand and began walking into the store.

That's what he thought. She had the secret weapon that would be used to retrieve that information—food. Her food.

***

"Huh? What did you say?" Ibiso asked.

"I said you were in your natural habitat back there. You were like a kid in the candy store," Rasheed said, as they walked back to her car two hours later.

Rasheed had spared no cost on what they needed. He was passionate about giving back which made her feel even worse about what she said about his charity meaning nothing. His care was genuine and pure. It was as though he was reliving his painful childhood, trying to make up for whatever he lacked.

"The kitchen is my natural habitat." She nudged him. "You know that. I get excited when I see things that could make my cooking easier."

They had picked out a state of the art stainless steel stove, a mega-sized refrigerator and a deep freezer that was perfect for a commercial kitchen. The stove was equipped with two convection ovens and a warming drawer. It was every cook's dream. The fridge, also stainless steel was huge and had compartments that varied in temperature according to what was stored in them. Ibiso dreamed of the day she'd be able to expand her restaurant and have something like that. Now all she had to do to finish the job was hire the right cooks. That would make the effort worthwhile.

"I know. I'm happy to be a little part of the smile on your face."

They reached her car and she to get out her keys when he placed his hand over hers to stop her.

"Do you have to go now? We could get a drink together."

"Let me think about it." Ibiso leaned against her car, crossed her arms across her chest and studied him for a few seconds. "Why would I want to do that? I came here to pay off some of my debt." The look on his face made it hard for her to contain her amusement.

"Come on, have mercy...I'm trying to get out of a hole here."

She laughed. The expression on his face changed to confusion before he relaxed and joined her.

She rubbed his cheek. "You were never in the hole, just teetering on the edge. I kinda like you, remember?"

He leaned into her, and rested his forehead against hers. Their silence spoke volumes despite the riot going on in her head. She reached up, wrapped her arms around his neck and hugged him.

"I'm sorry," she whispered in his ear.

"I am, too. I have things to work out, but please don't give up on me." The soothing baritone of his lowered voice so close to her face sent her heart racing.

A beat of silence passed between them. She cupped his face. His gaze at her was so intense that his eyes seemed to change color. "I'm trying, but you have to meet me halfway by opening up your heart to the possibility of letting go and surrendering to God. As you can see, this affects you and me, too."

He captured her lips and kissed her to seal the deal. "You're right."

"Rasheed Naetochi Danjuma, is that you?" the woman who owned the car parked next to Ibiso's screamed. They had been so engrossed in their discussion that they hadn't seen her come up. But apparently the woman hadn't been so engrossed in her own business that she noticed a man who had his back to her.

Rasheed turned around. From his slow motion moves, Ibiso could tell he knew her. The woman walked around to where they were and wrapped her hands around his neck. Ignoring the fact the Ibiso was standing there.

"Adaku. Hi, long time." Rasheed said as he tried to break loose from her grasp and create some space between them.

"It's been ages. Don't tell me that you came into the country and didn't bother to call."

Ibiso sized up the woman who had completely ignored her. She was almost as tall as Rasheed and was dressed in tight, skinny, white jeans and a casual t-shirt that she knotted at her back, revealing her navel and the ring that hung from it. Her skin was a light mocha shade which was several shades lighter than Ibiso's. Regardless of her attitude, the woman was drop dead gorgeous. It caused the green animal in her to rise. As though he read her mind, Rasheed turned to her.

"Ibiso, this is Adaku—"

"Iheme. Adaku Iheme, Miss Nigeria 1989," Ibiso said.

The woman flipped her hair around. Her eyes looked like there were about to pop out of their sockets. "That's 1999, sweetie."

Did this woman just call her sweetie like she was a groupie? Two can play at this game. "Oh, I thought you were much older." Ibiso knew the right year but couldn't resist. She knew she'd have to repent later.

"Adaku, this is my friend Ibiso Jaja." Rasheed completed the introductions. "We were just leaving."

"Okay, darling," Adaku lifted her hand to caress Rashid's face. "I'll call you." She then walked away without even looking Ibiso's way. Ibiso watched as she got into her Porsche and sped off.

"I apologize for her rudeness. Adaku is a spoiled brat," Rasheed said.

"Friend?" Ibiso asked.

"Huh?"

"Don't huh me. This *friend* has to go repent for her thoughts."

"It's like that?"

"Yep! Pick me up in the morning for church." She winked and

got into her car.

As she drove away, she glanced up at her rearview mirror, and saw Rasheed still standing there looking confused.

Serves him right for referring to me as a friend.

Chapter 20

"So, what do you think?" Rasheed asked as he ushered Ibiso back around to the living room where they had started the tour of his new home. Ibiso hadn't been to his home since he moved in. There hadn't been any time, which was why he was thrilled when she agreed to follow him back after church. He needed her approval on the final look. Why – he didn't know or rather he wasn't ready to admit it.

Even though Ibiso said she was fine, he had been kicking himself ever since he introduced her as a friend. She was more than that, but seeing Adaku had caught him by surprise. He called her later that evening and apologized for himself and Adaku. He had slept better, however, he remembered how her claws came out at Adaku's behavior. Ibiso was jealous. For him, it meant she cared for him far more than she let on. That was fine by him because he cared for her too, but wasn't ready to put labels on anything.

"I love it." Ibiso walked back into the kitchen.

Rasheed followed. He watched as she twirled around and admired all the appliances once again. She had since kicked off her shoes and was barefooted. Seeing her so carefree in his kitchen, in his home, made his heart swell. She fit perfectly. For a second, he could imagine her making meals for him and their kids in this kitchen. He shook his head at the thought.

Where did that come from? He and Ibiso were just getting to know each other. Besides he hadn't made up his mind on whether Nigeria would be a permanent thing for him. A lot could happen in a year and he wasn't ready to put his heart all on the line. Although as they spent more and more time together, he felt he no longer had a say in the matter. He couldn't stop thinking about her when they were apart and he yearned for more time with her when they were together. But that was it. He was *fond* of her. Love was nowhere in the cards for him. It did too much damage.

"I'm so jealous of this kitchen. No fair because you can't even boil water and you have such a kitchen." She crossed her arms and pouted.

Rasheed walked over to where she was leaned against the fridge. He drew her face up to his and kissed her pouted lips. "Sweetheart, you can use my kitchen any time. Now would be nice." He kissed her forehead and walked into the living room to turn on the television.

Ibiso twirled a strand of her newly twisted hair around her finger. "Hmm...I don't know. I was all willing to cook for you when I thought you were a helpless bachelor. But now that I know you have *friends* everywhere, maybe one of them could do it."

Rasheed threw his head back "Urghhh... don't start with that again. I told you Adaku is the daughter of my mom's friend. My mom introduced us when I visited home some years ago. Her hope was I would fall hopelessly in love with Adaku and get married."

Ibiso opened up the stainless steel refrigerator.

With nothing else to do last night, Rasheed had gone to the supermarket to stock up the fridge. Hoping Ibiso would come back here with him after church. Everything was working just fine and if he wanted it to continue that way, he had to change the topic.

"I guess the fact that she was a beauty queen didn't hurt." Ibiso took out some lamb chops, red and green peppers, and tomatoes.

Rasheed threw the remote on the couch and walked back into the kitchen. "Listen to me. Yes, I dated Adaku, but that's over. I haven't seen her in ages. You heard her yourself. I care about you and we are here now together. Now, can we drop it?"

Rasheed turned around and headed in the direction from which he came. Several drops of water touched his neck. He wiped it off and turned around. Ibiso had splashed water on him.

"Where are you going?" Ibiso asked.

"There's a soccer game on."

"Do you see the words personal chef written on my

forehead?" She went to the pantry door, got an apron, and threw it to him. She pulled out a knife and the chopping board. "Here, dice up half a pepper each. In my house if you wanted to eat, you had to work. Now govern yourself accordingly."

With a fake pout on his face, he got to work. The main game he wanted to watch was the next one. But Ibiso didn't have to know that.

Later, they were seated at the dining table finishing up the meal they prepared together. At first, Rasheed had a problem dicing the peppers the way Ibiso wanted. Her attempt at showing him the proper way was futile. Her beauty was breathtaking and the light fragrance she wore sent his mind in such a frenzy that he couldn't concentrate. At a point, she wanted to kick him out of the kitchen but he got serious, because he wanted to be right where she was. Even if it meant getting serious and paying attention.

The baked lamb chops with stew, spaghetti and veggie mix was superb.

"That was something else," Rasheed said as he put a spoonful of the fruit salad she made in his mouth. She was quick and swift with the knife, cutting up bananas, strawberries, pineapple, mango and guavas in record time.

"I'm glad you liked it."

"There is always something unique in your dishes. I've had similar meals..." He saw her raised eyebrow and quickly added, "I mean either in a restaurant or my mom's, but yours taste different. What's the deal?"

"Err, let me think about it...I thought about it. I'm not telling you what it is." She stood, picked up the empty serving bowl, and headed to the kitchen.

"Touché." He was tickled at her imitation of him. "Okay you got me. If you tell me, I'll tell you what Boma said."

"Promise?" she yelled over the running water.

"Yes."

"I don't trust you. You go first. Boma won't tell me."

"I'm hurt." He placed his free hand across his heart and placed the last dish in the sink.

Ibiso turned from the sink to look at him. It was the perfect opportunity for him to steal a kiss and he did.

"So?"

"She said I shouldn't pay any attention to your attitude. That you do that to people you like, and you like me a lot."

Ibiso mouth was open. "No she didn't out me like that."

Rasheed took paper towel and wiped off the table. "Yes, she did and after that she invited me to Port Harcourt for the twins' dedication."

The look of total disbelief on Ibiso face was priceless. For the first time she didn't have a smart comeback.

"Now your turn," Rasheed said.

"You ready for it? Are you ready? This will blow your mind...so simple yet profound."

He walked back to the kitchen and trashed the paper towel. He rubbed his hands together in anticipation. His eyes widened with admiration. He loved this playful side of her. "I'm ready. What's your secret? Unless...you're afraid I'll start cooking better than you. Then I get why you're stalling."

Ibiso placed an empty storage container on the counter. "Honey, even if I write a manual for you starting with how to turn on the burner, that can never happen. If you must know, the secret is I always put a scoop of ..."

"Of what?"

"Of love. A scoop of love." Ibiso picked up the pot of spaghetti and transferred the leftovers into the container. She covered it and placed it in the fridge. "Silence. You got nothing to say after my reveal? Or the profoundness has you speechless. I knew it."

"Are you serious?"

"Yes, I put in a scoop of love. A scoop is like a spoon but not as flat, it's deep. I put a deep dose of love and care into every meal I prepare."

Rasheed could tell Ibiso was waiting for a reaction, but words failed him.

She got another container and put in the remaining lamb chops. "Christ gave His all that He was willing to die for us, so when I cook I always give it my all. I value those who buy or taste anything I have prepared."

She began to pour the tomatoes sauce in the next container when Rasheed blurted out,

"That's the *corniest* thing I've ever heard. How you manage to turn almost everything into a Bible lesson stuns me."

They both busted out in laughter. He saw the exact moment the almost empty pot began to slip from her hand. He rushed to get it, but it was too late. The remaining contents spilled all over the bottom part of her dress.

Ibiso placed her palm on her forehead. "Oh no." She got some wet paper towels and tried to wipe off the huge stain. Instead of disappearing, it was expanding.

"Okay stop, you'll ruin it. Gimme a second." Rasheed strode to his bedroom. Seconds later, he came out with a pair of slacks and a t shirt. "Here, put these on, and we'll get that to the dry cleaners later."

Ibiso took them from him and dragged her feet into the half bath he had shown her earlier. When she was out of sight, Rasheed let out the chuckle he had been suppressing. *That's what she gets for making up corny stuff—a scoop of love. Yeah right.*

Chapter 21

The clothes Rasheed gave her swallowed her whole body. Ibiso must have folded the lounge slacks up a numerous times just to get them to stay above her ankles.

How could I have poured stew on myself? This is just a mess. She lifted up her hair to adjust the collar of the University of Edinburgh t-shirt he had given her. The clothes had that freshly laundered smell, but his scent lingered. The closeness she felt to him sent her senses racing. She had to take a minute to get her thoughts under control. She didn't want to get ahead of herself. She loved him, but wasn't sure he was there yet.

She looked down to ensure that she had secured the pants with the tie rope. Then she tied up her soiled clothes in a nylon bag and left the bathroom. She was startled by Rasheed's voice.

"Are you kidding me? Not again." He was sitting at the edge of the couch, shouting at the television.

Ibiso picked up her pace. "What is it?"

He looked at her and paused. His eyes roamed all over her. The heated glare caused her to fidget with the nylon bag in her hand.

"What is it? And you better not tell me you're screaming at those football players, because I ran out here thinking something else was wrong."

"You look so good in my clothes," he said, turning his attention back to the television.

Her heart rate accelerated at his remark but normalized when she remembered her mother's, "why buy the cow, when they can have the milk for free?" lecture.

"Don't get used to it." Ibiso walked over to her bag to retrieve her phone. Although she liked soccer, she wasn't in the mood for a game. She decided to occupy herself with social media until the game was over.

Ibiso leaned back on the arm of the couch and stretched her legs in the huge amount of space between them on the couch. Rasheed, who was now dressed in a casual, black, Ralph Lauren t-shirt and a pair of three-quarter length khaki shorts, hadn't flinched since.

Men and sports. She peered at the television and saw the players dressed in red and blue running across the field. Barcelona was playing the Real Madrid.

"So are you going to tell me why you were screaming?"

Rasheed looked her way for a fleeting minute, smiled, then turned back to the television.

"Sweetheart, I don't scream. But if you want to know why I was *shouting*, it was because one player bit another."

Ibiso sat up straight. "You mean bit as in like a dog? He put a person's sweat filled skin between his teeth? What in the world?"

"I'll tell you the whole sordid story, but let the game be over first – thirty more minutes." He stood, kissed her on the forehead and went into the kitchen to get a bottle of water.

Ibiso resumed her position and began logging into her social media pages.

It wasn't until Rasheed tugged her toes that she realized thirty minutes had passed. The timer on her phone indicated it was five thirty. She had been so engrossed in networking and updating her Facebook, Twitter and Instagram pages that the time just flew by.

"I should be on my way," she said, putting her phone to the side.

"Come on, stay with me a little longer. I forgot that the game was on today. Couldn't resist." He pursed his lips together and pouted. "I'll tell you about that player."

"That's now old news."

His eyebrows furrowed. "It was just thirty minutes ago."

"Is it by force? I don't want to know about the biter again."
She struggled to keep a straight face. His desperation was
charming.

"You must hear about him, *oh*." Rasheed teased. He inched
towards her like a lion after its prey. Ibiso tried to get up and run
but then tripped on the loose pants she was wearing and fell right
into his arms before they landed on the carpet. She thought he was
about to kiss her and she tried to get up. Instead he pinned her
down and started to tickle her. She laughed so hard that her sides
hurt.

Ibiso raised her hands in surrender. "Okay, okay tell me about
the biter. But then you have to watch Super Story with me."

"What is that?"

"A sitcom. It's my guilty pleasure."

"Deal."

Rasheed helped her up and handed her the remote. She
changed the channel and settled back into the sofa. She listened in
displeasure as he told her about the player on the Barcelona team
that was notorious for biting. Apparently the need to taste
another's skin overtook him in the height of tension. Ibiso thought
it was a joke, until he told her of other instances.

"He's supposed to play for his country in the world cup. I
hope he doesn't do that there," Rasheed said.

"The man might need psychological help. So what team is
yours because I want to know what boundaries not to cross?"

"Sweetheart, you can cross any boundary with me any time."

"Be serious and FYI, that's not happening so get your mind
out of the gutter."

Rasheed chuckled. "Madrid."

The theme song for her show started to play and she raised her
hand to silence him. He pulled her close and wrapped his arm
around her. Ibiso placed her head on his shoulder and
concentrated on the television.

Rasheed was still amused by the time the show ended. She was glad he watched it with her. She went into the kitchen and put together a trail mix snack. It consisted of peanuts, cashew nuts and coconut slices. When she got back, Rasheed had his laptop on his lap.

"What's this? Checking if you got an email from the procurement officer?" She handed him his bowl.

"Thanks. You know me so well. Yes, I am."

Ibiso knew that one of the biggest challenges Rasheed was facing at work was getting people on board who supported his leadership and all the changes he had ordered with human resources, IT, and now the cement plant. The company's largest source of income was its cement business. The plant was located at Lokoja which was about a three-hour drive from Abuja.

Danjuma Group was already the sole supplier of cement to big name construction companies in and outside of Nigeria and most Nigerian state governments. His next plan was to supply to Federal governments, starting with Nigeria and Ghana. To do that, however, he needed to upgrade the machines. He had charged the procurement officer with finding a vendor that would provide these newer ones.

"You know you told him to show you nothing but the best money could buy, so it might be taking a little time to vet all the vendors," she said.

"I guess you're right. The town hall I had with the people of Okpella was dominated with complaints about their water supply being contaminated. A big media stink is not what I need right now. I just want to bring everyone along when I'm making changes that may cut the workforce. Division at the top is bad for business."

Ibiso remembered how angry and determined Rasheed was to change the status quo when he visited the community where the waste from the plant was treated. Danjuma Group provided jobs, but the harm it was also doing was one thing Rasheed was determined to fix immediately. His decision, however, had been plagued with opposition since he proposed the idea of acquiring new machines. The upgrades would come with a possible reduction in the workforce. The machines he envisioned would work cleaner, be more efficient, and reduce pollution by eighty percent.

Ibiso sat by him and rubbed his back. "Honey, don't worry about it. Mr. Eke should be efficient for your father to have kept him. He would have everything ready by the deadline. He is on your side and will do well presenting to other members of senior management." Ibiso removed a wayward strand of hair from her face. "They should be glad that you're the kind of CEO that cares about their feelings or approval. Most CEOs don't. People are resistant to change. Especially when they think something better will cause them to be out of the manual work they do. But it's all in the presentation."

"Thanks, sweetheart. Pray for me...please."

Ibiso gasped.

"What?"

"You actually want to surrender this to God? I'm not going to ask why, how or when...I'm ecstatic." She grabbed his hand and they bowed their heads to say a quick prayer.

"So what are you doing this week?" Rasheed asked.

"It was going to be a busy one, but I moved some things around. Now I have just one corporate lunch to cater."

"Was?"

She rolled her eyes. "I've suspended any outside jobs until I get the center's kitchen and staff in order. I want to be done before I, or now *we*, go to Port Harcourt in a few weeks."

"You'll give up your gigs for me?"

"No, I'll give them up to get done being your work horse."

"You're going to milk this to death. You want me to feel bad, but I won't. You owe me." He threw a pillow at her.

"Very funny." Ibiso stood and tossed the same pillow back at him. "When I get out of the restroom, you're taking me home."

Rasheed picked up the pillow that had landed on the floor when the phone rang.

"It's Jabir," Rasheed answered the phone. Laughter was still in

162

his voice when he greeted his brother with a "Hey bro." He placed the phone on his lap and put it on speaker. Ibiso walked back to the couch and sat down.

"Stone Cold, are you laughing?" Jabir voice was agile and alert.

"Yes and behave, I have Ibiso here."

"Hey Jabir, long time. Sorry I couldn't see you before you left. How is Kamal?"

"Kamal is fine. It's cool. We'll see each other again. Besides, I know my brother was hogging your time. I'm glad he's with you and not—"

Rasheed cut him off. "Didn't I just tell you to behave? What do—?"

"Don't listen to him. And *not who*?" Ibiso asked, giving Rasheed a light punch on his arm.

"Ouch. Jabir, you don't know this adorable spit-fire I have here. Please don't cause any problems for me."

"Relax Ibiso, I'm just joking. You know you're my personal person. I'll tell you if my brother gets out of line," Jabir said.

They all chatted a few more minutes. Rasheed gave an update on how the business was going, his new house and the impending visit to Port Harcourt. Ibiso excused herself and went to the bathroom. She was at the door when she heard Jabir ask whether Rasheed had heard anything about Damisi lately. She wasn't answering her phone or emails. Rasheed hadn't, but from what Ibiso could deduce, Jabir was about to leave for Tanzania for a couple of weeks on a missions trip with Doctors in the Skies and wanted Damisi to know.

Rasheed told her Damisi was a friend of Jabir's who lived in Lagos. Ibiso knew Damisi as a newscaster turned television personality of Channel 151. Her and Jabir's relationship was not written in the stars because according to Rasheed, they had been at it for a while. Ibiso shrugged and entered the restroom and closed the door behind her. Jabir was a playboy and a breathtakingly, handsome doctor. God help the poor woman if she thought she could resist him for long.

Later that night, Rasheed parked his car outside her apartment. Ibiso gathered up her things and turned to him. "I had fun."

Rasheed slipped his hand around the back of her neck and drew her closer. "Me, too." He kissed her. "We should do this more often."

"I'd love too, but you know we're treading on dangerous ground. Next time we'll go out. Your house, my house, it's becoming a bad idea."

He exhaled deeply. "As long as we're together."

Ibiso was shocked at how easy it was for him to give in. She was thrilled they were not going to have a drawn out debate on this. She knew her limits and she had begun stretching them too far.

"You know what? I *really* kinda like you." She opened the door and walked toward the front door.

Chapter 22

Some days later, Rasheed was awakened by his cell phone ringing. He reached over and activated the call, "Good morning, beautiful."

He had assigned that ring tone to Ibiso.

"Morning, handsome. Don't tell me you're still asleep." Ibiso sultry voice caressed his ear.

Rasheed looked at the timer on his dresser. It was 6 a.m. The days of waking up at the crack of dawn were over with the move to this new apartment. Now he could make it to work in thirty minutes tops.

He sat up in the bed. "Actually I was. I don't have to wake up that early anymore. You slept well? Sorry for keeping you up so late."

He and Ibiso hadn't spoken since Sunday except for the exchange of texts messages. He had been working hard and so had she. But last night, he needed her help. The procurement officer had sent over the presentation Rasheed had been expecting. Although the numbers looked good, there was something about the set-up of the pitch that didn't look appealing. He sent it to her and they stayed on the phone for two hours while she displayed her marketing skills. She changed colors and fonts, reminding him of how they played on human emotion and grabbed attention. She also inserted an ice breaker which would help Mr. Eke ease into the conversation. She had been fantastic.

"Yes, I did. And 11 p.m. was not late."

"I've barely gotten five hours and I know you didn't get a lot of sleep either."

"I'm fine. Today is the big day. I called you to pray. Are you game?"

Rasheed was surprised and pleased at her request. But most of all grateful for it. "Yes and thank you."

"Father God, let this day bring us your unfailing love. Help us put our trust in you, Lord. Show us the way to go. In Jesus' name. Amen."

"Amen."

They spent the next few minutes exchanging details about their day before they disconnected the call.

Before he knew it, Rasheed was humming the U2 song, "It's A Beautiful Day." An emotion he didn't recognize propelled him up from the bed. He was happy. It wasn't the act he had put on almost every day since his father left so his family didn't have to worry. He was happy.

Later that morning, Rasheed sat at the head of the table in the expansive conference room and observed the way Mr. Eke delivered the presentation. Rasheed had already made up his mind, but wanted to see the reaction and opinion of others. At the table were senior departmental heads, Uncle Musa and Halima. Uncle Musa and Halima didn't run specific departments but often represented the company and handled special *ad hoc* projects.

Just as Rasheed expected, some were pleased with the change and were eager for its implementation while others were a little hesitant about rocking the boat as they put it. Rasheed was tickled at how well he had predicted each person's reaction. Ibiso had thought otherwise. She was determined to believe they would see the good in what he was trying to do.

Thirty minutes later, Mr. Eke was done and answering questions from the managers. Rasheed observed that while Uncle Musa—as expected—was against the change, Halima seemed to not have an opinion. He observed his sister closer. The words his mother had spoken to him the other day echoed back in his head. She was a victim, just like he and his brothers. She was right. Halima didn't ask for this, why make her pay for it?

She was friends with his brothers, especially Kamal, so he might as well try to at least be cordial. A relationship they could build later. He made a mental note to go to her office to talk to her after the meeting.

"Look, I disagree with spending this amount of money on this machine," Uncle Musa's voice brought Rasheed out of his reverie.

With Uncle Musa's outright objection, everyone thought it was a free-for-all forum to argue back and forth. Rasheed let it continue for a while then banged his fist on the table to call order.

"Lady and Gentlemen." Rasheed nodded in Halima's direction. She smiled. "If we don't make strides now to fix the pollution problem, we stand the chance of being sanctioned by the government. That is not going to happen on my watch."

"Ever since your father – my brother – died, you've been spending money with these your upgrades. You could use half that money to just give the leaders of that community and they would be quiet," Uncle Musa said.

Anger pushed Rasheed from his chair. "I'm glad you understand that he was *my* father, not yours. If he thought you could do a better job he wouldn't have sought me out, would he?"

Uncle Musa stood. He swung the oversized sleeves of his flowing *abgada* over his shoulders. Then he adjusted the cap on his head. "Are you talking to me like that?"

"Please sit down, Uncle Musa, and earn the respect I give you," Rasheed thundered.

Instead of sitting, Musa stormed out of the room. Rasheed stood and began to walk back and forth in the space behind his chair.

"The implementation of this new piece of equipment is not up for debate. The fact of the matter is that I could have made an executive decision to downsize the staff and install these machines. But I chose to lead differently." Rasheed looked around the room. Those that were in agreement nodded, the rest had a look of defiance but dared not speak now that their ring leader had left.

Halima's expression remained blank.

"That's what my father would have done, but it's a new day. If it's something huge and I have the time, I'll run it by you. Don't take it for granted." He paused. "Let me be clear, seeking your opinion doesn't equate to seeking your consent. Any questions?"

There was silence in the room. After a few moments, he continued. "As Mr. Eke said, the mercury pollution found in the village's river can be traced back to our plant. The machines will help with manufacture and silo clean up. Installation will be in the coming weeks. Any questions you have, direct them to Ms. Danjuma who will be heading the project. If there is nothing else, this meeting is over. Halima, please wait behind."

A few minutes later, everyone had left the room. Rasheed walked closer to where Halima was seated. She was a carbon copy of her mother, but the expression she had on her face reminded him of their father. Now that he thought about it, his father's eyes always had a sad, confused look behind them. He walked over and sat in the chair next to hers.

"How do I begin to apologize?" he asked. She opened her mouth to speak and he raised his hand slightly. "Don't say anything. Let me get this out."

She nodded.

"I have a lot of anger with the way our father did things in his lifetime. But I've come to realize through a very wise woman that you're a victim in this, too. So I'm saying, I'm sorry. For all those times you tried to get close to me and I shut you out. For every time we passed each other in the hallway or met in a gathering and I acted like you didn't exist, I'm sorry. The fact is you *do* exist and you are my little sister, no matter the circumstance. And as your big brother, I'm supposed to protect you. I know we won't be friends right away, but I'm hoping you'll accept me as your brother and we can try."

Rasheed stood and walked to the window. The serenity of the grounds always seemed to bring him peace. He turned around after a couple of moments and saw Halima saunter toward him. She stood in front of him for a moment, and then she wrapped her arms around his neck so hard that he almost stumbled. "Brother, please don't apologize. You don't know how I have asked Allah for you find it in your heart to accept me."

Rasheed was taken aback at the mention of Allah, but

remembered that she was indeed raised Muslim like her mother and their father.

He hugged her back and held her tight. He remembered what Pastor had taught this past Sunday about extending mercy and second chances. Rasheed knew of the Jonah and whale story, but this time it had been broken down to illustrate God's patience and willingness to extend mercy even when undeserved.

"I promise I'll do better," Rasheed said. "Now about this project – we'll do lunch tomorrow and I'll tell you my expectations. I've seen the work you've been doing on implementing many other programs around here. Much is at stake here and I trust you to do a good job."

He opened the door and ushered her out. The siblings engaged in small talk as they walked back to their respective offices on opposite sides of the floor. Rasheed was all smiles when he reentered his office. He took off his jacket and draped in on his chair. He loosened his tie a bit. He felt good about the way things were going in all areas of his life, business and personal. Thinking of personal, he had a call to make.

Moments later, Rasheed hung up the phone the second time with no response from Ibiso. He hit the messenger button on his phone and constructed a text.

Hey beautiful, how is your day going? Mine went just as expected. I can't wait to tell you about that uncle of mine. Call me back or I'll call you later tonight ~ R.

No sooner had he hit the send button when the door of his office swung open and a fuming Musa Danjuma walked in. *Think of the devil.*

Rasheed rose from his chair and stuffed his hands in his pockets. Uncle Musa, who was about five years younger than his dad looked older than his sixty-seven years.

"What can I do for you?" Rasheed asked.

His uncle began to pace the length of his office, his *abgada* flowing behind him like a parachute. Rasheed could hear him muttering some Hausa words and had no idea what they meant. Then Uncle Musa paused without warning and rushed toward him.

"Listen, young man. I don't need anything from you, but I have come to warn you."

"About?" *This man must think I'm sacred of him.*

"About disrespecting me."

"You haven't earned my respect."

Uncle Musa shook his head. "Look at this small boy taking to me anyhow. Anyway I don't blame you. I blame my father and my late brother. When your father went gallivanting in London all those years under the guise of studying and hooked up with your mother, we knew nothing good would come of it."

"But you saw to that, didn't you? So I don't understand your anger."

"I was the one that stood by my father all those years. I was the one who stayed in Nigeria to study just so he wouldn't be too heartbroken over your father. But did he see all of that when he brooded over him day and night until your father succumbed?"

Rasheed jaw clenched. He didn't want to be reminded of how his father had chosen all this over his wife and his sons. "I really don't need a history lesson. What do you want in my office?"

"Don't make yourself too comfortable. The only reason you're here is because my weak brother grew a conscience on his sickbed."

"Well, I'm here. So deal with it. I'm trying to tolerate you. Don't take it for granted."

"Are you talking to me?"

"I don't see anyone else in the room. Now leave."

"You might have your half-sister fooled about your intentions here, but not me. I'll not stand by and watch what my family has built go down the drain with your so-called changes." Uncle Musa turned to leave.

"One more thing," Rasheed said, causing him to pause. "The last time I checked, the same Danjuma blood runs through my veins. You and my grandfather might have been able to manipulate my father, but you do not want to test me."

Chapter 23

It was an unusually sunny day for late September. The weather in her home state was often unpredictable. It was supposed to be raining. Ibiso hoped the sun was an indication of how bright and enjoyable this trip would be. Looking outside the window, she trembled as the taxi got closer to the Le Meridian hotel in Port Harcourt. The Presidential suite of the hotel would be Rasheed's home for the next four days. Ibiso had heard of this hotel, but never been inside it. In fact, she hadn't been home in three and a half years, so a lot of Port Harcourt looked different from when she left.

Over the last weeks, she and Rasheed had worked hard to ensure that everything was done so they could enjoy this mini-vacation. The machines for the cement plant arrived on time and were installed some days ago without incident. She and Rasheed had celebrated with dinner at an exclusive restaurant in Abuja. It was a double celebration as they also rejoiced over the completion of the center project she had been working on.

Ibiso left Amina in charge of Bisso Bites and hired one more sales girl to help out. She was then able to concentrate on getting the center's kitchen ready faster than she had anticipated. The cooks weren't hard to train on the new variations of healthy snacks that she had developed.

Ibiso looked to her left and snuggled closer to the man that had stolen her heart. Rasheed wrapped his arms around her and smiled down at her. He stretched his neck from side to side and Ibiso laughed.

"Is something funny?" Rasheed asked.

"You've been stretching your neck since the flight landed. Was it so hard flying commercial?" Ibiso caressed his cheek with the back of her hand.

Rasheed opened his mouth to respond but was interrupted by the driver they had hired for the weekend asking a clarifying question about the hotel. Ibiso answered him and turned to Rasheed.

"I would have you know that before my life changed about six months ago, I rode on nothing but commercial liners." Rasheed twirled his finger around a stray strand of her hair.

Ibiso almost collapsed the day she overhead him telling Ireti to fuel up the Danjuma private jet for them to use to fly to Port Harcourt. She was going to have to deal with her brother's mouth about bringing a man home. She didn't want the added talk of her selling herself to a rich man. After much negotiation, Rasheed agreed to nix the private jet and settle for first class on a commercial airline.

"Oh, really now?"

"Yes, really." He took a breath.

Ibiso immediately knew what was coming. Before he could speak, she spoke. "I'll be fine. I'm kind of nervous, but I'll be fine. They *are* my family. What's the worst that can happen? We are not enemies. Things are just a little awkward between us. Besides, I want to talk to them first before I introduce you to them." Ibiso saw that her reassurance did little to ease his mind. But this was the way it had to be.

A few hours later, Ibiso stood outside her family home with her luggage in tow. She had left the hotel a little while ago after Rasheed was settled in. He had been working nonstop to be able to have this time off. So she made him promise he would use the opportunity to rest. Boma had a lot of activities planned for them, starting the following day 'til when they left Monday evening. She didn't want him to burn out.

Ibiso stalled for a few minutes. It was on these steps that Sodienye had called her a disgrace and her mother had wept that she no longer had a daughter when Ibiso decided to leave with the ex that she would no longer name. As she lifted her hand to ring the bell, the door flew open. On the other side of it was her mother—Sonia Jaja.

"Ibisowari Linda Jaja, how long are you planning on standing at the door?" her mother asked. "I heard when the gateman opened the gate for the taxi a few minutes ago."

"Good afternoon, mother," Ibiso said, dragging her luggage into the foyer of the house.

The two women hugged each other and proceeded into the living room.

"So how was the trip?"

"It was fine, mother. Do you mind if I go up and shower? I'll be right back." Ibiso inhaled deeply and exhaled slowly, trying to relax. She hadn't been happy in this house for a while. Memories of her dad engulfed her. She needed some time to regroup.

Her mother hesitated. "Sure."

Ibiso took her bags to what was once her room. Everything was the way she had left it. Minutes later, she had freshened up and made her way back downstairs. She was ready.

"I prepared your favorite. I hope it still is, since I haven't seen you in three plus years," her mother said, walking to the dining table.

Ibiso rolled her eyes and followed her mother. This was a record. Her mother waited a full thirty minutes before trying to make her feel guilty. At the table, Ibiso paused. It was set for three. That could only mean one thing – Sodienye was on his way. Just as she was about to ask, her mother confirmed her suspicion. "Let's give your brother a couple of minutes. He's running late. He should have been here when you got here."

"Anybody home? Mother, mother where are you?" her brother shouted from the living room moments later.

"We're in here, darling," her mother answered. Ibiso couldn't help but notice that the welcome he received was warmer than the one she gave her daughter whom she hadn't seen in "three plus years."

Sodienye entered into the room and it shrunk. A tear formed in the corner of Ibiso's eye. She missed her father so much and her brother looked exactly like him. His tall, rugged look was masterfully dressed up in a grey, pinstriped suit. His dark eyes met with hers and the smile on his face disappeared. His expression turned to disappointment. He ignored her and hugged their mother tight, rocking her back and forth. Ibiso wasn't sure whether he missed their mother who he probably saw the day before, or the little performance was for her benefit.

"Good afternoon Sodi," Ibiso greeted her brother. She could hear her own nervousness.

Sodienye walked over to his place at the table. "Hello Ibiso. I see it took Boma to bring the prodigal daughter home."

"Stop that. Your sister just got here. I'm sure she has been busy with her new found life in Abuja." Her mother began opening the covered dishes on the table.

The aroma of catfish stew and white rice filled the space. Ibiso loved catfish, especially point and kill. She remembered when she and her mother were closer, they would go to the fish farm every other Saturday.

They all sat down at the table and enjoyed their meal in awkward semi-silence. Her mother filled her in on the latest developments with the salon and spa she was opening. Ibiso wasn't surprised at her mother business choice. Since she retired as a nurse, she had been longing to do something else with her free time. She loved to pamper and be pampered so it was an obvious choice. Her brother, who was a top realtor in Port Harcourt, bragged about the latest deal he closed. Finally her mother asked about her restaurant. Ibiso was pleased. They *were* interested in her.

Ibiso began to narrate how the restaurant was faring. She observed her family. They were listening with keenness. Whether it was in pretense or genuine, she hadn't quite figured out. That was until Sodienye spoke, "Well, at least God smiled on you and gave you a second chance to make something of yourself."

"We thank God, oh," her mother said.

"Yes oh. 'Cause if you had come back with a plea for money, you would've been out of luck." Sodienye took a spoonful of rice.

Ibiso looked at him with confusion. How could he say such things then act like his words didn't hurt? She then remembered what Rasheed told her, "Don't let them push you around." Anger forced her up from her chair, almost knocking it over. "I have had it." Her mother and brother looked at her with surprise written all over their faces.

"Ibiso, are you okay?" her mother asked.

"No mother, I'm not. I made a mistake, fine. Show me someone who hasn't and I will show you Jesus Christ. I'm sorry for disappointing you and my brother, who is above reproach, with my decision to follow what I thought was love." Tears blinded her eyes. "I'm sorry I didn't become the big marketing exec you thought I would be. I'm sorry I followed Tokoni to Lagos against your wishes, but I'm changed. I asked God for forgiveness and a second chance. And my dear brother yes, He did smile on me and I have a thriving restaurant that I built from the ground up and I am proud of it. I haven't been here in three years because I wanted you to be proud of me. To see that although I made a wrong turn, I'm finally moving toward my destination. I use my degree to help my business and it is thriving. Have you even checked out my website since I told you about it?"

She looked at her mother and brother. Their eyes widened in surprise. She had gotten their attention and she was going to bring this baby home. She was sick and tired of being treated like an outcast.

"Sodi, you're supposed to be my protector since daddy died. Is this how you are protecting me? For the last time, I'm sorry. If that's not enough I don't know what else to do, neither will I try to figure it out."

Without waiting for their response, she left for her bedroom. With a start like this, how was she going to tell them about Rasheed? She plopped down on the bed, covered her face with a pillow and let out a muffled scream. A few minutes later, her mother came knocking on the door asking to be let in. Ibiso needed a reprieve so pretended to be sleeping and walked into her bathroom. This was not turning out as she had thought and there was only one voice she wanted to hear—Rasheed's. She dialed the hotel.

He was ever so attentive – listening without interrupting her once. He was upset that they had treated her that way, but he didn't try to fix it. Instead, he asked what he could do to make her feel better. She wanted to talk about anything but her family.

They talked about the center, then he gave her a great idea of starting her own web series with her V logs or a cookbook of her recipes. Ibiso got excited at his thoughts, but her mood changed when he talked about his impending trip to London to tie up loose ends with his job. She was going to miss him. She walked back into her bedroom and lay on the bed.

Before she knew it, they had talked for an hour and little by little, she drifted off to sleep while he crooned a melody in her ear.

The next sound she heard was the annoying ring of her cell phone. It was Boma. Without asking her permission, Boma ordered her to get ready. She was coming to take her out.

***

Later that day, Ibiso wiped her brow. She was grateful for the air conditioning in the Genesis Mall supermarket. It was a welcome reprieve from the sun she and Boma had endured in Mile 1 market, where Boma claimed her personal butcher had the best meat.

"Look Miss Thang, we have to hurry up before the evening rush of people getting off work begins." Boma tossed two large bags of Maggi and Knorr cooking cubes into her shopping basket. "Unless Abuja is now in America, I don't know why you are forming *ajebota* over a little heat."

"Don' hate on my *ajebotaish* nature," Ibiso replied. Boma always teased her for acting like she could endure no hardship.

The two friends laughed and continued shopping. Although the reception after the christening would be held in the upscale Barakah restaurant, Boma wanted to make sure she had food at home in the event that some guests followed them back.

Ibiso was ecstatic for her friend whom after three miscarriages and surgery to remove her fibroids had conceived and given birth to twins – a boy and girl. This was indeed a big occasion for Boma and her family.

"I'm glad you're feeling better," Boma said. "I don't get to see you much since you moved and I don't want anyone to spoil your day. I think your mother and brother were hurt and missed you. Although I must say they have a funny way of showing it."

"Thanks B. Sometimes I *jus tire* for them. If not for Rasheed's encouragement, I don't think I would have been able to stand up to them. But I had had it. My brother started from the minute he walked in the door."

Boma rubbed her friend's back, providing her a little comfort. The friends shopped for a couple more items and about half an hour later, they were at the register checking out.

"When do I get to meet this Rasheed?" Boma asked.

"Tomorrow. Tonight, I want to take him around the city, before I have to share him with all of you." Ibiso reached into her purse and pulled out some Naira notes for the items she had gotten.

She prayed her family let up a little bit because she planned to ask Rasheed to eat dinner with them tomorrow night. The items she bought were ingredients for pounded yam and Native soup. It was her brother's favorite and her hometown delicacy. Ibiso was counting on a little bribe to bring out the best in Sodienye.

"I've never seen you so happy. Even with what's his name, you still had some doubt and reservation behind your smile. But with Rasheed it's evident you're in love, my friend, and I'm so happy."

Ibiso looked out of the window of Boma's Jeep Grand Cherokee. She was still amazed at the fact that the backseat had car seats in it. Her mind drifted to Rasheed. She was indeed happy and content. She knew she loved him and was falling deeper by the day. She just hoped he realized he felt the same.

"Yes, I'm happy, but scared. I don't know if he feels the same. He cares, does all the right things, but love…I don't know," Ibiso said.

"He does. He might not have come to terms with it yet. No man on this earth will follow a girl to see her family if he's not vested. I know I'm the one that invited him, but he could have given an excuse and gotten out of it. You know I'm cupid's detective. I'll check him out when we double date tomorrow."

As Boma navigated them through Trans Amadi Road, Ibiso leaned back into the leather car seat. She was determined to enjoy her stay in Port Harcourt. Rasheed had come all this way with her and she was going to keep him as drama free as possible. The next day being Saturday, Boma and Dokubo had planned a full list of activities for them in the morning but in the evening, Rasheed was coming over for dinner. Her family was going to behave whether they liked it or not. But tonight, she wanted memories of her own with the man she loved in her home state.

Chapter 24

Right before the break of dawn the next day, Ibiso padded softly into the kitchen. She didn't want to turn on any lights as her mother was still asleep. So was grateful that all the furniture was still in the position she remembered. She didn't want to knock anything over. She poured herself a glass of water. She leaned against the refrigerator and a smiled as her date last night replayed in her mind. There was only one word to describe it... fantastic.

By the time Boma dropped her off, Sodienye and her mother were nowhere to be found. It was okay since she didn't want them ruining her night. She showered and changed into a print peplum top and a pair of black skinny jeans and made her way to Rasheed's hotel.

Rasheed who was dressed in all black, looked well rested. He was a sight to behold. The driver took them around the city. Just as she had hoped, the night lights lit up the city that was nicknamed the Garden City and it looked amazing.

After driving around for a while, they had dinner. On their way out, they saw a poster that advertised the stage play adaptation of Ola Rotimi's *The Gods Are Not To Blame*. Deciding they both wanted to see it, they rushed to the theatre and were just in time for the last showing. The play was so poignant. No matter how many times she had seen it, Ibiso cried every time. It was way past midnight before they kissed each other goodnight.

She walked into the adjourning formal dining room and looked at the clock on the wall. It was 6:15 a.m. Ibiso pulled out her smartphone and logged into her Bible app and sat down while the screen loaded. Isaiah 12:2 was the verse of the day. She read it carefully, then tapped on the screen to open the whole chapter. Her eyes focused back on verse 2...*surely my God is my salvation; I will trust and not be afraid. The Lord, the Lord himself is my strength and my defense, He has become my salvation.*

"For the dawning of a new day, I bless your name, dear God. Thank you Jesus for that confirmation," she prayed quietly. "Your anger has turned away from me and You have comforted me. I'll keep my trust in You, You are my strength. I know everything will turn out right in the end. In Jesus' name. Amen."

She leaned back and she closed her eyes. She welcomed the silence. Moments later, she opened her eyes to see her mother leaned against the doorway with her arms wrapped around her.

Ibiso flashed a faint smile. It was a new day.

"I'm glad to see you are in a better mood than yesterday." Her mother's commanding voice broke the tranquility. Her mother walked back into the kitchen without waiting for a response to her comment.

"Good morning, mother," Ibiso said. She finished her water and followed into the kitchen where her mother was fumbling with some pots. She put the glass in the sink, and turned around to see her mother staring at her.

"Ibisowari, sit down. Let's talk."

They both pulled out chairs at the small dinette in the oversized kitchen.

Ibiso's heart sank. She had been prepared to glide by the next three days without rehashing anything. It was a new day. After her cold welcome, she decided she'd let sleeping dogs lie. But it was apparent her mother didn't want that. Ibiso already knew this conversation could go one of two ways. Her mother would explain and defend her and Sodienye's stance or understand her side. Somehow Ibiso just knew it was the former, but the earlier she got this chat over with, the better.

"What's wrong?" her mother asked.

Ibiso turned around looking for who her mother was talking too. It couldn't be her because she didn't understand the question. "With who?"

"You. You got back here yesterday after three years away and acted so harshly," her mother said.

Ibiso laughed. "Mother, are you serious right now? I came in here thinking you would be proud of me. You've told me you had forgiven me but you watched once again as Sodienye made all those disparaging remarks about me. I defended myself and you're asking me what's wrong with me?" Ibiso put her face in her hands. A beat of silence passed between them.

"Okay, I'll tell you what's wrong with me. I miss my father. I miss him so much. Not only did his death leave a gap in my life, but it somehow gave Sodienye...and you, the license to treat me like an outcast because of one mistake. I didn't kill anybody. All I did was follow someone I thought was the love of my life. How is that so horrible? You're supposed to love me, no matter what." Ibiso began to cry.

After a few seconds, Ibiso felt her mother draw her near. Tears were streaming down her face too.

"My daughter, I was so hurt and angry when you left, because I could see that Tokoni didn't have good intentions toward you. You had just met him and barely a month later, he had convinced you to leave your family and move to a different city." He mother wiped her face. "My pain, Sodienye took personal. It's my fault for not stopping it earlier, but I think he felt pain too. We were all so close knit and you let that man tear us apart. You know how your brother dotes over you. That to him was as though you were rejecting his protection."

Ibiso had never heard it from their perspective before. Looking back now, she could see that she could have handled the situation better.

"I don't think your brother told you this, but he ran into Tokoni soon after you moved to Abuja. Tokoni taunted him about what happened between both of you. Your brother, not one to hold his temper, beat him up and that action landed Sodienye in jail for two days. He has found it hard to let that go."

Ibiso gasped. Now everything made sense. Her brother could use a lesson in humility and for that to happen, his ego must have been crushed.

"Mother, I'm sorry. The Ibiso of then and now are very different people."

Her mother's eye sparkled and she beamed. "For you to stand up to your brother, I believe you. He was quite impressed himself. I've missed you so much, my daughter."

Mother and daughter wrapped themselves in the warmest embrace they had shared in a long time. Her mother broke the hug, put her hands on Ibiso's shoulders and examined her.

"You look good. May I ask the reason behind the new you?"

Ibiso paused at first. They had just reconciled and she didn't think this was a right time to bring up Rasheed. But then if she planned on inviting him over for dinner, she might as well get it out of the way.

"I found Jesus and He sent me a man," Ibiso said.

Her mother cupped Ibiso's face in her hands and looked into her eyes. "Jesus was never missing. You were."

Ibiso lowered her eyes.

"Look at me. I'm so proud of you. Now put those culinary skills of yours to use and make us breakfast, while you tell me all about this man."

***

Sometime later, the kitchen had been restored and Ibiso put away the container of leftover egg stew they ate with boiled yams. Her mother had listened with care as she told her about Rasheed. When Ibiso got to the part about how he helped her with the restaurant that clenched the deal for her mom. She was sold.

"*Eh hen*, that's what a man should do – assist the woman he likes and not try to take the little she has," her mother had said.

Ibiso knew she was referring to the time she shared that Tokoni had asked her for a loan. If only she knew that despite her advice, Ibiso had given it to him in the end. Her mother wanted to hear more, but was meeting with contractors in the salon. Being the weekend, she was afraid that if the men didn't meet her there, they would turn around and leave without waiting.

Ibiso watched as her mother placed a call to her brother to cancel his plans for tonight and come over for dinner, not telling

him why. Ibiso didn't know what to expect from tonight, but
prayed everything went well.

I will keep my trust in You. You are my strength.

Many hours later, Ibiso and Rasheed arrived at the Marina.
Boma and her husband, Dokubo were already in line and waved
them over. Boma always loved to coordinate with her husband and
today was no different as both of them had on pink Polo t-shirts
and blue jean capris. The ladies hugged and Ibiso made the
introductions. The way Boma did a double take when she saw
Rasheed, Ibiso knew her friend was about to say something silly.
Just in time, the attendant came by and asked for their tickets.
Saved.

The yacht took six people each. Rasheed and Dokubo helped
the ladies into the boat. While the attendant gave instructions,
Boma pinched Ibiso. *He is fiiiiiiiinnnnnnnnnneeee,* she mouthed. Ibiso
giggled and turned her attention back to the attendant. She knew
how to swim but it never hurt to pay attention. The tour guide
used the first fifteen minutes to educate them about the historic
attractions they passed. He then allowed them to take in their
surroundings for the remainder of the thirty minute ride.

Ibiso walked to the other end of the boat and admired the
work of God. The ocean looked so beautiful – how it all stayed
within its boundaries was nothing but God. She felt Rasheed's
arms slip around her waist. She leaned into him and wrapped both
her arms around his waist. There were no words shared between
them. No need for it, as the unison of their heartbeats spoke for
them.

He had changed a lot since she met him. He was beginning to
enjoy and partake of her love for Christ. He had stopped drinking,
his mood was no longer unpredictable, and most of all he had
made strides to reconcile with his sister. One thing was left – he
hadn't confessed with his mouth and accepted Jesus as his Lord
and Savior. But she had learnt not to push, because he had to be
the one to want to make that decision. Until then, she had to keep
her feelings under wrap because they had to be equally yoked to
move forward. She had been there and was not going down that
road again.

Sometime later, Ibiso and Boma stood in the ladies room freshening up. The boat ride was over and they stopped by the mall to do some shopping and have lunch.

"I'm over the moon for you. Rasheed is almost as fine as my husband. And he loves you to pieces." Boma refreshed her eyeliner.

"Oh, so he is *almost* as fine?" Ibiso nudged her friend.

"See what you've done," Boma said, pointing to the line that now extended to her cheek.

"Good for you, saying my man is *almost* as fine." Ibiso ran some water on the edge of her handkerchief and wiped the unwanted line.

"You know what I mean. I'm so happy for you girl. I watched you guys all day. He couldn't take his eyes off you. I'm certain that he loves you." Boma inspected her eye once more.

"You think so?"

Boma reached for her friend's hands. "Joy cometh in the morning. This is your morning. Jesus put him in your life for a reason. You yourself say he has changed. It's a process and your love is helping him through all the pain and bitterness he had held on to."

"Thanks, sis. I'm nervous about tonight. Sodienye better not mess this up for me," Ibiso said.

Boma waved off her concern. "You and your mom have called a truce. You both can handle Sodi. Besides, he is your brother and will always protect your interests. If Rasheed is half the man I think he is, he's up to whatever Sodi brings his way. Now let's go eat, before all these side chicks think our men are up for grabs."

The ladies arrived just as the host was leading the men to their table. Ibiso and Boma stood by as the men pulled out their chairs. The conversation was light and concentrated on politics and the next day's celebration as the Asian chef prepared their meal before them. The artistry of his skill fascinated Ibiso as he flung knifes into the air and caught them. She and Boma giggled as Rasheed and Dokubo told the man to watch where he flung those things.

The waiter refilled their soft drink and water glasses as the chef served their meal. They continued their conversation with caution, not wanting to choke on the extra hot spice they told the chef to add to the rice. Ibiso picked up a piece of shrimp with her fork and fed it to Rasheed. They were lost in their own world.

"About tonight, I know you are just as headstrong as Sodienye. Please try to curtail the Danjuma fire...for me," Ibiso whispered.

"Sweetheart, I adore you and once your brother recognizes that, we won't have any problems." He brushed his lips against hers.

She furrowed her brow. "Please, I'm serious."

He winked. "So am I." He leaned in further and whispered in her ear, "So am I."

***

Later that evening, Ibiso cut up the last of the vegetables for the Native soup when she heard the front door chime. It must be her mom. She left her a message that she was running late but would be ready by the time Rasheed got here.

"Mother, is that you?" Ibiso yelled from the kitchen. There was no response. She wiped her hands and turned around to see who it was and came face to face with her brother.

Sodienye stared at her for a couple of moments, without saying anything. He then walked straight to the sink, washed his hands and took a piece of boiled cow meat from the bowl she had set aside for the soup. She didn't know what her mom had said to him, but there was something different about his demeanor. She recognized hurt, disappointment, and a twinge of defeat.

Although through different circumstances, Sodienye, just like Rasheed was forced to grow up way before his time.

"Look Sodi, I'm sorry for the disappointment and pain I caused you and mummy when I left. I'm different now and have worked hard to prove I can be something other than a spoiled brat." Ibiso waited for his response. When it was not forthcoming, she filled a medium size pot with water and put it on the stove to bring to a boil. It would be used for the pounded yam.

"I'm sorry, too. I've missed my baby sister because of my stubbornness. It was more about my pride and the fact I thought you rejected my care and as such, I thought I was letting dad down." Sodienye put his hand in the bowl for another piece of meat, but Ibiso smacked it away.

"Ouch."

The siblings laughed and Sodienye drew her close and hugged her. She had missed her brother so much.

"Mom, says we're entertaining a guest tonight. Tell me about him. Do I have to cork my gun?" Sodienye asked.

"I'm a big girl and much wiser. Trust me, please."

Sodienye looked at her a few seconds, then walked to the container of cashew nuts and scooped a handful.

"I hear he is the Danjuma heir. Money or not, his intentions have to be honorable." He popped some nuts in his mouth and peered at the contents of the large pot. "Besides, if he's the one that got you making my favorite soup, then I might be willing to ease up, but just a little."

"I appreciate it. By the way, I see you still haven't gotten yourself a girlfriend."

"I have, but nothing serious. What's your point?"

"Because you're always here eating, so I assume no one has agreed to cook steady meals for you yet." She laughed.

"Ha, ha, ha. Very funny. For your information I had a date I cancelled tonight to accommodate your little dinner." He stretched his hand toward the door. "I can go oh... better stop me now."

Ibiso laughed and picked up the bowl of assorted meats and fanned the steam in his direction.

He inhaled the aroma and then smiled. "Okay, okay I'll stay."

***

Rasheed studied the clothes strewn on the bed and contemplated a traditional or an English look for tonight's dinner. Opting for a traditional mix, he selected a black casual dress shirt and Ankara print pants and black loafers. He strolled across the room and picked up his phone. He flipped through – no emails that needed his immediate attention. He dressed and picked up the key and left the room.

"Oga, your swagger na die o," the driver said as he opened the back door of the Mercedes Benz SUV. Rasheed patted his back and smiled. Accepting the man's compliment, he entered the back seat and pulled out his phone. He sent Ibiso a text alerting her that he was on his way. Before he put the phone back in his pocket, her reply came through. *Can't wait.*

"Oga, na madam Ibiso house *we dey go?"* the driver asked, peering at him through the rearview mirror.

"Yes, you know the way, right?"

The driver nodded and pulled out of the hotel parking lot.

Forty-five minutes later, Rasheed walked down the pathway to the Jaja's front door. He rang the bell and the door was answered seconds later by Ibiso. She left him astounded by her beauty. Ibiso looked amazing in her burnt orange, fitting top and blue jeans. He was surprised by the effect she had on him since he had been with her almost all day.

They greeted each other and then he kissed her on her cheek, cautious that this was her family home. After stepping inside, Ibiso walked ahead of him into the family room. He couldn't draw his attention away from the sway of her hips. She stirred something in him and it wasn't just physical.

Within seconds, they turned right into the living room. It was a large space and had the feel of his mother's home. It was decorated in beige and crème colors with large paintings adorning the walls. His nostrils were tickled by the enticing aroma coming from the kitchen. He could tell Ibiso was at work. That woman cooked everywhere she went.

"Rasheed, meet my family – my mom and brother, Sodienye." Ibiso made the introductions.

"Good evening, Ma," Rasheed bent his head slightly to greet her mother.

"Good evening, Rasheed. How are you? Have a seat." She pointed to the chair in between her and Sodienye who stood and was walking toward him. Rasheed knew he was sizing him up.

"Sodienye. Nice to meet you."

"You, too." Sodienye extended his hand and Rasheed placed his in it for a brief handshake.

An awkward silence ensued which Ibiso broke by announcing, "Let me get us something to drink." She retreated into the kitchen.

The minute Ibiso was out of sight, the interrogation began. With each answer, Mrs. Jaja's resistance toward Rasheed waned. By the time Ibiso returned with the drinks, her mother was calling him "my son."

Sodienye, on the other hand, continued to watch him with hesitation. It wasn't until Rasheed confirmed his relation to Kammy, the famous soccer player that Sodienye smiled for the first time. Rasheed made a mental note to thank Kamal and give him less slack about his chosen path.

"Dinner is served," Ibiso announced. Her eyes twinkled with relief. Rasheed knew she was nervous because of her past relationship and he understood.

Soon, they were gathered around the big, dark wood table that sat six. With hands joined, Sodienye said grace and they sat down to eat. Rasheed had never seen Native soup that looked this good and since Ibiso was the chef, he knew it would taste as good as it looked. Ibiso dished out food for each of them before sitting down to hers. The conversation during dinner was comfortable – from sports, to current affairs, to inquiry about adjusting to working in Nigeria.

"Thank you for helping my daughter with her restaurant. That had been a dream of hers for a long time. Although we would have preferred for her to have her restaurant here in Port Harcourt," her mom said.

"Mother..."

"I'm glad she chose Abuja," Rasheed said, his eyes focused on Ibiso.

"I bet you are," Sodienye said.

Although they were cordial, Rasheed had a knowing feeling that before he left tonight, he and Ibiso's brother would have a talk. A much needed one.

After dinner, Ibiso declined his offer to help with clean up. Her mother helped her instead. As they walked to the living room, Sodienye asked if he wanted to have a tour of the compound.

"Sure," Rasheed replied. It was the perfect cover for a man-to-man talk.

Moments later, they were walking down the short trail that led to a garden on the other side of the house. Once they were at a safe distance, Sodienye turned to him.

He stuffed his hands in his pockets. "I don't believe in circling the car park."

Rasheed folded his arms across his chest. "Me neither."

"Good, that's something we both agree on. Now let's hope we can agree on something else."

Rasheed titled his head. "Which is?"

Sodienye's expression hardened. "Ibiso's happiness. My sister is clearly smitten by you and she loves hard. If anywhere in your subconscious, you're not sure about her, then I suggest you make a clean break with her, now rather than later."

Rasheed's nose flared in agitation. Sodienye had just implied he was somehow like Tokoni. "Smitten belittles what we share."

"What do you share? What exactly are your intentions?"

Rasheed was not about to bare his soul to her brother when he hadn't told her how he felt first. And that was because he wanted to be sure. He didn't want to hurt any woman the way his dad had hurt his mother.

"My intentions are honorable and we share something very special," Rasheed said in a tone of voice that gave an indication of finality. The only person he owed any other explanation was Ibiso.

"While I appreciate your protectiveness as her brother, since I met your sister, her happiness has been my number one priority."

Sodienye observed him for a while. "Okay Danjuma, I promised my sister I would let up. But hear this, I let her ex get away with what he did to her, but it won't happen a second time. I'm entrusting her to you." He stretched out his hand for a handshake.

Rasheed gave him a slow smile and accepted his peace offering. "You won't be sorry."

An odd feeling came over him as he came to the realization that he would do the same for Halima given the chance. He made a mental note to call and check on her in the morning.

***

The next morning, Rasheed watched in total admiration as Ibiso—who looked so elegant dressed in silver-toned, lace attire and a navy blue head tie—fulfilled her godmotherly duties. She turned and glanced his way. She had been doing that since yesterday after he and Sodienye got back from their walk. She had asked him several times what they discussed and he told her it was big brother code. Her pout at his response got her a kiss on the lips.

Applause from the congregation brought him back from his thoughts. He looked up and saw the twins raised up in the air by their father and mother as they introduced them as new members of the body of Christ.

The rest of the service went without event. The pastor gave a short sermon about parents and godparent responsibility in the life of a child. The ushers collected offerings and there was a lot of singing and dancing.

After the service, people hung around to exchange greetings and take pictures. With their arms around each other, Ibiso introduced Rasheed to a couple more people—old classmates and acquaintances as well as friends of her family.

"You were a hit with everyone," Ibiso said, as they strolled to the car.

He opened the back door and helped her inside. As he walked

190

around to the other side, he turned on his phone that had to remain off during the church service. He entered the car, put his hand behind her neck and drew her face close to his.

"The only person I want to be a hit with is you." He captured her soft lips with his. The kiss deepened and would have continued if the driver didn't feign a cough.

"Oga, where we dey go?"

Ibiso gave the driver directions to the restaurant.

Soon after, Rasheed's phone began to buzz from incoming email and messages. He pulled Ibiso close and hung his arm around her shoulder knowing that once they arrived at the reception venue, there was no telling when they'd have time to be together again for the rest of the day. The following day, they'd be heading back to Abuja.

He scrolled through his messages until he saw one that made his heart stop. He sat up straight. Before he could finish reading the message, a phone call came through. It was Ireti. He answered it.

"Ha. Thank God. Sir, I've been trying to reach you. There's big trouble in Lokoja. The private jet is waiting for you at the Port Harcourt airport. I also have a driver waiting to drive you to Lokoja. The villagers refused to talk to anybody from the company but you."

"What's going on?" Rasheed listened attentively, his brows furrowed in confusion. Anger seeped through his clenched fist. He thanked her and ended the call.

Rasheed turned to Ibiso. "I have to leave for Abuja now."

Chapter 25

The day Zayd Danjuma walked out of their lives, Rasheed swore to himself that failure would never be an option for him. His primary goal had been to prove that he was capable of being something and taking care of his mother and brothers without their father's help. This was the third day of negotiations with the villagers of Okpella and it hurt to admit that on his first major project at Danjuma Group, he had failed.

Rasheed drummed his fingers on the table as the lawyers spoke in the local dialect which he didn't understand. Waiting on a translation made him antsy.

By the time he arrived in Lokoja three days ago, things were worse than he thought. There had been one death as a result of what the villagers believed was pollution from the plant. They had barricaded the plant and the office in protest, halting all work. Overnight, they had taken their anger a step further by vandalizing the place. From the initial assessment, it would take a fortune and lots of labor to put things back together. The money that would be lost in the meantime from weeks of closure would also be a huge hit.

After a few minutes, Rasheed stood and walked outside. He needed some air and a little time to think to plan his next move. He leaned against the wall post and his phone buzzed. It was Ibiso. He looked at the screen for a minute and sent her to voicemail. He wasn't in the mood or the frame of mind to talk right now. He had given her the abbreviated version of what happened on Sunday night when he got to Lokoja, but hadn't talked to her since then. She was one distraction he couldn't afford right now. Truth be told, she was the kind of distraction he couldn't afford period.

He had known better than to let the relationship between then become so serious at such a crucial point in time. He should have been more focused. Love. The feeling he had fought so hard to avoid had snuck up on him while he wasn't paying attention. He had seen what love could do. He, of all people, knew of its potency. He had seen it do a number on his mother. How a simple emotion made such a vibrant woman lose all sense of purpose – her reason for living – was still foreign to him. And so up 'til now, he had avoided love at all cost.

As Rasheed began to beat himself up mentally, the double doors swung open. It was Mr. Eke and the independent engineer they had hired to inspect the machines.

"Sir, we have a problem," Mr. Eke said.

Rasheed's eyes went from one man to the other. His brows bunched as he observed their demeanor. "What is it?"

"The machine that was installed wasn't the one I ordered. It was an imitation," Mr. Eke whispered.

Rasheed looked toward the engineer for confirmation. The man nodded, his mood somber.

Rasheed's jaw tightened, his fist balled. "That means that—"

"Yes, sir. It means that we're to blame for what happened to that young man." Mr. Eke finished for him. His face was downcast.

"But how can that happen? The only people that where here during the installation were you, some engineers and Halima. How could that happen under your watch?"

"No sir, as the project coordinator, Ms. Danjuma told me she would meet with the vendor when they delivered. I insisted on staying since I was the one that had been working with them. She sent me back to Abuja to get something." Mr. Eke paused. "I was back here the next day, but the machines had already been installed. When we tested them, they looked the same and everything was fine but now this other engineer is saying they're not the same thing. This machine didn't come from the vendor we hired. "

"So a young man died because you were incompetent? Do you know how much it's going to cost to fix this damage? Not just money, but the loss to that family?" Rasheed asked. His teeth clenched as he struggled to suppress his temper. They weren't in a secluded area and negotiations were going on in the room next to them. He now knew that his company was responsible, but there was no reason for anyone else to know that. None of this made any sense to him. He needed to get to the bottom of this.

Rasheed sneered at Mr. Eke's insinuation. Halima couldn't have knowingly allowed this to happen. They had talked every day during the installation and she had said everything was going on fine. As part of his attempt to forgive and let go, he didn't want to smother her. Especially after seeing other projects she had managed.

Something here just didn't add up. When he inquired about her on his way here, her secretary told him she had been out sick. A quick call to her mother confirmed it. He would not have bothered her under normal circumstances, but he needed to know what in the world had happened.

Rasheed dismissed the men, but not after he asked for a full report to be placed on his desk in Abuja by morning. He pulled out his phone and called his driver. He needed answers and needed them now. He'd leave the lawyers to tidy up while he made his way to Abuja.

***

Three and a half hours later, Rasheed stepped out of the car. He yawned. His body ached, telling him that the four hours of rest it was getting every night wasn't cutting it anymore. Rest would have to wait. Failure had never been a sweet pill for him to swallow. He rolled up his sleeves as he walked across the parking lot into the office building. It was past closing time but he figured some people should still be there. He'd run up to his office, pick up a file, and head over to his stepmother's house to see Halima.

He got into the elevator and immediately rested his head against the steel panel. He tried calling Halima again to let her know he was back in town, but there was no response. Just as he was about to put the phone away a text from Ibiso came through.

I'm worried about you. Call me. Ibiso.

Rasheed began to compose a response when the doors opened. He heard raised voices coming from one of the offices down the hall. As he inched closer, the voices became louder and recognizable. It was his Uncle Musa.

The man is a born trouble maker. I wonder who he's having a problem with now. Rasheed moved toward the voices. His heart beat a little faster as the voice of the person he was talking to became more familiar. *Halima? What was she doing here? Wasn't she ill?*

"But I told you I was no longer a part of this. He was acting like my brother, being nice to me. Now look where your plan had led us - to the death of a young man. Death...death, I can't have that on my conscience." Rasheed heard Halima say.

"My dear niece, money can buy anything. You know Rasheed is a like a foreigner, so he'd be more than willing to settle the villagers and get this behind him."

Rasheed heard Uncle Musa pause, and then he continued after a few moments. "The important thing here is that the damage has been done. Let's see him speak his way out of this." There was some more silence then Uncle Musa continued. "Coming in here and acting like the people here before him were stupid. He was never supposed to be here. Now his reputation and the losses he will incur are well worth it."

There was silence. Rasheed wanted to go in, but restrained himself so he could know what he was dealing with. After a few moments, the extended calmness began to unnerve him. Rasheed placed his hand on the door knob when he heard Halima said, "Okay, you got your revenge, Uncle. Please, no more."

"No more what?" Rasheed walked into the office. His teeth hurt from clenching them so hard. His nose flared as he looked at both occupants in the room.

There was silence for several minutes as his uncle and sister, visibly shocked, exchanged glances.

"I thought you were in Lokoja," Musa Danjuma said.

Rasheed kept his eyes on Halima. She avoided looking at him as she twisted her fingers. She was squeezing them so hard that Rasheed thought they might fall off. Her body language told him all he wanted to know. Disappointment slammed his body. How could he have been so vulnerable?

Rasheed ignored Uncle Musa and continued to stare at his sister. "Halima, no more what? If you don't answer me, both of you will be talking to the police." He waited. "Now I'm going to ask you once again, no more what?"

After a few seconds, she raised her head and looked at him. Her eyes looked glossed over with traces of tears. He wasn't falling for it. He needed to know what he was up against here. He lifted his hand and ran it over his head. He watched as she moved from behind the desk and came to stand in front of him. Then she knelt in front of him and raised her eyes to meet his.

"Brother, I'm so sorry. I can't even explain it. Uncle Musa—"

"Young woman, I better not hear my name in this conversation. After all, you are the project head, not me. Since you felt compelled to talk, do that, but leave me out of it."

"Tell me what's going on," Rasheed thundered.

Rasheed saw Musa pace in the corner while Halima used the next ten minutes to tell him how Musa had convinced her to sabotage the project by firing the initial vendor and hiring one that was well known for producing low grade machines.. She admitted to being the one that told Mr. Eke and the engineers to leave and come back the next day. She also admitted to turning the other way as Uncle Musa got the plant manager on board with the plan. They didn't envision that a man would lose his life as a result of their scheme. When she was done, she began to cry.

Rasheed's body shook with anger. He left her kneeling and walked over to her desk in silence. He picked up the phone and dialed. "Get me security."

"For who? Me? Young man, didn't your mother teach you how to respect your elders?" a defiant Musa asked.

"Don't you dare talk about my mother."

Halima got up and walked over to Rasheed. "Please, I didn't mean to do it, but Uncle wouldn't let up."

He brushed past her and walked to the window. He put both hands on the large windows and bowed his head. His back was to them. Halima's sobs and Uncle Musa's huffing were the only sounds in the room. He turned around when he heard the door open.

Two security personnel dressed in grey and black entered room. "You called for us, sir?" one of them asked.

"Escort this man to his office, watch him pack, and take him outside. If I see him here again, you both will lose your jobs. He is no longer allowed on the premises," Rasheed instructed.

After an initial struggle, Musa left with the men.

Rasheed turned to his sister. "Come Monday, I want you to report to Mrs. Niyi in the Lagos office." Rasheed saw the alarmed look on her face, but he was not fazed. "I'll let her know you'll be starting there immediately. I no longer trust or want you here in Abuja."

"Logistics? I don't know the first thing about it," Halima pleaded.

Rasheed walked to the door. "You'll learn. Just the way you learned to sabotage me."

"You can't do this to me. I don't know anyone or anything about Lagos. You can't do this to me," Halima cried.

"If I see you here come Monday, I'll forget we share a last name." He opened the door and walked out.

***

Ibiso rinsed her hands and tore open the large bag of turkey cuts. She rinsed the pieces and placed them in a large basin and then using her measuring spoon, she spiced the pieces with thyme, curry, salt, red pepper and seasoned salt. She looked at the clock hanging on the wall. It was eight p.m. She had sent Rasheed a text almost four hours ago and yet no reply. Since she got back, she hadn't been able to talk to him. Either his phone was turned off or it would ring without an answer. What happened to her fairytale? She knew he had some serious issues at work, but that wasn't enough for him to not call her. She missed him so bad it hurt.

Ibiso exhaled loudly. She would have dropped everything and gone over to see him. But she had spent the last two days preparing for an event she was lucky enough to land. Her clients were a new company located in the heart of Abuja and they were sponsoring a leadership conference for their employees. Bisso Bites had been contracted to prepare breakfast, lunch, and dinner for over one hundred and fifty people. Amina called her when she was in Port Harcourt to give her the news that she had won the bid. Without delay, Ibiso called in the girls that she had on standby and was glad when they obliged.

She had been on work mode for some days. So was Rasheed, but this was inexcusable. Immediately after the conference the following day, she was going to get an explanation. It was the weekend, so there would be no avoiding her.

"Are you okay?" Amina asked. She insisted on staying with Ibiso since she decided to marinate the turkey tonight.

"Yes, why wouldn't I be?" Ibiso asked.

"Maybe because you've been beating up the turkey in the name of mixing it together," Amina washed her hands and dragged the basin away from Ibiso.

"I'm fine. Just got a lot on my mind. Thank you for waiting with me." Ibiso washed her hands, wiped them off with a paper towel, and took off her apron.

"It's no problem. I can't leave you here alone, especially since I haven't seen Rasheed here recently."

"Me neither." Ibiso murmured. "Let me get the plastic wrap." She walked into the storage unit. The ladies worked in silence for the next hour, chopping up the vegetables and fruit.

For the attendees, Ibiso wanted to have an English and Nigerian breakfast option. Toast, sausages, scrambled eggs, potatoes, egg stew and boiled yam. For lunch, she'd also have a mixture of both types of cuisines. Dinner would be comprised of light sandwiches which she was going to sub-contract from another caterer. Since she didn't have a lot of time, she'd skip the in between snacks. Even though they gave her little or no notice, there was no way she was going to turn the contract down. She'd just find a way. And she did.

Ibiso got home close to midnight. She was tired, but ready for tomorrow. She showered and slipped into her silk pajamas. She tied her hair and placed the cup of tea she had made on her dresser. She needed to be up earlier than usual tomorrow so reset her alarm. As she sipped her tea, she skimmed through her Bible, too tired to concentrate on any verse. It was no use. She put it away. Her heart leaped in excitement when she heard the buzz of a text message. Her enthusiasm was erased when she saw it wasn't from Rasheed.

Hey sis, haven't heard from you in some days. Hope everything is okay. Miss you. Sodi.

Ibiso smiled. She loved that the relationship with her family had been repaired. She quickly composed a response telling him she was fine and about the big event she had to cater tomorrow. She sighed in despair. Just as the relationship with her family was getting stronger, her love life was in shambles. Couldn't she ever keep both going at the same time?

***

Saturday morning, Rasheed was thankful that he was waking up in his own bed and not the hotel he had called home for the last week. After this encounter with Halima and Uncle Musa on Wednesday, he drove back to Lokoja the next morning. He gave the lawyers the go ahead to settle for more than what the villagers asked for. He was not going to put the company at risk by admitting guilt, but his conscience wouldn't allow him to keep fighting them when he knew it was his fault. He fired the plant manager and instructed Mr. Eke to get the right machine from the original vendor they had planned to do business with.

For the next couple of weeks, they'd have to work overtime to double up on the repairs if they had any chance of at least fulfilling some of the orders that were placed months ago. He planned to spend next week working from the Abuja office, then the week after back in Lokoja until things normalized.

He left his bedroom, turned on the news, opened up the curtains, and walked into the kitchen to prepare breakfast.

As he boiled water for custard, his mind drifted to Ibiso and their unfinished business. He didn't want to hurt her, but right now he couldn't be distracted. It was that distraction that led to the disaster the company was now in.

How could he have let his guard down and let this happen? All the Danjumas had ever done was to inflict pain on him and his family. First, his father now, Uncle Musa and Halima. If he had remembered that, he would have been able to anticipate anything. The one job he had, he had messed up all because he had begun to let his heart rule his mind. He allowed himself to get caught up in the forgiveness and second chance sermon his mother and Ibiso sold to him. The only reason he bought that, knowing what he knew, was because he had allowed love or whatever it was he was feeling to cloud his judgment.

However, he still owed Ibiso an explanation. He had contemplated sending her a text last night, but later decided against it. The least he could do was call her, after all the messages she had left him.

"Hello," Ibiso said, after the fourth ring.

"Hi," Rasheed said.

She never waited this long to answer his call. She was angry and he couldn't say he blamed her.

"How are you?"

"Good." Her response was curt. "I know you didn't call me for small talk so..."

"We need to talk—"

"You think?"

"Are you busy today? I was wondering if you'd like to meet me at the center when you're done at the restaurant. I haven't been there in a while." Rasheed knew using the center was pretty low, but he needed a lifeline. What he was going to do with it, he wasn't quite sure, but he needed it.

"I can't do today. I got a lot on my plate." Her voice was distant.

Rasheed knew her schedule on weekends. He knew she could make it if she wanted to, but right now he knew she didn't. "What about later? Let's meet at our joint."

She remained silent.

"Please."

"Fine. I'll see you by six." She hung up the phone before he had a chance to say goodbye. That was the most awkward conversation he had ever had with her. He had hurt her. She deserved better and despite what he thought, he couldn't give it to her.

***

The nerve of him. If not for the Holy Spirit, whom she had just talked to before Rasheed's call, she would have told him off. In a way she hadn't done in a long time. How could he do this to her?

She peeped into the kitchen and greeted Amina and the girls before making her way into her office. She didn't have to volunteer today and the restaurant was only open until five p.m. She hung her bag on the rack and powered up her laptop.

How could he ignore her for a week? Her calls and texts went unanswered. He didn't even let her know what was going on and then had the nerve to call her for small talk. The only reason he contacted her now was because the crisis was over. At least that's what the news reported. A settlement had been reached and they were going back to business as usual. She had turned the channel the previous day when Rasheed was giving a statement to the press. She was so angry that he left her in the dark, but her heart melted at the mere sight of him.

Despite the love she had for him, she felt déjà vu from her previous relationship. Tokoni was so focused on work that nothing else mattered when there was a crisis. He would shut her out and become harsh in his speech and actions. With no one else to carry his frustration out on, she would become a target—verbally.

Rasheed on the other hand, was not aggressive, but complete silence was just as bad. Both men were driven by the same success demon for different reasons, but the results for her were the same—a hurting heart. She had been dumped by one of them but that was something she wasn't going to allow to happen a second time.

Ibiso was still brooding some hours later when she closed the restaurant for the day. She headed down the highway for her meeting with Rasheed. Her heart and mind had been in a battle all day on whether she should have been more understanding. Rasheed was new in the country. He had just inherited his father's company which was a huge responsibility. She would at least listen to what he had to say. She owed it to herself.

***

Rasheed ordered two glasses of Zobo and walked back outside to the balcony where he'd wait for Ibiso. She had called him a few minutes ago and said she was on her way. She loved this place that served suya and other assorted snacks. He often teased her about liking so much junk food when she cooked healthy. Her explanation of wanting someone else to cook for her once in a while made sense.

The waiter brought the cold drinks and he was just about to take the first sip when he felt a hand rub his shoulder. He turned around to see Adaku. She smiled and sat in the empty chair.

"What are you doing here?" he asked, quietly thanking God Ibiso hadn't arrived.

"Hello to you too. So rude…but I'll ignore it since I know from the news you've been under a lot of stress lately," Adaku said.

"I'm sorry. Hi." Despite her manipulative ways, Adaku had been his friend once. No need to be so hostile.

"Apology accepted. I'm here on a date. Ben is ordering our drinks."

"Ben Sebu?" Rasheed asked. He didn't know his old classmate was back in Nigeria from Australia. Last he heard, he had a thriving medical practice there.

"Yes, the same one." Adaku narrated how she ran into him while at the gas station earlier and since they were both free decided to come here for drinks and suya.

"So is everything well in Danjuma world now?" she asked.

Rasheed hesitated, but then saw genuine concern on her face. "Yes, all is well."

"I was shocked to hear it though."

"Why?"

"Rasheed, you and I dated for a while and what I hated most was the way your job took precedence over everything. How this happened on your watch floored me." She paused and looked around. Rasheed assumed she was looking for Ben.

Adaku laughed. "I guess your church girlfriend got you sprung. You're losing focus." She rubbed his hand in a mocking gesture. "Your brothers need to give you another nickname because Stone Cold is turning into mush."

This was the Adaku he knew – manipulative and snobbish. He studied her for a few moments. She did have a point though. He had let down his guard and let this slip by him. Anger snapped in him. "We're friends, and I'm very much in control of my business and have my feet on the ground." His voice was raised several notches higher than he intended.

Adaku raised her hands in mock surrender and stood. "Okay, okay. I'm just checking." The next words out of her mouth were silenced by the appearance of Ben and Ibiso. The group exchanged pleasantries after which Ben and Adaku went to their table.

The tightness in Ibiso's jaw and the daggers in her eyes told him one thing. She had overheard their conversation. What part, he wasn't sure. He stood up to pull her chair out. When he touched her, she flinched.

"Do not touch me." Her voice was iced over.

Now he was pretty certain that she had heard everything. How could he have let Adaku get such a rise out of him?

"Ibiso, please listen—"

She sat down and leaned in. "No, you listen. I can do the whole stand by your man routine, but I don't have the time or energy for confusion. This…is it."

He watched as she stood, straightened her shoulders, and walked away. He needed to go after her. His heart told him as much, but his head rebelled. Besides how would he explain his way out of what he said? Maybe this was for the best.

Adaku made him so angry with her insinuation. He wanted to

be angry with her, but then again, she might just have done him a favor. He should have stuck to what had worked for him all along—avoid long term relationships and focus on work.

Rasheed sat back down. He sipped his drink and nodded as his plan developed in his head. He'd focus, get this company running smoothly, and then go back to the UK. Now all he had to do was get his heart back under control and in alignment.

Chapter 26

"So you are not going to tell me what's going on?"

Rasheed wedged the phone between his ear and his shoulder and threw an additional piece of clothing into his suitcase. He had been on the phone with his mother for fifteen minutes and now his patience was wearing thin. Why couldn't she just accept his information?

In the week since his break up with Ibiso, or rather since she broke things off with him, he had buried himself in work, but the pain was still there. He woke up each day and had to will his heart to get with the program. He didn't have time for love or any serious commitment. It wasn't like he was the marriage type, so where would it lead anyway? He had seen what love did to people. What guarantee did he have that he wouldn't end up doing the same to Ibiso?

Abuja had become too small for him and he needed a break. The stars must have been in position with the moon because his boss in the UK called. He needed a favor.

"Mama, nothing is going on. My boss in the UK needs me. He had always been fair to me, so I want to help him." He picked up his sleeveless kaftan and contemplated whether to take it or not. Deciding not to, he placed it on the bed.

"Aren't you supposed to be on a leave of absence? Why can't someone else do it?"

"Yes I am. But he asked me. Mama I'll be gone three weeks tops." Despite his leave of absence, Rasheed jumped at a chance to get away for a while.

"What did Ibiso say?"

Rasheed remained silent. He didn't know what she would have

to say because he didn't tell her. A clean break was always the best.

"Mama, please let it be. Ibiso and I are no longer together." He heard his mother let out an exaggerated sigh. He knew she had a Bible verse and a sermon prepared. There was a honk outside. The taxi taking him to the airport had arrived. His mother's message would have to wait for another day.

"I have to go now. I promise I'll be back soon. Ireti has all my numbers and the managing director is in charge. I love you, mama."

"Wait. *Nna biko*, please, what happened? You were so happy."

Rasheed hated making her worry over him. But he had spent most of his life worrying about her and his brothers. He needed this time away for him.

"Nothing you should be worried about. I call you when I get to London."

Before she could utter another word, he disconnected the call, closed his suitcase and walked out the door.

***

Ibiso parked her car in the only vacant space left. She hated doing her hair on Saturdays but had to cancel her Thursday appointment because one of the girls called out at the restaurant. She lifted her hand and scratched her head. *I'm getting tired of this natural hair. I'm one step from getting a perm.* She knew she wouldn't do that though, all she needed was a good wash and conditioning.

She walked into the salon. The air was saturated with a mix of burnt hair, ultra sheen and shampoo. Although the place was packed, her stylist was waiting for her.

"Hey lady," Ibiso said, dropping her book and purse.

"Hey, right on time. I'm glad you could make it this early. I have a full day," Gladys said. She had been her stylist since Ibiso moved to Abuja. Ibiso sat down and Gladys removed her scarf.

"Seven a.m. is early, but I'm glad you could fit me in."

"What do you want done? I know you need a wash and conditioner."

"Yes, wash, conditioner, and Bantu knots."

Moments later, Ibiso was seated under the steam dryer. She opened her book and tried to find her place. After staring at the page for a few seconds, she closed the book. As was the case for the past week, she was having a hard time concentrating. Since she ended things with Rasheed, she had gone from tears as a result of the pain in her heart to regret that she may have acted irrationally, to anger that he let her go. How dare he make her feel so good one minute, and act so indifferent and confused the next?

She got out her iPod and tucked in her earphones. She scrolled through her playlist and selected the song that had now become her feel good song—*Nobody's Supposed To Be Here* by Deborah Cox.

The lyrics penetrated her soul as she hummed along... *When I turn around, again love has knocked me down. I'm sad to say love wins again. So I place my heart under lock and key...but I turn around and you're standing here.*

Two hours later, Ibiso paid and inspected herself in the mirror. She loved it. The style enhanced her cheek bones. Her phone rang as soon as she unlocked her car. She smiled and activated her hands free set.

"Hey you," Ibiso said.

"Hello?"

"B, can't you hear me?"

"I can, but I'm scared."

"Why?"

"Err... you just broke up with your boyfriend and you're sounding too happy," Boma replied.

"Aren't you the one who told me that joy is attainable even when the clouds are grey?" Ibiso could remember the Psalm 94:19 verse in her sleep. *When the cares of my heart are many, your consolations cheer my soul.* She had been down this road before.

"I know. I'm glad. But wait oh, Rasheed still hasn't called?"

"No." Ibiso turned her car down the four lane road leading to her restaurant.

"What are you going to do?"

"Do what I've done for the last three years. Live my life and run my business. I was here before Rasheed came to Abuja."

"This hurts my heart. What is wrong with him *sef?*"

Ibiso giggled at her friend's dramatics. She was such a romantic. "Boma, why are you drinking Panadol for another person's headache? Let it be."

"But you love him…"

"Yes, I do, but it's not enough. One person's love does not a relationship make."

"I know he loves you too. Can't you just call him?"

"You of all people know I've been down this road. Rasheed has to realize it for himself or it's no use. *I no fit, abeg.*"

Both friends remained quiet for a few moments.

"I'm coming to Abuja so we can have a girl's weekend," Boma announced.

"And leave the twins? No, how about this – I'll come home soon for a girl's week?" Ibiso didn't need her friend watching her every move and feeling pity for her when she wasn't feeling pity for herself. All she felt was hurt, but she would do her best to get over it. Maybe Rasheed was just put in her path for a season and that season had passed. If not, then everything would work out, but he had to make the first move.

"Okay, cool. Let me know so I can plan."

Ibiso heard the cries of her godkids in the background. "Go take care of the kids. I just got to the restaurant. Talk to you later."

By the following week, Ibiso wasn't doing so well. Despite her efforts, her mood had changed after church the previous Sunday. A newlywed couple had their thanksgiving ceremony that day. The sermon was centered on true love and how growing old together was only possible when the couple practiced forgiveness and God's kind of love. Unconditional.

Her heart ached. There was a time when she dreamed that she

and Rasheed would end up in happily ever after. When she got home later, in a moment of weakness she called his cell phone. There was no response. The call went straight to voicemail.

The next day, Ibiso called his office, convincing herself she wanted to make sure he was okay. When Ireti told her he had gone to the UK and wasn't sure when he would return, Ibiso felt like her heart was being squeezed by a vice. How could he just leave? When the call ended, she felt a weight on her chest depriving her lungs of oxygen. In that moment, her resolve to put him behind her was stronger than ever. Some days were good, some days were bad, but every day was a new day.

Chapter 27

Rasheed turned on the artificial gas fireplace in the bedroom of his London apartment. He rubbed his hands together while he waited for the effect to kick in. Despite his padded gloves, his fingers were numb. It was a wet and cold Friday night and he had been stuck on the highway in horrible traffic. He had no one to blame but himself. He could have been enjoying cool mornings and sunny afternoons in Abuja instead. It was the first week in November and he had been in London a week longer than planned.

Satisfied with the heat from the fire, Rasheed walked into the bathroom. He needed a hot shower. He turned on the water and let it run a while. Once hot, he stepped in and let the droplets bring his body temperature back to normal.

Minutes later he wrapped himself in an oversized towel and stared at his reflection in the mirror. The lines that furrowed his forehead refused to disappear in spite of the relaxing hot shower he just had. He had done his best to run away from the truth by diving into work, but he was now coming to the realization that he had failed miserably. No matter how hard he tried, Ibiso's face was wedged in his head and as hard as it was to admit, his heart. The thought excited and scared him at the same time.

He walked into the bedroom, changed into a pair of lounging slacks and a t-shirt, then strolled into the kitchen to put on the kettle. He opened the fridge to bring out the creamer when he saw the Heineken that he had stacked up. He stretched his hand to grab one.

"I need something stronger," he muttered.

Ibiso's face came into his mind's eye. He closed the fridge and turned his lips up in a half smile. He remembered the day he promised her to wean himself off alcohol. He had changed and given up things because of her – like his Sunday golf games had been replaced with church.

He gave himself a mental shake to avoid visiting the past. Their breakup was for the best. He must have been crazy to think otherwise. He had watched his mom give up her whole heart to his dad – an action that had destroyed her. He was not ready to let go of his heart, not to her and not to Jesus. It was all he had left, all he had control over. He couldn't give that up. In an act of defiance, he turned off the kettle and opened the bottle of Heineken.

He walked over to his laptop to check his emails. One had come from the managing director of Danjuma Group. He browsed over it, hit the reply button, and gave additional instructions.

His cell phone buzzed. For a moment his heart leapt in excitement. Although he knew Ibiso didn't have his UK number, somehow he still expected to hear her voice on the other end of the line. With disappointment, he answered the call. It was his friend Jide. Rasheed remembered he hadn't spoken to Kene or Jide since the three friends had gotten on a three-way phone call and Rasheed informed them of his decision to fulfill the conditions of his father's will.

"What's up, man?" Rasheed greeted his friend.

"I didn't expect you to answer the call. What are you still doing here? I can't believe you're still in town."

"One question at a time, and didn't I tell you I have some business to wrap up?" Rasheed leaned back into his recliner and took another sip of his beer. If he knew his friend well enough, there was an inspiring speech percolating in his head. Rasheed sank his body deeper into the chair. He might as well get comfortable.

"It's one thing to lie to me, but if you're telling yourself that, then there's a problem. No scratch that, there is a bigger problem."

"Man, I have no idea what you're talking about," Rasheed said.

"Kene told me you ran away from Abuja some weeks ago. I tried to call but couldn't reach you. Since I flew back here yesterday on *real* business, I'm coming over to tell you," Jide said.

Rasheed shook his head as though Jide could see him through

the phone. "Man, I'm tired. I was just about to go to bed."

"Yeah right. Just make sure you open the door when I get there."

Rasheed's response was muted by the sound of a dial tone. This was going to be a long night. If he was going to endure a lecture, he might as well have a snack to go along with it.

Half an hour later, Rasheed opened the door to his grinning friend. In silence, he stepped aside as Jide entered his apartment.

"Since when do you cook or have anything in this house to eat?" Jide asked as he inspected the spread of kebabs that were on the center table.

"Are you saying you've not eaten in my house before?" Rasheed turned on the television. He surfed for a minute looking for something interesting while his friend entered the kitchen. He settled on the news.

Jide came out seconds later with a bottle of fruit punch soda. "Oh, I forgot your woman is a chef. Did she teach you how to cook before you ran away?"

"I didn't run away."

"Keep telling yourself that."

For the next couple of minutes, the men ate amidst light chatter. Jide caught Rasheed up on the reason he was in the UK, while Rasheed filled him in on the happenings in Danjuma Group and the project he was closing out here.

"Sounds to me like you're done. So why are you still here?" Jide asked.

"I'm not completely done. And like I told you, I just needed to get away and think for a bit." Rasheed wished Jide would drop it. He hadn't been ready to hear this sermon from his mother and he wasn't ready to hear it now. He knew they meant well, but they didn't understand. No one did.

"You've been gone for a month. You had a good thing going with Ibiso. You were the happiest you've ever been. What are you so afraid of?"

"I'm not afraid of anything. The whole thing started to get complicated. Then add all this Jesus stuff," Rasheed said. That was all he was willing to share. The fact that he was fighting his love for her would be his secret. It was an emotion he wasn't willing to entertain.

"Jesus stuff…" Jide's eyebrows shot up, demanding an explanation.

Rasheed hesitated, and then he realized a clarification would be the quickest way to get done with this topic. So he decided to indulge him so they could move on.

"Yes, surrendering and living for Jesus was part of Ibiso's package. It's just not for me." Rasheed snickered as he imagined thought clouds hovering over Jide's head.

"I know you're dying to say something, so out with it. And then, we're *not* going to talk about this again."

"For an educated man, I'm amazed at how stupid you sound." Jide stood up and paced in front of the television for a couple of seconds.

"What are you talking about? You're a man of faith, but I don't have you breathing down my throat every second about forgiveness and love that expects nothing – all which I have to do to walk the Christian walk."

"You're right. I blame myself for cosigning your bitterness all these years." He walked back to his seat and sat. "Your dad left when you were ten. You're now thirty-six, and it's time to let it go. I'm not belittling your pain, but you haven't let it stop you on anything else you've tried to accomplish. Why now? I'm not saying forget it, but let it go."

"I have let it go. But there is nothing that says I can't be cautious. Look what almost happened to the company. When I'm with Ibiso, I feel things. Good things, that encourage me to let my guard down, see the good in people – even those I know can hurt me. That's dangerous."

"Things like this happen in every family or company. If you've truly let go of your hurt, you won't be blaming it on Ibiso or the fact that she is encouraging you to live for your Maker." Jide took a sip of his drink.

A beat of silence passed between them.

Jide spoke first. "I remained passive when I knew the truth. The minute I gave my life to Christ, I should have witnessed to you, instead of allowing you to continue to spiral down this path."

Rasheed stood, picked up the empty platter, and took it to the kitchen. Jide followed. Rasheed placed the platter in the sink and turned around. Leaning against the sink, he faced his friend who was seated on a stool in the corner.

Jide said, "Man, don't be a fool. Ibiso loves you and all she's trying to do is help you live free. That freedom only comes from the knowledge of Him."

"I know she loves me." Rasheed bowed his head. Although Ibiso hadn't said the words, with all he had put her through he knew she did. He saw it in her eyes. The same look his mother had before everything went south.

God help me. I love her, too.

"The Jesus stuff, as you call it, is not the real reason you're pushing Ibiso away. Until you realize that what happened to your mom was her own path to walk and not yours, you won't be able to accept the love anyone else is trying to give you. Love is scary and messy. God has given you a good thing. Fix this before it's too late," his friend finished.

Jide looked at his watch. "I have an early appointment tomorrow, so I gotta get going."

Rasheed remained silent. Jide patted him on his back and left.

Rasheed ran his hand over his head. His heart ached at what he knew to be true and the fear that it might already be too late.

***

"Omg. Omg." Ibiso gripped the piece of paper in her hand so tight that it threatened to tear under the pressure.

She read the letter again, savoring every delicious word, making sure she didn't miss a noun or verb that might convey a different meaning. She shot up, clutched the letter and then knelt. She didn't care about what the hard cement floor of her office would do to her knees – she had to praise her Lord.

"Father, who am I that you are mindful of me? Yet you come through for me time and time again. Thank you, thank you, and thank you."

Ibiso stood and screamed again in excitement.

Amina came rushing in. "You'll scare the customers. What is it?" she asked.

Ibiso danced around her desk to where Amina was standing. She handed the letter to her friend/head cook. She waited as Amina scanned the letter. She got the reaction she was waiting for when Amina's eyes bugged out. They looked like they were about to fall out of their sockets.

"How? I don't understand. The Women's Summit is in two weeks. Two weeks. How are we going to pull off catering to a hundred and fifty women for two and a half days?"

Ibiso stopped dancing. The truthfulness of Amina's statement dampened her mood. Then she remembered that the God that brought this job to her would make a way for her to complete it. He didn't do things half way.

"God will make a way. When I got the letter this afternoon, I thought it was a mistake, so I called the office of the organizers." Ibiso took the letter from Amina.

"What did they say? It's strange that they'd wait this long to award a contract when the event is just two weeks away."

"Well according to them, the hotel they had given the job dropped out."

"Do you believe that story?"

"No. So I asked around and apparently, the hotel failed their health inspection even after a second test. But here's the kicker. Remember that company we catered to their board members a while ago?"

"Ermm…what's their name oh… Xanter LLC."

"Yes. One of the board members is on the planning committee

and remembered Bisso Bites. Seeing that we already put a bid in, she pushed for us to have the job. Something about helping small businesses for women." Ibiso walked back to her desk and sat. She raised her hand to the heavens. "As I repeat the story to you, it sounds strange, but that's exactly what they told me. How God did it I can't say, but He did."

Ibiso was in dire need for some sign that God was still looking out for her. The last couple of weeks had been hard for her emotionally. She needed something good to happen and when God showed out, He did it big because she still couldn't fathom how a one million naira contract had just fallen into her lap.

The ladies fell into a long silence.

Ibiso shuddered. She had so much work to do. According to the contract, Bisso Bites was to serve dinner on Friday evening, a full course Saturday and breakfast on Sunday. This was a huge opportunity. Now she just had to figure out how she would pull this off. First she had to make a call to Boma; the trip to Port Harcourt would have to wait.

Amina slipped out of the room, promising to stay late so they could start planning. Ibiso plopped down on her chair. *Lord, I need your help. I have absolutely no idea where to start.*

Two weeks later, Ibiso and the ten contract workers she hired, held hands for a brief prayer in the back room of Trans Hills Conference Center. After the final, "Amen" she directed them to their stations while she made her way to the back of the room. She wanted to get a clear visual that everyone was being taken care of. All the ladies where dressed in black pants, white dress shirts, and a fitted black vest with the Bisso Bite fork and knife logo. She, on the other hand, had on a black and white polka dot dress underneath her white chef's jacket with the same logo on the upper left hand corner.

The gold, green, and grey colors that adorned the conference room wasn't a palette Ibiso thought would go together, but it did. She admired the way the event planner had put the room together. The stage was decorated with bold, mixed flowers. There was a balloon arch at the registration table and a DJ that played soft music in the corner. The round tables for the participants were decorated with gold linen table cloths and set up to seat ten women each.

Minutes later, having inspected each food station for the final time, Ibiso glanced at her watch. It was 6 p.m. The guests started to trickle in. Her phone buzzed. She glanced at the screen and it was a text.

Hey girl! First day of the conference, I know you're excited and it's about that time. Don't fret, He that begun a good work will finish it. Call me when you get home. ~Boma.

Ibiso smiled her heart full with love for her friend and sister that was always there for here.

It was 10 p.m and the evening had gone without a hitch. The ladies worked with precision when it came time for dinner. They had practiced a lot the previous week and everything flowed accordingly.

The last of the guests was filing out as Ibiso packed up the last container. With any luck, she would get three hours of sleep since she had to be up early to make sure breakfast was served by 8:00am.

"Ms. Jaja."

"Yes." Ibiso turned around and her eyes met the lady who had hired her. Standing beside her was Rasheed's mom and another lady.

"Good evening," Ibiso greeted Rasheed's mother and her friend. Then she turned to the lady that had hired her. "Thank you, Madam, for giving me a chance. I hoped everything was to your liking."

"It was great." The woman said. "When I saw your restaurant on the list, I immediately remembered you for your impeccable service. Your work spoke for you."

Ibiso saw admiration in Rasheed's mother's eyes. It was the same look her son had when he complimented her cooking.

The woman then pointed to Rasheed's mother, "I see you and Mrs. Danjuma know each other. She wanted to know who was responsible for tonight's delicacies. This is Mrs. Iheme."

217

"Yes, we do. My daughter, how are you? You did a great job tonight." Rasheed's mother said. Her friend echoed her sentiment.

"I'm fine, ma. Thank you." Ibiso felt her cheeks flush. She had no idea Rasheed's mother was one of the participants. But it made sense considering she had been administrator of the city's major school district before she retired.

Another lady came from behind to compliment tonight's service as well. As the woman was leaving, she dragged the lady who had given Ibiso the job away, leaving Rasheed's mother and her friend.

There was an awkward silence. Ibiso had no idea what to say. She had talked to Rasheed's mom a handful of times. She didn't want to ask of Rasheed because she didn't know how much or what he had told her. She had spent the last month getting herself together and didn't want to go back.

Rasheed's mother took out her phone and checked it. Ibiso assumed she was checking for missed calls or messages.

"Ma, may I pack something for you to go or for your driver?"

She smiled at Ibiso. "No, my dear, thank you. My driver didn't bring me. He's ill."

"Oh, I'm sorry to hear that. Do you need a ride?"

"You're such a nice young lady. No, but thank you. My daughter is on her way to pick us up," Mrs. Iheme said.

"Besides, you have to be here early in the morning. We're looking forward to it." Rasheed's mother smiled.

Ibiso opened her mouth to speak when her eyes connected with the woman who refused to go away—Adaku. She was dressed down in jeans, a simple t-shirt, and a pair of sneakers.

"Mummy, Aunty, sorry I'm late. I was halfway across town when I got your call," Adaku said. She turned to Ibiso. "Hello, so you were the cook here tonight."

The way Adaku said the word cook was planned to get a rise out of her. Ibiso decided she wasn't going to bite. Since Rasheed hadn't fought for her, he wasn't worth going to war with another woman for.

"Hello Adaku," Ibiso replied, her voice devoid of any emotion. She should have known when the other woman was introduced as Mrs. Iheme that she was Adaku's mother. Rasheed did say they were friends. How could a perfect day end up so wrong?

"Are you ready to go?" Adaku asked.

"Yes, we are so tired," Adaku's mother replied.

"Good night, my dear. We'll see you in the morning." Rasheed's mother drew Ibiso in for an embrace.

No you won't. Ibiso planned on doing her job and avoiding any contact with Rasheed's mother, her friend or Adaku.

"Good night ,ma," Ibiso replied and the women walked out of the opposite exit.

As she rolled out her items to the lobby, Ibiso made a mental note to buy her ticket to Port Harcourt. Once the job was over, she was going home to be with her own family and friends, people that loved her and were not confused about it.

Chapter 28

It had been three agonizing weeks since Jide had come to see him. Rasheed had spent half the time wondering how he was going to redeem himself and the other half in fear that it was too late for redemption. He had tried calling Ibiso once and his call went straight to voicemail. When he tried again a couple of days later, it was turned off. Where could she be? Was she all right?

He stretched his legs out in front of him as he sat in the lounge area of Heathrow International airport. He needed to get some rest, but was too wired to even do that. It was amazing what determination to get back to the woman one loved could do. He had worked day and night to finish the project, and then he tendered his formal resignation. Now he was waiting to board his flight to Lagos. He would've gone straight to Abuja to see about Ibiso, but knew he had other business to handle—his sister.

"Ladies and gentlemen, we are about to start boarding for flight 843 headed to Lagos. We would like for all those that have small children to get ready to board," the airline personnel announced.

Rasheed watched as a couple dragged their twins away from their video games and got their luggage together. Twins. He hadn't spoken to his brothers since last Sunday. He'd call when he got back to Abuja. The announcement for first class passengers was made and Rasheed began to wheel his luggage down the narrow walkway when his phone rang.

"I was just thinking about you," Rasheed said to Jabir.

"Good thoughts? I've been thinking of you too. And it wasn't good."

"Why?"

"'Cause you're acting like the same man you've spent your life trying not to be like," Jabir said.

Rasheed got to the plane and was shown his seat by one of the hostesses. He tucked his laptop overhead and settled in his seat. His jaw tightened. "Say that again, because I don't believe I heard you."

"Yes, you did. Bro, come on. You always said that daddy was a coward for not fighting to be with his family. Letting his father dictate what he did. But you're doing the same thing because the man is dictating your life from the grave."

"What are you talking about?" The only thing Rasheed told his brothers was that he was back in London for a job. He had told them it didn't work out with Ibiso. Jabir didn't preach to him then, so what happened for him to deserve the sermon now?

"Talked to Mama yesterday. She was upset."

"Why? I talked to her this morning and she didn't say anything."

"Yeah, she decided not to interfere, but I guess running into Ibiso made her think about your "stupidity" as she calls it."

Rasheed buckled his seat belt and signaled for the hostess. When she appeared, he asked for a glass of water. His mother hadn't said anything to him. When did she see Ibiso? Why didn't she say anything?

"So what happened?"

"I don't know. Last week, she was with Adaku and her mom at some conference, so was complaining about how you let two of them get away."

Rasheed closed his eyes and leaned his head back. That couldn't have been good. He knew Adaku would have done everything to rub the fact that she was closer to his mother in Ibiso's face. He had no one to blame but himself. He had to fix this.

"I gotta go. I'll call you when I get to Lagos," Rasheed said.

"Good luck. According to mama, it might be too late. She said Ibiso didn't even ask of you."

***

Ibiso stretched out on the queen-sized bed in her Port Harcourt bedroom. She had arrived three days ago and this was the last day of her four day weekend getaway. The effects of the whirlwind of last week's conference on her body had all but disappeared. Her days had consisted mostly of sleeping, lounging around the house and eating. Boma had also come by every day to take her shopping or sightseeing. Ibiso wasn't into the latest trends but a little retail therapy had turned out to be a good thing. She turned her head and saw the shopping bags from last night's spree in the corner.

Today she was going to spend the whole day with her godkids before she left for Abuja in the morning. First order of business when she returned was a photo shoot for a small lifestyle magazine. They wanted to feature her restaurant in their Yummy Cuisine of Abuja section. Ibiso still couldn't believe it. Her...a magazine.

Ibiso turned over and pulled the covers over her head and whispered a quiet "thank you" to God. Everything had gone better than she could have imagined for herself. She reached over to grab her phone. She needed to access her Bible app, but remembered that she had lost her real phone or left it in her apartment in her rush. The Nokia flip phone she held in her hand was a quick replacement until she got back home - new number, no contacts. She replaced the phone on the dresser. The only number she needed was to her restaurant and that she knew by heart.

Although she longed for a few more minutes of slumber, a whiff from the kitchen gave her a reason to get up. She spent the next couple of minutes in prayer and worship, and then detangled herself from the sheets, put on her robe and made her way to the origin of the aroma.

She entered the kitchen and saw Sodienye at the kitchen table concentrating on the plate of food in front of him.

Ibiso walked over to the stove where her mother was turning the contents of another pot.

"Good morning, mother." She peeked into the pot and saw that her mom was making *Oha* soup.

"Good morning, my love. I hope you slept well." Her mother's eyes roamed from the scarf on Ibiso's head to the cotton robe she had on. "You haven't showered yet?"

"Nope. I'm here strictly for relaxation. Besides Boma is coming by later. I'll shower then," Ibiso replied. She looked over to her brother who hadn't said a word.

"Sodi, morning. What are you doing here? Don't tell me food brought you? Don't any of the women that hang around you know how to cook?"

"You're teasing your brother. When he starts, better be able to handle it," her mother said.

"Ah mama, hold on now. Let me finish this food first, then I'll be then be able to match her word for word." He winked at Ibiso.

Ibiso knew that wink meant there would be no mercy.

"Okay bro, my bad." Ibiso took the plate of yam and vegetable porridge her mother handed her and blessed it.

Sodienye stood and took his plate to the sink. He kissed his mom on the cheek and turned to Ibiso.

"Sis, I have a deal to close this morning. See you later, right?"

"Yeah, I'll be back by evening. Remember you're taking me to the airport tomorrow."

Her mother walked over and kissed her on her hair.

"My baby, you know it's always hard for me to see you leave again. Christmas is in three weeks. Will you be back?"

Ibiso didn't know the answer to that question. She had no idea what she was going to do for the holidays. Normally, it was down time for her restaurant so she planned for the year ahead. Six weeks ago, she and Rasheed had planned to split the time between Abuja and Port Harcourt for Christmas and New Year's.

"Yes, mother, I'll be back." Even though she wasn't sure, there was no need ruining the nice atmosphere.

"You wouldn't have to shuttle back and forth if you seriously consider what we discussed," Sodienye said.

Ibiso smiled up at him. "Sodi, I can't just pack up my restaurant and move it to Port Harcourt."

"I don't see why not." He opened the jar of crayfish his mother handed to him and set it on the counter.

"I told you this prime space just became available. I could loan you money and we put a down payment on it. I ran into it when I was closing on another deal for a client. The agent is a friend of mine and I told him I wanted it." He looked at her with anticipation.

Ibiso exhaled. She didn't want this to be another wedge between them. The space was fantastic, spacious, her dream come true, but she didn't want to run away again. She had done that before with Tokoni.

"Don't pressure your sister. I'd love to have her home but as long as she visits more often. I'm fine." Their mother picked up her tea cup, turned off the burner and left the kitchen.

"The allure of a new, bigger place is tempting but…"

"You would be closer to me and you know mother misses having you around. I promise not to interfere. I get your need to do things on your own. Just don't ask me to stop protecting you."

"I'll think about it," Ibiso said.

"You do that. And I still owe Danjuma a phone call. He didn't keep his word."

"Sodi, please let it be." Ibiso finished her juice and walked to the sink.

All her brother wanted was to protect her, which was why she hadn't told him everything about her breakup. Just that they needed time apart. Right before she left Abuja, the center's director inquired if she and Rasheed would attend their open house next week. Apparently he'd be in the country then.

Ibiso wanted to hear his voice so bad, but she knew this was for the best. She had done the right thing in letting go. She loved Rasheed to bits, but not at the expense of her salvation and her heart. Any future they had would always be shaky if he couldn't get himself together. She wasn't willing to put herself through that again.

As they walked out of the kitchen, Ibiso loosened the sash of her robe. She had overfed. "I'm going to have to be careful with mother's cooking."

"As long as you're staying with her, good luck with that."

Ibiso walked her brother to the door. "And your house is better?"

"Yes, because I'll keep you busy. There's a lot to do around the house, cooking, cleaning..." He stepped out of the house.

"You see why I won't move back. I'd become your maid. Bye." She playfully slammed the door and headed inside in search of her mother.

***

Later that day in Lagos, Rasheed tucked his cell phone between his ear and his shoulder and waited for the Amina or someone from Bisso Bites to pick up the phone. He had been trying to reach Ibiso since he got into the country three days ago. His phone calls went straight to her voicemail. He had spent the day before trying to convince Amina to tell him where Ibiso was or give him another number to reach her. She refused both requests. He must have a big X marked by his name and pasted on the wall of Bisso Bites because this wasn't the Amina he was used to.

Rasheed sat on the bed in the room Kene had offered him. It was soft, but he hadn't been able to enjoy it. As much as he tried to rest, sleep escaped him. He found himself awake all night replaying the events of the last several weeks in his head. How could he have been so stupid? For the first time in years, he longed to hear clear instructions from God. He now knew that that was the only way he could begin to fix the mess he had made of his relationship with Ibiso and get his life back on track. Starting with confession of his sins and asking God to come into his heart. Ibiso had said it was as simple as that.

He dug his hands in his suitcase in search of something suitable to wear. He settled on a pair of dark blue jeans and a green checkered dress shirt. There was a brief knock on the door and it opened.

Kene walked in and handed him a cup of coffee.

"Morning, man. Thanks," Rasheed said as he took the hot cup.

Kene wouldn't hear of him staying in a hotel and had given him a room in his four bedroom house in the Ikeja area of Lagos. The house was modern and posh, exactly Kene's taste, but it lacked the feminine touch Ibiso had put in his apartment. He hung up the phone.

"Still no luck?"

Rasheed took a sip of the steaming beverage. "No and I'm bordering between worry and irritation."

"You know you don't have a leg to stand on, so just take whatever Ibiso dishes. It's your fault."

"I know. She has a way of just..." Rasheed shook his head.

Kene snickered. "You're funny. You go silent for six weeks, and then you come back and want her to be waiting. Don't be surprised if she's moved on."

"Not you too?"

"Yep. I head the committee that thought that was an idiotic move. So, you ready to go to your sister's?"

"In a minute." When he had arrived in Lagos, Halima was traveling to secure a new client. On her return, he had toured the Danjuma offices and was quite impressed but what he had to say to her now had to be done in private. She had invited him to lunch.

"Okay, I'll drop you off so you two can talk, then I'll spend the day with my dad and his wife."

Kene's birth mother had passed away when he was twelve years old. Soon after, his father remarried. An action that caused father and son to be estranged for a couple of years. Although it had taken a while, Kene had since warmed up to his stepmother.

"After all these years, you still call her his wife?" Rasheed chuckled.

"That's what she is, right?" He smiled, opened the door, and walked out.

***

Hours later, Kene turned his car into the gated community where Halima lived. Soon, both friends walked up to the front door, rang the doorbell and waited.

Rasheed was taken aback when Halima, dressed in a simple cut red dress with white polka dots, opened the door. She looked different without her hijab on. In fact, this was the first time he was seeing her auburn flowing hair. His kid sister was quite a beautiful young woman.

"Good afternoon, brother," his sister said. Her tone was low.

"Hi. This is my friend Kene. Kene this is my kid sis, Halima."

"Hi." Kene stretched out his hand and Halima placed hers in it. He gave her his charismatic smile and if Rasheed didn't know any better, he'd think that Halima had just been captivated by Kene's charm. Her eyes had a hint of admiration in them. The handshake seemed to last a moment too long. Rasheed cleared his throat and Kene let go of her hand.

A strange overprotective feeling came over him. She looked so vulnerable, giving him another reason to dislike that fact that she was in Lagos all by herself. She opened the door to usher them in.

"I'm afraid I have to leave, but it was nice meeting you," Kene said. "Call me later, man."

"Nice meeting you, too," Halima said, and walked into the house.

"Okay, thanks," Rasheed replied.

He locked the door and walked over to the one of the seats in the corner that she had ushered him to. Unlike Ibiso, his sister was more minimalistic with her color scheme. A black and white theme ran throughout the living room. The only colors were provided by the throw pillows on the sofa.

"You look nice. Different."

She bit her lip and avoided eye contact. Rasheed could tell she was nervous. She stood, "Lunch is ready. Do you want to eat now?" Her eyes avoided his.

"No, sit. Let's talk. I have something to say." He paused and waited for her to look up at him. "I'm sorry."

Halima remained silent. Her eyes questioned him, waiting for answers he wasn't sure how to give.

"Sis... is it okay if I call you that?" he asked.

A nervous smile played on her face. "Of course..."

"I've been so angry for so many years, but then I decided to forgive and trust. You betrayed that trust. The good news is that after an autopsy, it was revealed that the young man didn't die from our pollution. He had other health problems. But that doesn't negate the fact that you connived with Uncle Musa to sabotage me."

Tears fell down her face. She walked over to her the corner of the mantle that held a 42 inch LCD television and retrieved some tissue from the box.

After dabbing her eyes, she said. "Rasheed, I was very angry with daddy's will. I was the one who was here for him, but that didn't stop him from talking about you and the twins all the time. When he went looking for you, and was not received, I had to work extra hard to make him see that I could do anything that the sons that no longer wanted him could. But I never met up, and then the will was the final straw. Uncle Musa took advantage of that and I let him."

Rasheed saw her eyes dance with tears and wanted to just pull her to him. He could see more so now that she had suffered just as he had. While he wondered how his dad could abandon them, Halima had spent all her life to measure up to a picture of perfection that didn't exist.

"I've wanted for so long to have a relationship with you and the twins. While the twins at least talked to me, you looked at me with so much hate." She sniffed.

"I'm sorry. It was my misplaced anger." He closed the gap between them and hugged her while she cried.

"I'm so sorry. I'm really not a bad person. I haven't been able to rest, thinking about that young man," she said.

Rasheed held up her face with his index finger. "Somehow I knew that little girl I met when I was eleven was not a bad person."

"You saw me when you were eleven?"

Rasheed held her hand and walked to the sofa. He sat and she sat next to him. He told her about how he first found out that he had a sister. As he told the story, her expression changed several times from regret, shame, to empathy.

"Thank you for giving me another chance to be your sister. You won't regret it."

After lunch, they settled down to played chess. Rasheed was glad that at least one of his siblings loved the game. His brothers hated it, so he only got to play with Kene or Jide.

"You have a nice place here. I'm surprised you didn't get something bigger," Rasheed said.

"Bigger? Why? You think I'm one of those spoilt rich girls? Brother please, my mom made sure I was well grounded. 'You're going to somebody's wife someday. No man wants a spoilt woman', she would say." Halima mimicked the way her mother spoke.

She placed a bottle of Vita Malt in front of him, and then stared at the chess board for a minute before making her move.

Rasheed let out a hearty laugh then took a sip of his beverage. That was precisely the way Aisha, his step mother sounded.

"So is it true?"

"Is what true?

"The spoilt rich girl bit?"

Rasheed scrunched his eyebrows together and shrugged. "I don't know. I guess so. I wouldn't want a spoilt woman on my hands. So your mom is right."

"Speaking of which, how is your girlfriend? We never got introduced, but everyone in the office knew of her."

Lifting his head, he stared at her. His heart tightened. "She's not my girlfriend. Not any more..."

"You're kidding? That's too bad. Well, whether it's your fault or hers, if that's regret I see in your eyes, then you should be looking for her and not here playing chess with me." She paused. "Before it is too late. Someone else would recognize what you didn't and you'll regret it. Sound familiar? That's what happened to our father. Before he realized it, it was too late."

Chapter 29

Monday morning, Ibiso shifted again in the passenger seat of her brother's car as he drove her to the airport for the second time in two days. The day before, she had waited in the airport for two hours before her flight was finally cancelled due to bad weather. She was sad to be leaving, but she was also excited. She had gotten her physical rest and after the sermon yesterday, her mind was right as well.

All that was left was for the ache in her heart to stop. It had increased in the last few hours as she prepared to head back to Abuja. However the promise from Psalm 73:26 gave her comfort. *My flesh and my heart may fail, but God is the strength of my heart and my portion forever.*

Four hours and two more flight delays later Ibiso and her brother were still at the airport. She was restless. He, on the other hand, was still able to work on his Samsung Galaxy, so he didn't seem bothered. She stood and adjusted her skirt for the umpteenth time. She walked up to the front counter to check on the status of her flight again. She couldn't spend another day in Port Harcourt. She had a business to run and an interview to give.

Minutes later, she was back with the same response that she had gotten each time, "We are waiting for the plane to come in."

Her brother tucked away his phone. "Ibiso, sit down. You should be used to the aviation system in this country by now."

"I can never get used to it. This getting used to things that don't function as they should is our problem as a people." She plopped down on the chair beside him in the waiting area.

"Since you're not running for office, make your voice heard in the next election by voting," he said. He rubbed her shoulder. "So, did you like restaurant space I showed you?"

The previous day on their way back from the airport, Sodienye took her to another expansive restaurant space. She was in shock at its magnificence. To sweeten the pot, it was located smack dab in the middle of one of the busiest intersections in Port Harcourt. The space had a sprawling kitchen, two back offices and the dining area was divine. The power in that area was pretty steady, but there was also a generator house at the back that was set to power on automatically. Sodienye had once again offered to be a silent partner, but this time with a clause stating that she could buy him out when she wanted to.

The business woman in her wanted to sign the lease immediately. She had friends and family in Port Harcourt so it wouldn't be difficult picking up momentum. However, she had run away before because of a man and was not going to do it again.

"I loved it as you know, and I wish I could have signed the lease. Especially since you are going to help me out," she said.

"But?"

"But, I can't. Under different circumstances, maybe," she said.

Ibiso watched Sodienye's mood turn contemplative. He was seldom at a loss for words, but she saw the effort he was making to ensure he said the right thing.

"Sis, I can't believe I'm going to say this, but I understand." He raised his hand to silence her when she opened her mouth to speak.

"Hear me out. All of a sudden, you show up for a four-day weekend. I've been silent and let you do your thing, but don't forget I'm your big brother and I know you well. You told me something, but I get the feeling that that's not the whole story. In as much as I want to protect you, and my reason for asking you to come back home might have been selfish, you're a big girl. If you ever decide to relocate, I want it to be because you are tired of living in Abuja and want to come home. Not because I want to shield you from some guy. At first I couldn't stand Danjuma, but it was obvious to everyone at the christening that you two loved each other. I have to admit, we guys can be irrational sometimes. Just try to work it out."

Ibiso couldn't contain the emotion that was about to envelop her. In that moment, her brother spoke to her just as she knew her late father would have. Her eyes welled you with tears, the tightness in her throat blocked the words from coming out.

"You know I can't do the tears. Come here." Her brother drew her close and she hugged him tight. She only let go when the announcement for her flight was made.

She stood up and gathered her oversized handbag and carry-on suitcase.

"Here take this." She handed her brother the bag that contained cooked soups and stews that her mother had packed for her. Even though she protested, her mother still forced her to carry them with her. "Take, so you don't have to keep disturbing mother. This should last you a while."

"I see you're funny, but hey, I never turn down food." He walked her to the boarding area. "Look sis, one wrong move from that knucklehead guy and you give me a call. I'll be in Abuja to move you back myself."

He kissed her on the cheek and turned to leave.

***

The next day, Ibiso stretched her arm to silence her alarm. After hitting the snooze button for the umpteenth time, she knew it was time to get up. The flight home last night took a toll on her mentally and physically. After the numerous delays, the plane ended up being overbooked. Instead of the window seat she paid for, she ended up being seated between a woman, her crying toddler, and an oversized man who could have done with more room. By the time she got to her apartment, her head felt like a rock band resided there and her body just longed to stretch.

Despite the pain however, she found herself replaying the conversation she had with her brother at the airport. What astounded her most was Sodienye's turnaround. She'd have thought he'd be out for blood. The outcome was Rasheed's appearance in her dreams and the fun times they did have together.

In fairness, when she thought about it in retrospect, she too had a part to play in their breakup. She was in it, but not fully, always waiting for the other shoe to drop because of her last experience. Everything Rasheed did had been compared to Tokoni. Could she have been more understanding and hung around? Yes. But at the first sign of trouble she bolted. However, she couldn't stick around for a man who didn't even know what she was to him. Love – yes she loved him. Desperate and stupid, no – she was not.

She reached over for her Bible, and then remembered it was in her suitcase that was somewhere in the living room. She searched her handbag and retrieved her Kindle and opened up the You Version app. Her reading plan today took her to Psalm 119:114 *You are my refuge and my shield; I have put my hope in your word.* She opened the full chapter and read it in its entirety. It was the confirmation she needed that she was on the right path in sticking to the Lord's word and His commands. No more compromises. Rasheed had to come to her whole or not at all. Wholeness could only happen by him giving his life to God and every other thing would be fine. She said a silent prayer that Rasheed would come to the realization of God's love. However, she was comforted in understanding that whatever happened, the peace the Psalm promised would heal her heart.

Ibiso got out of the bed and turned on her radio to her favorite gospel station, then walked into the living room to retrieve her luggage from where she left it last night. Returning to the bedroom, she unpacked, separated her dirty clothes into a pile that she'd drop off at the cleaners and a load she'd wash during the weekend.

After a quick shower and wardrobe change, she went in search of breakfast. Her cupboards were bare, so she put together a meal of oatmeal and fruit for breakfast. On her way out, her eyes caught her phone in the corner.

So that's where I left it. The battery must be beyond dead. It was. She plugged it in, threw the loner phone in her laptop bag, picked up her laundry and left.

***

Rasheed tried to work but his mind was far away. He kept glancing at the clock that hung in the corner of his office. He hadn't been able to concentrate on anything since he got back to Abuja two days ago. Upon seeing him in person, Amina had admitted that Ibiso was in Port Harcourt. His patience was wearing thin waiting for her to return. A couple more days of this and he'd hop on a plane to go get her. He wondered why her phone was off. Amina did nothing to ease his worry as her response each time was, "I can't say, but she'll be back soon."

Rasheed was tempted to call Sodienye but remembered that they weren't what he would call friends. With all the promises he made to the guy, how would he explain that he didn't know where his sister was? That would be a dead giveaway that there was trouble. Or had Ibiso already spilled the beans to big brother?

"Sir, you have a call on line two," his secretary's voice came through the buzzer and jarred him back to the present.

"Who is it?" he asked.

"He said his name is Sodienye Jaja."

Rasheed's instincts told him this wasn't a friendly call. He wasn't ready for this especially since he hadn't seen Ibiso. He understood Sodienye's concern being a big brother having just reconciled with his sister. However, whatever was going on with Ibiso and him was his business.

He sucked in a deep breath. "Put him through and hold all my calls. If my 2 p.m. conference call is ready before I'm done, please come in and interrupt me."

Rasheed exhaled and picked up the receiver. "This is Rasheed."

"Danjuma, I know you're a busy man, so I'll get straight to the point. When you came to Port Harcourt you promised me that my sister's happiness was your number one priority. That promise has been broken and she is not happy. The gods must be working in your favor because for some insane reason, I sent her back to Abuja instead of keeping her here. Don't make me regret that decision."

"Ibiso is back in town?" Rasheed asked.

Sodienye's silence was the confirmation he needed. He also knew that the man on the other end of the line wasn't going to let go until he was pacified.

How long had she been back? Why hadn't she tried to contact

him? Then again, he left her with no reason to.

"Sodienye, I know what I said. And while I respect the fact that you care about your sister and her welfare, you have to understand that this is between she and I," Rasheed said. His voice was tight. If everything went accordingly, Rasheed planned on being the only man issuing any kind of warnings where Ibiso was concerned.

"I gave you that autonomy before and you blew it. She is my sister and I told you she loves hard. Fix it or move out of the way."

Rasheed could hear the venom in the other man's voice. At this point he knew that there was no reason to debate him. He had only one mission, wrap up his conference call and go and search for Ibiso. Also despite his anger, Rasheed knew that Sodienye meant well to call him. For that he owed the man a thank you.

"I will and thank you for trusting me with your sister."

"Don't thank me yet. Good luck."

Hours later, Rasheed pulled off his headset and picked up his jacket to leave. The call had gone so well and there was a huge possibility that he would supply cement to the Ghanaian government. This would be their third international partnership.

He placed his hand on the door knob when he heard commotion outside his office door. He picked up his attaché and moved towards the outer door. He opened it to find Adaku arguing with Ireti. When she saw him, in swift strides she walked to him and entwined her arm in his.

"Rasheed darling, I've called you several times."

He peeled her arm from his. "I've been out of the country."

"I know darling, but I also knew when you got back. I have people you know." She giggled. He didn't pay any attention before but now he realized that her giggle sounded like a frog being squeezed to death.

Rasheed said goodbye to Ireti and ushered Adaku towards the elevators. There was no need for the whole office to know about his personal life. He should have known not to use Adaku to try to get rid of his feelings for Ibiso. After he and Ibiso broke up, they had gone out to dinner twice before he realized she thought more of it than he did. He had been paying for that decision ever since. She could be counted among the reasons he left the country, but that all ended tonight. He'd dismiss her and head to Ibiso's house. There was so much they had to talk about.

Once the door to the elevator closed, Adaku became more aggressive. She rubbed her body against his. He knew she was trying to get some kind of reaction from him. He set his attaché down and held her at arm's length.

"Adaku stop it." His voice was forceful.

"Rasheed, we've been playing this game for a while, don't you think it's time to give in? We're good together," she pleaded.

The desperation in her voice and eyes almost made him pity her. But he knew her and couldn't let his guard down.

"I'm so sorry if I've led you on, but this won't work."

"Why? Ben and I didn't work out. You and the church girl are through. What's the problem?"

"Her name is Ibiso and I 'm sorry for making you believe there was something between us when there isn't."

Adaku remained silent. She dropped her head. Seconds later, she lifted her teary eyes and moved towards him. "You can't blame a girl for trying." She paused. "Let's say goodbye right, a kiss for old times."

Without hesitation, Rasheed said, "No."

Adaku raised her hands to cup his face. As he tried to break free the elevator door opened. There stood Ibiso. Her mouth hung open as he struggled for the words to say. The hurt in her eyes made his heart clench. Soon that hurt was replaced by rage emitting from her eyes. He had never seen her so angry. In that moment he knew that any chance of reconciliation was going to be a million times harder. Harder, but not impossible. That hope propelled Rasheed forward. He turned around and glanced at Adaku, rage tearing through him. He'd handle her later. Now he had to get to Ibiso.

***

Thank God for flat sandals and side stairwells, Ibiso thought as she opened the door to her apartment forty-five minutes later. She threw her keys on the center table, pulled off her shoes and went into the kitchen in search of something to drink. She sat at the dinette with a cold glass of Fanta.

Before Rasheed could get out of the elevator she slipped through the side stairwell and waited there for a few minutes. She needed time to calm down and pick her face off the floor. Then she gathered herself and continued down the stairs to the parking lot. She started her car and headed in the direction she should have headed the minute she got off work—home.

What was she thinking? In the morning, her resolve was strong. Then Amina had to continue harping about how many times Rasheed had called looking for her. She began to second guess herself. She still stood by her earlier convictions until she was on her way from the dry cleaners and heard a commercial for the Danjuma Group cement. The old irrational Ibiso took over, or it was the love in her heart she had tried so hard to suppress. She didn't know which, but she turned her car around and headed to his office.

Ibiso took another sip of her drink and sighed. She picked up her glass and headed to the bedroom. She started to peel off her clothes as she remembered the look on Rasheed's face. It told her that he had an explanation. But it was one she didn't want to hear. What was the point?

Besides, if she allowed Rasheed close to her, the tears would flow and that she wouldn't allow. Not in front of him. That would be beyond pathetic. What was she thinking? How could she think that Rasheed had missed her as she missed him or even loved her? It was evident that he was still playing games and she had had it. In the safety of her room, Ibiso let the tears stream down her eyes as the sight of Rasheed and Adaku took residence in her thoughts.

Chapter 30

Rasheed was confused. How could she have disappeared so fast? After searching the parking lot for the second time, he went back in to make sure the receptionist didn't see her.

His phone rang. He answered immediately, thinking it was Ibiso. "Where are you?"

"*Oga*. It's me Ireti."

"Yes, what is it?" Rasheed's eyes roamed around, hoping to catch a glimpse of Ibiso.

"Mr. Danladi tried to reach you after you left the office. He requested you call him immediately."

Mr. Danladi was the new manager of the Lokoja cement plant. Ireti briefed him about the emergency—the villagers were making demands again and picketing the site. Rasheed thanked her and disconnected the call.

He knew his irritation was visible when he made a call to Mr. Danladi. After a quick chat, it was evident that his presence was needed. He couldn't send the operating manager because he was out of the country on vacation. And it was too much of a short notice to tell anyone else. Since the site manager was new and wasn't up to speed on the history Danjuma Group had with the people of Okpella, Rasheed would have to make the three hour journey to Lokoja himself—tonight.

He looked at his watch. With the way the roads were, he'd have to get going now in order to be back before midnight. He wouldn't be able to see Ibiso right now, but she should count on them settling this tonight. No matter the time. How could she run off like that?

He made his way to the parking lot again. Once he was settled in the back seat, he called Ibiso's phone. This time it was ringing, but she was not answering. He disconnected the call in annoyance and placed a call to his mom.

"Mama, I have to make a quick trip to Lokoja. I'll be back tonight," he said when she answered the phone on the second ring.

On her inquiry, he filled her in about the latest happenings at the plant.

"*Nna*, it's late. Please if you can't make it back tonight, wait until morning," his mother said.

"I'll make it back." Nothing was going to keep him away. He had come to learn that a vital part of his existence hinged on Ibiso and he was not letting her run away a second time. "I'll call you when I get in." He disconnected the call.

"Benjamin, we're going to Lokoja, Call your wife and let her know," Rasheed told his driver. He leaned back in the leather seat of and waited for his driver to make the call. As the driver turned the car out of the parking lot, Rasheed picked up his phone and typed a text to Ibiso.

Things didn't quite go as planned. It was 6 p.m. the following day before Benjamin pulled into the parking garage of Rasheed's Abuja home. It took an overnight stay and two meetings with the local government chairman and village leaders to get everything back on schedule. The deal his company had with the villagers concerning clean up and payout for the previous damages was back on track. There was a mistake in the funds payout that triggered outrage and demonstration. Now that business was back in order, it was time to take care of his personal life.

He hadn't gotten a reply from Ibiso last night and right now he was irritated by her stubbornness. Rasheed knew she could be strong-willed, but this was driving him crazy.

He caught a glimpse of the painting of Jesus with his hands outstretched that Ibiso had given him hanging in the corner. He stopped in front of the painting and stared at it. For the first time, he looked at the picture with intent. At the bottom was an inscription that read, *"Come to Me, all you who labor and are heavy-laden and I will cause you to rest."*

Rasheed murmured the line, then said it out loud a second time. He repeated the line a couple more times while he walked into his bedroom to freshen up from his long journey. As he showered, he kept repeating the verse over and over in his head. He bowed his head under the hot water and allowed the jet stream to massage his body. His body became limp. It was as if it was surrendering just as his mind and emotions followed. He was tired. For over twenty-five years he had tried to do it all by himself – be strong so his mother wouldn't have to worry about anything, he and his brothers included. And keep up a front so his brothers wouldn't be exposed to the pain he was exposed to. That anger and hate played out in his relationships and quest for success, until Ibiso.

She changed everything for him. He cringed at the thought that she probably compared their relationship to the disaster with her ex. Now, coupled with what she saw yesterday, he would have to do some serious groveling to fix it. But as she would say, nothing is impossible with God. With his face lifted to the ceiling, he said, "Help me out, Jesus. I'm counting on you."

An hour later, Rasheed, dressed in a dark blue pair of jeans and a grey print Ankara shirt got into his car with one mission in mind: get Ibiso Jaja back.

***

Ibiso couldn't focus. She looked at the empty moving boxes she had brought home with her earlier that day and sighed. The latest episode of Super Story was playing on TV, but she couldn't settle down to enjoy it. She hadn't reorganized her home in three years and her emotions needed an outlet. She wasn't going to sit around and mope. She planned on boxing up some stuff for charity.

She looked around the living room, not sure where to start. She gave up and walked into the kitchen and put the kettle on. *Some tea might help.*

She leaned against the counter while she waited for the water to boil. Her phone buzzed alerting her to a text. It was Boma.

Have you called him yet?

No. There's no need to. Ibiso replied.

So you're just going to act like you didn't see him yesterday with that Looney Tune and continue with business as usual?

Ibiso took a picture of the boxes and sent it to her friend. *Yep, business as usual. I'm rearranging my house.*

Huh? Are you sure you're okay? When I get out of this library I'll call you.

Kk, Ibiso responded.

Ibiso was glad for the little reprieve. Boma was studying for her doctorate degree in psychology and often went to the library because as she put it, "Dokubo won't let me rest." Ibiso was so happy that at least one of them was "getting some."

Her insides stirred and goose pimples riddled her body when she remembered how she and Rasheed had to take a step back so many times to not cross that boundary. The whistling sound from the kettle jolted her back to the present.

With her hot mug in hand, Ibiso walked back into the living room. She had to get some packing done today. The charity would come by to pick up on Friday. That was two days away. Ibiso went over to the bookcase that housed her print books and CD collection and started separating them from old to new. She saw her Heather Headley CD and decided to put it on.

I need some music to get this thing moving. She lowered the television as the soothing melody of the single, "In My Mind" filtered into the room. Ibiso worked in a steady rhythm, packing up the books, CD's, DVDs and pictures while singing, *"if you love something you've got to let it go. And if it comes back it then means so much more. But if it never does, at least you would know it's something you had to go through to grow..."*

A knock on the door made her stop. It was almost 9 p.m. She smoothed down her clothes, secured her head tie, and walked to the door. There was the knock again. "Who is it?"

Rasheed's voice came booming through. "Me. Open up. We need to talk."

***

Rasheed raised his hand to knock again when Ibiso opened the door. His eyes held hers hostage as she stepped aside to allow him enter. She looked so good in her V-neck, fitted t-shirt and shorts. He was almost tempted to chuck propriety and reach out and grab her. Then his eyes caught a glimpse of the boxes in the corner.

Rasheed crossed the room. With each step his jaw tightened. "What's going on?"

"What are you doing here?" she countered. The look in her eyes was heated with indignation.

He was determined not to be phased. He inspected the boxes and turned around to face her. "Answer me, what's going on?"

"*See me see wahala.* You have some nerve asking me that question." She picked up her half empty mug and walked into the kitchen.

From the looks of it, she was packing. *Where was she going? Was she going to leave without talking to him first?* Rasheed followed her into the kitchen and found her rinsing out her cup. The water continued to run over the already clean cup. He walked over and turned off the faucet. Ibiso turned around slowly. Her eyes were downcast. He lifted her face with his index finger.

"Ibiso, what's going on?"

She flung his hand away. Rasheed could see the pure fury in her eyes. He wasn't going to back down.

"Why do you care?" Ibiso walked back into the living room. She folded her hands across her chest and stood in front of her television. "I'm packing—"

"I can see that? To go where...?"

"Nowhere. I'm making a charity donation."

"Oh." He wasn't sure whether his relief was visible or not. Quite frankly, he didn't care.

"Drop the act. Pretending that my move would be devastating after a two month silence is a little over the top," she said.

"Cut it out."

"Why? Truth hurts, huh?" She walked over to the boxes and started throwing DVDs inside one of them.

A sense of loss overcame him. Was it too late? Panic moved his strides across the room. He grabbed her by her arm and turned her around to face him.

"I don't want to fight. I came over here to apologize."

Her eyes travelled from her hand to his face. She raised her brow. "For? Look, spare me. I don't have time for this. I have to be done with this by Friday."

"Not happening. Not until you hear me out. Sit down for a couple of minutes, please."

"No…You men are all the same. How stupid of me to think you were different."

Something snapped within Rasheed. How dare she compare him to that clown? He pulled her to the other side of the living room and sat her down, before taking his place next to her.

"Don't ever compare me to your ex again." He hesitated, expecting her to respond. She didn't. That meant only one thing, she was tired of fighting him and he was glad because so was he.

"Sweetheart, you came to my office yesterday after two months because you wanted to see me. What did you want to say?"

"Nothing," she quipped.

He turned her around to face him, and then cupped her face with one of his hands. "Okay, fair enough. But I have something to tell you."

Ibiso remained silent. He could tell she was still rattled, but at least she was giving him a chance to explain.

"For the past two months, I've been miserable. I threw myself into my work to escape facing reality…"

"Which is?"

"That I'm totally in love with you."

She stood up forcefully.

"Love? Do you know the meaning of the word?"

"I didn't until now. Please sit."

"Rasheed, I told you about my past. With that knowledge, love should have made you want to protect my heart." She plopped back down on the chair.

"But I couldn't love you how you deserved to be loved when I couldn't accept God's love for myself. I was afraid."

"Of what?"

"Of ending up like my mother." Rasheed saw the puzzled look on her face. "Growing up, I watched her go through hell because she loved so hard that she couldn't come to terms with the fact my dad left. I vowed then not to put myself in a situation where I'd have the slightest chance of being like her." He waited from a reaction from Ibiso but got none. "Then you happened. You gradually took me from everything I knew and had come to believe. When we got back from Port Harcourt and everything was crumbling, it took me back to my childhood and my vow to remain focused and not give in to love. So I panicked and sabotaged it. For that I'm so sorry."

Ibiso bowed and put her head in her hands. Rasheed saw the tears streaming down her cheeks. His heart ached at the sight of her tears and the knowledge that he put them there. He wanted to grab her and hold her close, but hesitated. Seconds later, she raised her head and looked at him. He lifted his finger and wiped the tear from the corner of her eye.

"Please say something," he urged her.

"I hear the words you're saying, but my head can't let go of the hurt my heart is feeling."

"Sweetheart, you're the one always preaching to me about forgiveness and letting go. I'm sorry. I'll do whatever it takes to make it up to you."

She cracked a smile. "I've told you before, you can't be using Jesus stuff when it suits you then dumping it when it doesn't. Forgiveness and letting go are Christian principles."

"About that…"

The expression on her face turned to dread. "Yes, what about it?"

Rasheed told her about Jide's visit in London which got him thinking and led him to open his heart and surrender to God. Although she hadn't said she was willing to give them another chance, the expression on her face as he narrated his story gave him hope.

Ibiso playfully swatted him on his shoulder. "And you thought it best to keep me in the dark? Why didn't you call me?"

He rubbed his shoulder in feigned pain. "Ouch woman. I tried calling you several times."

"Oh…"

"Oh what?"

"I left my phone here while I was in Port Harcourt." She stood and folded her arms across her chest. "What about Adaku?"

He wrapped his arms around her. "What you saw was a goodbye. I was leaving to see you when she showed up. Ibiso, I love you with everything I am and I'm convinced that you still love me." He brushed his lips against hers – something he had been dying to do since he walked in the door. "I can't say I'm a bow-tie wearing church boy now, but I confess Jesus Christ as my Lord and Savior giving me a feeling that's actually freeing." He smiled.

"Yes!" Ibiso pumped her fist in the air.

He pulled her closer. "I desperately need you in my life."

"You do, huh?"

"Yes," he confirmed.

"About that…I was made an offer I almost didn't refuse."

His eyebrows furrowed. "Explain."

Ibiso told him about how her brother wanted her to move back and offered her a new space and money as an investor. "You know, especially since I'm big time now."

"I heard you were a hit at the conference. Well done." He paused. "And you ran into my mother and her friends."

"Thanks. The chick that refuses to go away," Ibiso said. Both of them knew she was referring to Adaku.

"Back to your brother, I hope you gave him a definite, 'no thank you'."

"Umm…I don't know."

Just as she began to respond, his mouth swooped down on hers. He broke away abruptly and whispered. "So what were you saying about leaving again?"

"I was saying I don't know because Sodi did offer a good deal…"

Rasheed assaulted her lips again, drowning the words she was about to speak. When she started to respond, he drew away again. "I didn't hear you, sweetheart. You have to speak up."

"You're not being fair." She smiled and tried to pull away but he stopped her. "I love you too, more than words can express, and I'm not going anywhere."

"That's my girl." He gathered her into his arms. Half the mission was accomplished. He had the second half to go.

A long while later Rasheed looked down at Ibiso, who had fallen asleep with her head in his lap. He had helped her pack up one box before they called it a night. He stroked her cheek softly, as the last nine months ran through his mind. He loved her more than life. He vowed to spend the rest of his days treating her the way his dad had failed to treat his mom. *The tears she shed today were the last she'll ever cry, so help me God.*

The little velvet box in his back pocket poked him. He hadn't proposed earlier because they had things to iron out. But he wasn't leaving here without making her his wife to be. When he bought the ring before leaving London, he wasn't sure what to expect, but knew that if cupid smiled on him and gave him another chance with Ibiso, he wanted to be ready. He checked his watch, it was midnight. He shook her gently. If he didn't get going, there was the possibility he'd sleep here. And with the longing running through his veins, that wouldn't be a good idea.

"Sweetheart, wake up. I have to go."

She stirred and got up, her half shut eyes travelled to the wall clock. "It's late. I worry about you driving back at this hour."

"I'll be fine. Trust me. Staying here, even if it's on the couch, is not an option."

He got up and pulled her up. He guided her to her bedroom, turned down the covers and tucked her in. He kissed her on her forehead and knelt beside the bed.

"Ibiso, my life would not be complete without you in it. The thought of almost losing you causes my heart to ache." He removed the box from his back pocket and opened it.

Ibiso shot up to a sitting position.

"I've been carrying this around since I got back into the country, hoping that I'd get a second chance. Will you marry me?"

Ibiso reached out and cupped his face. "*In na son ki* and of course I'll marry you."

Rasheed smiled at her proclamation of love in Hausa language. She must have learnt it recently. He slipped the ring on her finger, and then gave her a quick kiss, not trusting himself to do more.

He stood and headed out of the bedroom. At the door, he turned around. "Sleep well *da son* and by the way, I'm not staying engaged for more than sixty days. So do whatever you need to do...."

She threw a pillow at him. He ducked, winked at her and said. "I love you, too. I'll let myself out."

Epilogue

Exactly two months and a day later, Rasheed and Ibiso sat side by side in the Danjuma jet. Destination: the Maldives. The events of the last two months were a blur and Ibiso was so happy that for the next two weeks she'd get to unwind with the man she loved and adored.

True to his word, Rasheed was not willing to accommodate anything that caused the marriage rites to exceed two months. After sharing the news with his family, they informed hers. Ibiso's mother couldn't contain her joy that her daughter was happy at last. She was prouder that Ibiso held on to the hope that God would send her the right person in due time.

The week after he proposed, Rasheed was baptized at the Overcomer's Chapel, where he became a member. Ibiso would never forget that day he was submerged and came out a new being. Her heart swelled with love and admiration. She was so grateful to God that Rasheed had found his way back to the Father, accepting the salvation He offered through Jesus Christ.

Right after that, the traditional ceremony was held in Port Harcourt, leaving her ample time to prepare for the church wedding in Abuja. She was so grateful to have Boma and Halima come and help her put together the intimate ceremony. They didn't want the media involved. The only media personality present was Damisi Ndungu. Jabir, her new brother in-law, had pleaded with her to allow Damisi access.

Ibiso became teary eyed when she recalled the events of yesterday. Rasheed stood with his two brothers and his friends, Kene and Jide by his side. His custom made, white tuxedo fitted his body perfectly. She was sure that she saw a tear fall from his eyes as Sodienye walked her down the aisle. After days of endless internet searches with Boma, Ibiso settled on a strapless, Cinderella wedding gown. It was as though the gown was made for her.

Everything was perfect, even the intimate reception afterwards. She and her new husband danced slowly to "All of Me" by John Legend. They gazed into each other's eyes, taking in all the lyrics of the song. Ibiso could feel their souls joining together as one. She remembered whispering to God to always be in her home and show how she could be the best wife, mother, and business woman.

Mother. She blushed when she remembered how despite the detail of her wedding dress, Rasheed had no problem taking it off last night. When they consummated their love, it was magical, just as she had imagined it would be.

"I hope I'm the one putting that smile on your face?" Rasheed asked but silenced her response with a kiss. The kiss started off sensual then progressed to a hungry onslaught.

They came up for air a few moments later. "You taste good." Ibiso used her finger to wipe the lipstick from her husband's lips.

"So do you, but you haven't answered my question."

"Yes honey, you are."

"I intend to put one on there always. You came into my world and turned it inside out. I am a better man for knowing you." He caressed her cheeks.

"Aww...honey. You say the sweetest things. I'm thankful you're part of my world." She looked at her wedding ring. Lifting her hand and extending it in front of her face, she grinned. "As stubborn as you were, I can't believe I am now Mrs. Ibiso Danjuma."

Rasheed smiled as he continued stroking her hand. "We Danjuma men know how to get what we want," he said with a wink. "And we have excellent taste in women."

From her interactions with the twins, Ibiso knew that just like her husband had, they believed that love or commitment wasn't in the cards for them. But she of all people knew that if her husband was any yardstick to go by, all the Danjuma men needed as the true love of a strong woman. She wondered which of the brothers would be the next to wait for their bride at the end of an aisle.

Ibiso grinned. "It's hard to argue with that. I'm worth my weight in gold."

Laughing, Rasheed pulled her close. "Come here, you vain woman." As his lips settled on hers, Ibiso sighed. Life is beautiful when you add a scoop of love to it.

THE END

Discussion Questions

- Do you think Rasheed's mother exposed him to too much at a tender age?

- Have you ever put your dreams on hold because of a relationship? Does it depend on the level of commitment in the relationship?

- Should Rasheed's father have given his mother anything in the will? Or was the fact that he was trying to right by their sons enough?

- Rasheed's mother was of the opinion that "by now" he should let his anger go. Do you think she belittled his pain?

- If hate or dislike for another person drives your actions have you truly let go?

- What do you think of Rasheed and Ibiso's first encounter?

- Considering her past, do you think Ibiso overreacted to Rasheed taking care of her rent?

- Do you think Rasheed was too harsh in his handling of the Halima situation?

- Rasheed's friend, Jide, blamed himself for co- signing Rasheed's bitterness for years. As a practising Christian, what role do you play in calling your friends out when you know they are doing wrong?

- Ibiso was a chef, who is the master in the kitchen in your house?

Other Titles By Unoma Nwankwor

An Unexpected Blessing

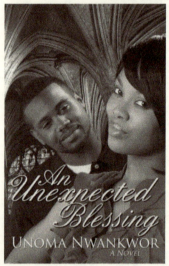

Personal banker, Feranmi Adewunmi has done well for herself in diaspora by any standards. But by her parent's calculations, she should be married by now. And they had the right man for her. For Feranmi, being single wasn't a crime and so she came up with the perfect plan to beat them at their own game. All she needed was a man.

CEO of Montgomery Construction, Alex Montgomery was back in Atlanta. His primary focus was rebuilding his business after an unfortunate incident in Chicago changed his life forever. A chance meeting with Feranmi turned that plan upside down. The pain she caused him in school was still fresh in his mind but so were the feelings that never died. Now she needed a favor.

For Feranmi time was running out. Her parents would be visiting soon and she still hadn't found the perfect Nigerian man. Alex was her only option, after all how hard could it be? What they weren't prepared for was an attraction they couldn't ignore. Will they lean on the Lord for guidance or insist on being in control? Will his guarded dark past confirm her fears? Or will love prevail the second time around?

An Unexpected Blessing is a novel of love, forgiveness, and being open to God's plan in your life. The best blessings are often unexpected.

BUY: http://goo.gl/sszGYz

The Christmas Ultimatum

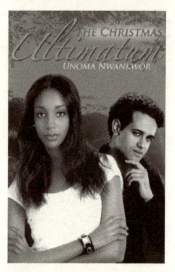

Freelance journalist, Olanma Obinze, just landed the interview of a lifetime. She didn't like the commercialism of Christmas, so the trip to Dubai was the perfect destination and it was happening at the perfect time. She'd get to escape the Christmas hoopla; and the big paycheck once the article was sold would ensure she didn't have to go crawling back to her father for money.

Abayomi Rice was in charge of scheduling interviews for his grandfather, but would only grant Olanma's request if she accepted his ultimatum—a trip half way across the world to Cape Town, South Africa.

Olanma wasn't falling for the charm of a recovering playboy and a rich one at that. But with her plans going up in smoke before her eyes, Olanma must decide whether to give in to the ultimatum or leave empty handed. Who said it was the season to be merry?

BUY: http://amzn.to/1y0a9dN

When You Let Go

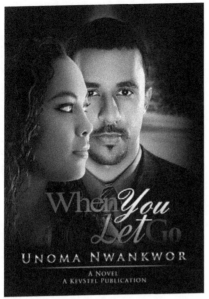

An answered prayer. An unforeseen betrayal. A family healed by grace.

Amara and Ejike Dike had been married for six glorious years. Amara was convinced Ejike, was the perfect gift from God. Loving, charming and very easy on the eyes. They had a beautiful life. Well, not so beautiful. Amara's inability to bear children made her feel like a less than the perfect mate for her husband. Then after many years, God lifted her faith and had finally heard her cry. The Dikes couldn't be happier.

A surprise visit from Chinelo, Amara's long lost cousin, turns Amara's world upside down and threatens to turn her once-perfect existence into ashes.

Ejike loved his wife with a passion. They shared a burning desire and faith in God that burned deep. However Chinelo's appearance would open a Pandora's Box that had purposely been kept shut. Faced with the loss of all she holds dear, Amara finds herself at crossroads. Would she lean on God's sustaining grace to let go and travel the rocky path to forgiveness? Or would she throw everything to the wind and walk away?

When You Let Go is a novel about people who know what the

Word of God instructs but struggle with actually doing it when the chips are down

BUY: http://amzn.to/1sMLGqg

CPSIA information can be obtained
at www.ICGtesting.com
Printed in the USA
LVHW031507300719
625872LV00002B/205